"Are you planning a trip to Italy in the near future?" Markos asked.

To his surprise, she didn't acknowledge him or respond to his question.

"I'm Markos Morretti."

Tatiyana stared at his outstretched hand as if it was covered in germs and raised her book into the air. "I don't mean to be rude, Mr. Morretti, but as you can see, I'm very busy."

"I deserve that. I was rude earlier, wasn't I?"

"Yes," she replied, vigorously nodding her head. "You were."

"I'm sorry. I'm working on an important deposition, and sometimes when I get caught up in a case, I lose sight of everything else."

"Then why are you wasting your precious time talking to me?"

"Spending time with a vivacious woman is never a waste of time," he said smoothly. "And I'm curious to hear about your trip to Italy."

"Why? Do you moonlight as a travel guide when you're not in court?"

"I do for beauties with freckles."

His heart inflated with pride when Tatiyana laughed.

Dear Reader,

You asked for Markos Morretti's story, and here it is! The smart, debonair attorney doesn't do relationships or believe in true love, but his feelings for Tatiyana Washington—the wisecracking beauty with the big personality and outrageous sense of humor—can't be denied. And Markos will do anything, including hiring her to be his receptionist, to get close to her.

Burned by love in the past, Tatiyana wants nothing to do with the opposite sex, but Markos breaks down her walls, one slow, sensuous kiss at a time. The odds are against them, but Markos proves that he can be trusted with her heart.

Look for the final book in the Morretti Millionaires series coming soon. Thank you, reader-friends, for your constant encouragement and support. There's no me without you!

All the best in life and love,

Pamela Yaye

Seduced
BY THE BACHELOR

Pamela Yaye

HHARLEQUIN® KIMANI™ ROMANCE

Recycling programs
for this product may
not exist in your area.

ISBN-13: 978-0-373-86489-8

Seduced by the Bachelor

For questions and comments about the quality of this book please contact us
at CustomerService@Harlequin.com.

HARLEQUIN®
www.Harlequin.com

Printed in U.S.A.

Pamela Yaye has a bachelor's degree in Christian education. Her love for African American fiction prompted her to pursue a career in writing romance. When she's not working on her latest novel, this busy wife, mother and teacher is watching basketball, cooking or planning her next vacation. Pamela lives in Alberta, Canada, with her gorgeous husband and adorable but mischievous son and daughter.

Books by Pamela Yaye

Harlequin Kimani Romance

Pleasure for Two
Promises We Make
Escape to Paradise
Evidence of Desire
Passion by the Book
Designed by Desire
Seduced by the Playboy
Seduced by the CEO
Seduced by the Heir
Seduced by Mr. Right
Heat of Passion
Seduced by the Hero
Seduced by the Mogul
Mocha Pleasures
Seduced by the Bachelor

Visit the Author Profile page
at Harlequin.com for more titles.

This book is dedicated to sisters everywhere.

Bettey Odidison (my smart, beautiful sister), thank you for being my confidante, my sounding board and my biggest cheerleader. You are one of the greatest gifts God has ever given me, and I love you with every fiber of my being.

Chapter 1

Tatiyana Washington was having the week from hell, and hoped for her family's sake things didn't get worse. The main breadwinner in her household, Tatiyana feared what would happen if she suffered another financial setback in August.

Speed walking through Los Angeles International Airport, Tatiyana considered her recent string of bad luck. On Monday, she'd lost her favorite pair of earrings, *and* her lucrative executive secretary position at the largest software company in the state. On Tuesday her Jeep had died on Hollywood Freeway, and that morning she'd overslept for her 9:00 a.m. flight to Tampa. It was a mad dash to get to the airport, and if not for her cousin Everly weaving her battered Passat in and out of traffic like an emergency vehicle with its lights blazing, she'd still be stuck on the I-105.

Spotting gate 55A at the rear of the terminal, Tatiyana picked up her pace, expertly dodging children and weary-looking travelers clutching coffee cups. Everything was riding on this four-day trip to The Sunshine State, and she couldn't afford to miss the flight. Consulting the monitors, she noticed Flight 74 to Tampa was delayed and sighed in relief. *Finally, something's going my way!* Tatiyana approached the airline desk with confidence, convinced she was doing the right thing even though it was a lie.

"Good morning," greeted the customer service agent, glancing away from her computer screen, her hazel eyes bright with interest. "How may I help you?"

Tatiyana read the brunette's name tag and smiled brightly. Surfing the internet last night had uncovered important information about Markos Morretti, and she wasn't going to blow this opportunity. "I need a *huge* favor." Tatiyana spoke in a hushed voice, as if she was about to spill her guts, instantly seizing the agent's attention. "My boy-friend's on the nine o'clock flight to Tampa, and I want to surprise him. Can you work your magic and seat us to-gether?"

"I'll see what I can do, Miss. What's your boyfriend's name?"

For effect, Tatiyana glanced around the waiting area, cupped her hands around her mouth and whispered, "Markos Morretti."

"Markos Morretti?" she repeated, his name falling from her mouth in a breathless gush. "The divorce attorney with the bedroom eyes?"

"The one and only. That's my baby, and I can't wait to see him! Is he here?"

The attendant bobbed her head. "Mr. Morretti walked inside the Boeing 738 five minutes ago, and when he strode through the terminal, women whistled and waved. I don't blame them. He's so dreamy I almost fainted when he smiled at me—"

"I know the feeling," Tatiyana interjected, hoping to win favor with the attendant by indulging in girl talk. She'd do anything to achieve her goal, including fabricating a story about a red-hot relationship with the celebrated at-torney, and spoke in a girlish voice to prove she was head over heels in love. "I melt every time Markos kisses me."

"I bet. He's gorgeous, and he smells good, too…"

To speed up the process, Tatiyana slid her photo ID across the desk and inquired about the delayed flight. LAX was swarming with disgruntled employees and travelers so loud she couldn't hear herself think. The sooner Tatiyana got to her first-class seat and made friends with Markos Morretti the better. She'd never met the divorce attorney, but after seeing his picture with Mayor Glover in the *Los Angeles Times* weeks earlier, Tatiyana made it her mis-sion to not only meet him, but befriend him. Markos was going to help her, whether he liked it or not, because no one messed with her family and got away with it. Tatiyana

was going to make sure Mayor Glover did the right thing—
even if it meant tipping off the media about his one-night
stand with her twenty-two-year-old sister.

"Why didn't you board the flight together?"

Tatiyana snapped to attention. Good question. "We had
a spat yesterday, and we haven't spoken since. That's why
I'm here. To apologize for hurting his feelings. I didn't
mean to."

"Sounds serious," she said, leaning forward, her hands
pressed flat against the desk.

Dabbing at the corners of her eyes with her fingertips,
she played the role of the distraught girlfriend to the hilt.
"We ran into my ex at a movie premiere, and Markos accused me of flirting with him. I still can't believe it. Why
would I want him when I have a loving, romantic man who
treats me like gold?"

"Why, indeed," she agreed, her tone filled with awe.
"From what I've read in the tabloids, Markos Morretti is
everything a woman could want. Handsome, successful,
romantic, and—"

"Amazing in bed—" Feigning embarrassment, Tatiyana
broke off speaking. "Oops, I've said too much. I better
board the flight before my loose lips get me into trouble."

Hearing her cell chime, Tatiyana opened her leather tote
bag, retrieved her iPhone and typed in her password. She
had a new message from her mom, and seeing the image of
her niece warmed her heart. Tatiyana had been gone only a
couple hours, but she already missed Allie. The nine-month-
old was the center of her world, a bright, bubbly baby with
curly hair and chubby cheeks. Cuddling with her niece was
the best part of her day. But when she saw Jantel curled up
in bed, staring off into space, her good mood always fizzled.

"You're all set. You're in seat 1C, next to your boyfriend."

Resisting the urge to dance around the desk, Tatiyana
cheered inwardly, grateful her plan had gone off without a
hitch. "Thank you, Mercedes. You're the best!"

"It was my pleasure."

"I'm going to email the airline, and tell them what a great employee you are."

"I appreciate that Ms. Washington."

"No problem," Tatiyana said with a wink. "We ladies need to stick together, right?"

"If you grab your things, I can escort you to the plane."

Panic flooded her body, rooting her six-inch heels to the floor. What if the attendant said something to Markos? What if she was exposed as a liar and hauled off the plane by airport security? Swallowing hard, she ignored the butterflies swarming her stomach and dismissed the attendant's offer with a flick of her hand. "I'm a frequent flyer. I know the way."

"I insist." The attendant took off at a breakneck speed, leaving Tatiyana no choice but to follow her. Inside the tunnel, she fluffed her short, fizzy hair and adjusted her uniform. "Markos has two younger brothers," she said, checking her appearance in a tiny, handheld mirror. "I saw a picture of Romeo and Enrique Morretti in *Hello* magazine a few months ago, and they're total hotties. I'd love to meet them. Have you?"

"No, not yet. We haven't been dating long, so I'd appreciate if you didn't say anything to Markos about our relationship. He's a *very* private man, and I don't want you to upset him."

"I won't say a word. I know how to act around celebrities. I'm an aspiring actress…"

Everyone is in this town, Tatiyana thought, nixing an eye roll.

"No worries, Ms. Washington. I'll be professional and polite."

Thankful her cover was still intact, Tatiyana wore a grateful smile. Following the attendant, her heart drumming inside her chest, she hoped her hair and makeup were still perfect. Normally, Tatiyana wore sweats when she traveled, but this morning she'd gone all out. Fake eyelashes, lush curls that flowed down her back, gold accessories to complement her Chanel outfit and peep-toe sandals. Markos Morretti had a penchant for model-types, with long hair and slim figures, and since Tatiyana wanted to catch his eye, she had to look her best.

"Here we are," the attendant said, gesturing to the aircraft. "If it's not too much trouble, I'd love to meet Mr. Morretti…"

"Thanks for everything." Anxious to meet her attorney "boyfriend" for the first time, Tatiyana waved and marched onto the gleaming Boeing 738 as if she owned it.

"Morning," greeted the flight attendant, giving her the once-over, his interest evident in his toothy grin. "Right this way, Ms. Washington. Let me show you to your seat…"

Tatiyana expelled a nervous breath. She could do this. *Had* to do this. Her family was depending on her. Lying went against everything she believed in, but what choice did she have? Her sister was depressed, and she was scared of losing her forever.

Her gaze landed on Markos Morretti, and she stopped abruptly, couldn't move. Tatiyana heard a gasp fall from her lips and slammed her mouth shut. He was a living, breathing men's ad, and seeing him in the flesh was a shock to her system. Blood surged to her girly parts, warming her body with desire, and her heartbeat roared in her ears.

In her haste to meet him, Tatiyana tripped over her feet. To avoid falling headfirst into his lap, she braced her hands against the wall and straightened her wobbly knees. Tatiyana gathered herself, then adjusted her clothes. To her relief, the other first-class passengers were too busy on their electronic devices to notice her blunder, and Markos—the devastating piece of eye candy—had his eyes closed, earphones in and a pensive expression on his face. He wasn't paying her any attention, but he would. Men always did when she turned on the charm, and Tatiyana was looking forward to seducing the Italian bachelor. He had smooth, olive skin, chiseled features and thick lips. Lips made for kissing and sucking and exploring between her legs—

"Here you go." The flight attendant gestured to the window seat with a nod. "If you need anything, push your call button and I'll be here in a flash."

Stepping over Markos's long, outstretched legs, Tatiyana swung her tote bag toward him, hoping to wake him, but he didn't move. How was she supposed to seduce him when he didn't even know she was alive? What if he slept the entire flight? Then what?

Sitting in her seat, she was impressed by how spacious and attractive the cabin was. Tatiyana had never flown first-class, and had had to use some of the money in her savings to afford the pricey ticket. Her gaze landed on Markos again—for the second time in minutes—and her mouth dried. Tatiyana smelled perfume on his clothes, a charming blend of fruits and spices, and wondered if everything she'd read online about his dating life was true.

The pilot came on the intercom, warmly greeting passengers to Flight 74, but Tatiyana was so distracted by Markos's presence that she couldn't concentrate on what the pilot was saying. Tatiyana couldn't remember ever being this attracted to a guy, this taken with anyone, and fanned her face to cool down her overheated body.

Studying his profile, she heard Lena's words in her ear and smiled to herself. Her mother was right; Markos *did* look like a movie star. Weeks ago, Lena and Jantel had gone to his swanky, downtown law firm, but the meeting had been a waste of time. Markos refused to help, insisted the mayor would never cheat on his fiancée and promptly kicked them out of his office. To add insult to injury, his receptionist had handed them a three-hundred-dollar invoice on their way out the door. Tatiyana didn't learn about the meeting until she'd returned from a road trip with her friends days later. No matter. Tatiyana knew what to do, and this time *she'd* be calling the shots, not the slick-talking attorney with the bedroom eyes.

Tatiyana buckled her seat belt and crossed her legs. She hated flying, and hoped a flight attendant would be around soon with a complimentary glass of champagne. Her first-class ticket had cost more than her montly mortgage payment, and Tatiyana planned to get her money's worth. She was going to have seconds and thirds of everything, especially dessert, and smirked when she remembered the conversation she'd had with her mom at dinner last night. "Eat your belly full," Lena had advised, adjusting her crooked, auburn wig. "Hell, at that price, the airline should give you a doggie bag *and* a bottle of Sangria!"

Fond memories came to mind, filling her heart with love. Her mother was bossy, and always had to have the last word, but she was the glue that held their family together, and Tatiyana adored her, faults and all. Suffering from postpartum depression, Jantel couldn't care for her daughter, Allie, so she'd moved her sister and niece into her house. A week later, her mom came to visit and never left. Lena ensured everything ran smoothly at home and doted on her only grandchild. Pounding the pavement for work, Tatiyana could attend interviews, knowing Jantel and Allie were in good hands. Her friend, Daphne Kostopoulos, owned a staffing agency, and gave her hours every week. Tatiyana missed her lucrative position at Pinnacle Microsystems, and was anxious to find another one, but first, she had make nice with Markos Morretti—the attorney who'd swindled her mom out of three hundred dollars—and persuade him to help her kid sister.

Within minutes, the plane was at cruising altitude, flying high above the clouds. Watching Markos on the sly, Tatiyana considered introducing herself, but sensed it wasn't the right time. He opened his briefcase, took out a leather-bound notebook and flipped it open. Pen in hand, he wrote furiously, only stopping to tell the flight attendant what he wanted to drink. "I'll have a coffee with a double shot of Bailey's, two sugars and a dash of espresso."

Sensing this was the opportunity she'd been waiting for, Tatiyana spoke up. "I'll have the same, but with a double shot of espresso."

Markos glanced to the right, staring intently at her. Tatiyana wanted to introduce herself, but she couldn't get her mouth to work. Remembering what was at stake, she conquered her nerves and offered her hand in greeting. "Hi," she said, wearing her brightest, most dazzling smile. "I'm Tatiyana Washington."

He nodded but didn't speak. *Jerk*, she thought, put off by his cold demeanor. Markos gave her a blank look, making her feel small and insignificant, and Tatiyana wished her happy-go-lucky self hadn't introduced herself first. Sensing some reserve in his manner, she toned down her excitement and spoke in a softer, quieter voice. "And you are—" she prompted.

"Working," he snapped.

Embarrassed, her cheeks flushed with heat, she forced an apologetic smile onto her lips. "Not a problem. Sorry for bothering you—"

"Thanks." Returning to his document, he picked up his fancy diamond pen and resumed writing, scowling as if she was a pesky fly he couldn't get rid of.

Shocked by his rudeness, Tatiyana realized she'd never disliked anyone more than the curt divorce attorney, and made up her mind to get even with him before Flight 74 landed in Tampa. Deciding to play it cool, Tatiyana slipped on her sunglasses and settled back into her seat, pretending Markos didn't exist. It didn't work. She couldn't stop stealing glances at him, watching him on the sly as he typed, and when their arms inadvertently touched and desire exploded inside her, Tatiyana feared she didn't stand a chance against Markos Morretti.

Chapter 2

Markos Morretti glanced around the first-class cabin, searching for an empty seat, but couldn't find one anywhere. *Dannazione*, he thought, dragging a hand through his short, black hair. *I'm screwed.* He had motions to read and depositions to write, but everything about his seatmate was a distraction. Her floral fragrance, her bubbly, effervescent vibe, how she danced around in her seat to the music playing in her pink earbuds, her pretty, melodious voice.

Staggered by her beauty, all Markos could do was stare. She was stunning, well-put together in a white shorts set, bejeweled sandals, and a gold ankle bracelet that drew his gaze to her silky, brown legs. Her outfit screamed, "Look at Me," and Markos did. He couldn't stop undressing her with his eyes. He had an erection growing inside his boxer briefs, and the dark-skinned beauty was the reason why. *What's wrong with me? Why am I sweating a woman who looks like trouble? Who's probably broken hearts in every state?*

Markos felt guilty for snapping at her, but he couldn't bring himself to apologize. It wasn't Tatiyana's fault he had a heavy caseload and an incompetent paralegal. The motion was riddled with spelling mistakes, and he had no choice but to revise the document Izzy had written. He made a mental note to have a stern talk with her when he returned to LA on Monday. He'd hired her as a favor to her mother but regretted it the first time Izzy Braunstein waltzed into his office an hour late, complaining about her boneheaded boyfriend.

Telling himself not to worry about it, Markos shook off his negative thoughts. His job was challenging, fast-paced and stressful at times, but he was a damn good attorney, and he was proud of his winning record. He spent his days meeting with potential and existing clients, drafting court documents, consulting with his staff and going to court. Although Markos loved his job, he needed a break. His brothers and cousins were en route to the Oasis Spa and Resort as well, and he was looking forward to their guys-only weekend.

Markos picked up his notebook determined to finish his work. Hired to represent the biggest pop star on the planet in her divorce, Markos knew the high-profile case could increase his popularity, and devoted all of his free time to plotting and strategizing how to win. The divorce proceedings had dragged on for eighteen long months, and he was growing tired of the case. But when he got into a heated argument with the opposing counsel in June, and the jerk threw a cup of water in his face, resulting in a courthouse brawl, Markos vowed to crush his opponent no matter the cost. His critics called him ruthless, claimed he was motivated by money, fame and power, but Markos didn't care. He was a Morretti, and Morrettis ignored what the haters said. He gave a 100 percent to every case, regardless of his client's net worth, and refused to let anyone outsmart him in court.

Like his thoughts, his eyes wandered to Tatiyana, instead of his notes. Tatiyana met his gaze, stared right at him. Sparks flew, proving their chemistry was real, and not a figment of his imagination. Markos felt an immediate attraction to her, a spark that couldn't be denied, and struggled to keep his hands in his lap and off her curves. His gaze dipped from her face to her cleavage, resting at her bosom. Her animal-print scarf gave her ensemble a touch of class, but he fantasized about her naked, on his lap, riding him—

She sang in a low voice, snapping her fingers, rocking her body from side to side.

Markos plucked at his striped shirt. Dancing around in her seat, having a party for one, Tatiyana reminded him of a video vixen in a music video. Too bad she was probably high maintenance. One look at Tatiyana told Markos everything he needed to know. Skilled at reading people, he suspected she was materialistic and decided to keep his distance. Markos didn't want what Tatiyana was offering. He was tired of women throwing themselves at him, and wished he could meet someone who didn't want anything from him.

Still, he was intrigued and couldn't stop staring at her.

"Excuse me." Standing, Tatiyana stepped past him, heading up the aisle as if it were her own personal runway. Her scent overpowered his senses, sending his thoughts into overdrive. Leaning to the right, he admired her captivating strut, curious if she had a boyfriend.

His eyes flickered over her curves, cruising down her hips with deliberate intent. She strode toward the lavatory, giving him a terrific view of her from behind, tempting him to break the rules. Sweat clung to his skin, drenching the back of his short-sleeve shirt. Long after Tatiyana disappeared into the bathroom, he was thinking about her—her smoky eyes, her toned, slender shape, her mesmerizing walk, how her aura and physical beauty drew him in.

"Sir, are you finished with your lunch? I hope everything was to your liking…"

Markos straightened and regarded the flight attendant, hoping she didn't see him ogling Tatiyana's backside. "Yes, thanks, everything was great."

To get his mind off Tatiyana, Markos stared out the window. The sky was clear, powder blue, and instantly calmed his mind. Hanging out with the guys was the perfect antidote for his stress. These days, all Markos did was work, and he couldn't remember the last time he'd cut loose. He had an active social life, but none of the women he was dating excited him. He kept females at a distance, hadn't gotten close to anyone since Emme left, and didn't plan to.

Thoughts of his ex-girlfriend flooded his mind, and Markos wondered if the pain in his heart would ever subside.

Someone whistled, drawing Markos's gaze to the front of the plane. Tatiyana was back, a sight to behold with that radiant, effervescent smile. A child raced up the aisle, slamming into Tatiyana, and she rocked back onto her heels. She dropped her purse, and its contents spilled onto the floor, flying everywhere.

Unbuckling his seat belt, Markos bent and picked up the items at his feet, handing them to her. Their fingers touched, brushing ever so lightly against each other. Tatiyana thanked him, but he could see the contempt on her face and knew she had her guard up. Her eyes bored into him, leaving him feeling vulnerable, exposed, as if she could see into his soul.

After he helped her pick up her stuff, she sat down, picked up the book on her seat and flipped it open.

"Italy for Dummies?" he said, unable to hide his amusement. "Are you planning a trip to Italy in the near future?"

To his surprise, she didn't acknowledge him or respond to his question.

"I'm Markos Morretti."

Tatiyana stared at his outstretched hand, as if it was covered in germs, and raised her book in the air. "I don't mean to be rude, Mr. Morretti, but as you can see I'm *very* busy."

"I deserve that. I was rude earlier, wasn't I?"

"Yes," she replied, vigorously nodding. "You were."

"I'm sorry. I'm working on an important disposition, and sometimes when I get caught up in a case I lose sight of everything else."

"Then why are you wasting your time talking to me?"

"Spending time with a vivacious woman is never a waste of time," he said smoothly. "And I'm curious to hear about your trip to Italy."

"Why? Do you moonlight as a travel guide when you're not in court?"

"I do for beauties with freckles."

He smiled when Tatiyana laughed.

Her bracelets clanged as she swept a hand through her hair. The words *Sister's Keeper* were tattooed on the inside of her wrist in small, fine script, and Markos was curious about the intricate design. "That's an interesting tattoo. Are you a twin?"

"No." The light in her eyes dimmed. "My sister's five years younger than me, but I've always taken care of her and I always will. She's my heart."

"I feel the same way about my siblings. I'd do anything for them," he said, meaning every word. "Are you from LA, or just passing through?"

"I was in town visiting relatives," she explained. "I'm originally from Bridgeport."

Markos saw a message pop up on his iPad, guessed it was one of his clients, but ignored it. He wanted to know more about Tatiyana, not read emails. "Have you been to Tampa before? Or is this your first time?"

"No, never, but Dalton loves the city, so I'm in good hands."

"Dalton? Is that your husband?"

"No, my best friend. We met in college, and we've been inseparable ever since."

Suspicious, Markos probed further. "And you're sure he's not your man?"

"I'm positive," she said, giving him a puzzled look. "Why don't you believe me?"

"Because you're stunning, and I bet men chase you down for your number 24/7."

"You're quite the charmer, Markos. Doesn't Mrs. Morretti mind you flirting with other women? I would if you were my man."

If you were my wife, I wouldn't need anyone else. He dismissed the outrageous thought with a shake of his head and answered her question. "I'm not married. Law is my first and only love, and that will never change."

"Spoken like a true attorney," she teased.

"Are you a model?"

"No, I'm an executive secretary at Pinnacle Microsystems."

Impressed, he nodded. "Great company. I have several friends at Pinnacle. Do you know anyone in the marketing department?"

"No, it's a huge company, and I like to keep to myself. I'm super busy with school right now, so I don't have time to socialize with my colleagues outside of work."

"What are you studying?"

"I'd love to work in the non-profit field as a program director or manager, so I decided to get my business degree," she explained. "But enough about me. Let's talk about you. Are you traveling to Tampa for work or pleasure?"

"Hopefully, both. Are you free tonight?"

"No. We're going to the R&B Summer Jam at Applause Nightclub, but you're more than welcome to join us. Divas are performing, and I can't wait to see them perform live!"

"Who?"

A puzzled expression wrinkled her features. "The female rap group?"

"Sorry. Never heard of them."

"Are you kidding me? Were you living under a rock in the nineties?"

"No, in Italy," he explained, warding off bitter memories. "My parents separated, and my brothers and I went to live with my grandparents until the divorce was finalized."

"That must have been a very difficult for you. I grew up without a father, so unfortunately I know what it's like to experience hard times. It's tough." Her expression was sympathetic. "But don't worry. I'll buy you their greatest hits album for Christmas!"

Markos laughed out loud. He liked her. What wasn't to like? A ball of energy, she was able to capture his attention despite everything he had on his mind. As expected, Tatiyana was far more interesting than his paperwork. She regaled him with stories about her childhood, her love of pop culture and her small, close-knit family.

"Where are you staying this weekend?" he asked. "With your friend, or at a hotel?"

"Dalton lives in Orlando, so we're staying at the Oasis Spa and Resort. It's the Rashawn Bishop Charity Golf tournament, and I'm going to win it all. Just watch me."

Markos admired her confidence. Tatiyana was as witty as she was beautiful, and he had to see her again. "Small world. I'm staying at the same resort, and I'm also attending the tournament."

"Then we'll be seeing each other a lot this weekend. Should be fun."

"Let's exchange numbers. Maybe we can have a drink one night."

"I'd like that. You seem like a cool guy, and I have a feeling Dalton's sister is going to love you. She *loves* Italian men, especially handsome ones."

Markos groaned, hanging his head as if overcome with despair. And he was. Sick of people hooking him up. He wished they'd quit sending needy, marriage-crazed females his way, and leave him alone. "I have the worst luck. I can't go anywhere without someone trying to set me up."

"Trust me, I'm an expert at reading people, and Genevieve is exactly your type."

Amused, a grin tugged at his lips. "What's my type?"

"Smart, independent and successful, right?"

"*You* certainly fit the bill."

"I'm looking for Mr. Right—"

"Look no further. I'm right here."

Tatiyana scoffed, with a loud, sarcastic laugh. "That's what they all say until someone younger and prettier with bigger boobs comes along."

"I'm not a player. Never have been. I'm an honest, upstanding guy who enjoys long walks in the park, shopping on Rodeo Drive, dining at five-star restaurants and Jill Scott."

"Good God," she said, her tone filled with awe. "You *are* my dream guy!"

Her girly, high-pitched giggles filled the air. Markos sensed her interest in him and knew he was saying and doing all the right things to impress her. He'd score her cell phone number by the time they landed in Tampa, and a date, no doubt about it.

They talked nonstop during the in-flight movie, laughing and cracking jokes. They had a lot in common, but what shocked Markos most were her insightful comments about the business world, her knowledge of Wall Street and politics.

"To be honest, I don't put much faith in politicians," Tatiyana confessed. "They'll say and do anything to get elected, but once they're in office, they forget about the promises they made to their loyal constituents. We need leaders who'll stand with the American people, and unite the country, not divide it."

"That's a tall order, don't you think?"

"No. If the government invests in education and health care, and provides better training to police departments, I think things would drastically improve. Especially for lower-income families and impoverished communities."

"Well said, Tatiyana. I wholeheartedly agree." Markos raised an eyebrow. "Are you sure you're an executive secretary? If I didn't know better I'd think you were a community activist."

Tatiyana smiled, and Markos did, too.

"It's hard to believe we just met. I feel like we've known each other forever. It's so easy to talk to you."

"I was thinking the same thing," he confessed, echoing her thoughts.

"It feels like we're old friends catching up at our high-school reunion."

"That's because you're an exceptional conversationalist. You're articulate, well-read, and you have an opinion about everything."

Tatiyana frowned, arching an eyebrow. "Is that your way of saying I talk a lot?"

"No, that's my way of saying I'd like to see you again."

The flight attendant appeared. "Can I interest either of you in a glass of Cabernet Sauvignon?"

"Absolutely." Tatiyana helped herself to a flute from the flight attendant's tray, two bowls of nuts and a warm hand towel. "Thanks, Miss, I'll buzz you if I need something else."

"And you, Mr. Morretti?"

"I shouldn't. It's too early in the day to be drinking."

"Get one," Tatiyana urged. "You only live once, right?"

"It does smell good," he conceded, licking his lips, his mouth wet with anticipation.

"It *tastes* even better…"

Markos swallowed hard. He couldn't stop thinking about kissing her, and wondered if her lips tasted as good as they looked.

"It's not going to kill you to have one drink," she said, popping a cashew into her mouth. "Everything in moderation. That's my personal philosophy, and it governs everything I do."

"Good point." Markos grabbed a flute off the tray and raised it in the air. "To Tampa."

They clinked wineglasses. Time stopped, and everything around them ceased to exist. They stared at each other, as if they were long-lost lovers reuniting after years apart, and instinctively Markos took her hand in his. She was a vibrant, young woman with a wicked sense of humor *and* a terrific pair of legs—and Markos couldn't wait to feel them around his waist. And he would, once they arrived at the Oasis Spa and Resort.

Chapter 3

Oasis Spa and Resort, a luxurious hotel known for its world-class amenities and picturesque views, was located in a sprawling, gated community thirty minutes from downtown Tampa. Strolling from his executive suite to Prime Steak House Markos took in his surroundings, noting the vibrant flowers and towering palm trees shielding the grounds. The resort had it all—an 18-hole championship golf course, swimming pools, tennis courts, acclaimed restaurants known for their delicious menus and a renowned spa. Popular among A-listers with time on their hands, and money to burn, the resort was filled with sports legends, actresses, reality stars and social media darlings snapping selfies at every turn.

Prime Steak House was packed, filled with laughter, conversation and casually dressed diners. The moment Markos stepped into the restaurant, he spotted the Morretti clan seated in a secluded corner, away from the other patrons. His body tensed, and the smile slid off his face. His cousins, Demetri, Nicco and Rafael, and his brothers, Emilio and Immanuel, weren't alone; they'd traveled to Tampa with their wives. It was obvious the couples were madly in love; they were whispering, cuddling, even feeding each other.

He cocked an eyebrow. Markos was shocked by his brothers' behavior, was blown away by their public displays of affection. They looked proud, too, as if they had the perfect lives, but Markos knew better than anyone how fast things could change. One minute it was candlelight dinners and weekend getaways, and the next it was screaming matches, separate bedrooms and divorce court. For their sakes, he hoped it wasn't the latter, but Markos didn't put much faith in relationships. They didn't last, and he had the broken heart to prove it.

Absent from the group were his youngest brothers, Enrique and Romeo. Based in Italy, they both worked nonstop, preferring to make money than spend it. Days earlier, he'd called Enrique to find out his travel information, but his brother said he was too busy with his media company, Icon Productions, to attend the charity golf tournament. He'd tried to persuade him, but there was nothing Markos could say to change his mind. Romeo had given him the same spiel yesterday. A brilliant investment banker, with foresight and ingenuity, he owned everything from real-estate properties to upscale restaurants, spas and fitness centers. In spite of his recent health scare, Romeo was still the hardest working person in his family. At thirty-one, he'd accomplished incredible success in his career, and Markos was proud of him.

Cheers and laughter filled the air. He heard his sister-in-law Sharleen giggle, and watched as Emilio kissed her passionately on the lips. *So much for our guys-only trip*, he thought, contemplating whether or not to return to his suite. He had a meeting with a Hollywood actor on Tuesday morning, and Markos didn't want to be ill-prepared. The Oscar winner wasn't just another client; he was also a friend, and Markos didn't want to let him down. Being a partner at LA Family Law was an honor, a goal he'd had since he started at the firm ten years earlier, but it wasn't enough. Markos had political aspirations, dreamed of being the next mayor of LA, and hoped to make it a reality during the next election.

His stomach groaned. The décor in the steakhouse was simple, nothing to write home about, but according to his siblings, the food was outstanding. Markos was starving, hadn't eaten anything since arriving at the resort two hours earlier, but he'd rather eat alone in his suite than watch his brothers and cousins fawn all over their wives. He didn't want to be the third wheel, and feared he'd die of boredom sitting with the love-struck group playing kissy face—

Ducking out of the restaurant, before his family could see him, he strode down the walkway, noting the pop star seated on the patio signing autographs.

Hearing a voice full of warmth and life, Markos glanced over his shoulder, searching for the owner with the exuberant laugh. His gaze fell across the woman in the bold, colorful outfit, and his feet stopped. *Tatiyana.* She looked hot, good enough to eat, and Markos was starving. Hungry for her lips, desperate to taste every inch of her body. He liked everything about her appearance—the sleek ponytail, her crimson lips, her flirtatious, come-hither smile, how her dress skimmed her thighs—and couldn't tear his eyes away from her.

An idea came to him, the answer to his problem. He'd ask Tatiyana to be his dinner date. The executive secretary had "It," the wow factor, and arriving at the steak house with the leggy beauty on his arm was sure to not only turn heads, but also impress his family.

Markos tried to catch her eye, but Tatiyana was too busy chatting to notice him. Holding center court, surrounded by men in golf attire, it was obvious she was in her element. Which guy was her traveling buddy? Were they really just friends and nothing more?

In a stroke of good luck, Tatiyana waved at her admirers and sashayed off, switching her hips, her ponytail swishing back and forth. As she stepped past him, Markos reached out and caught her arm. Surprise, then anger darkened her features. Tatiyana gave him a blank stare, as if he was a stranger, and Markos released her hand. Four hours ago she was talking his ear off, and now she didn't know him? *What gives?* Markos didn't know what game Tatiyana was playing, but he didn't like it. Still, he didn't leave. He wanted the pleasure of her company tonight, and he wasn't returning to the restaurant without her. Markos wore a disarming smile, but Tatiyana seemed immune to his charms, regarding him with a narrowed gaze. "We meet again."

Tatiyana fluttered her eyelashes, her expression coy. "Markos, right?"

"It's wonderful to see you again. Great dress."

"Thanks," she said, doing a twirl.

"Where are you rushing off to?"

"To see you, of course."

Her innocent, wide-eyed expression made Markos laugh. She smelled of roses and tropical fruit, and her sweet, heady fragrance tickled his nostrils. The blood drained from his head, shot to his groin, and his erection stabbed the zipper of his white slacks. Sex was his favorite pastime, the only activity ever worth skipping dinner for, and Markos craved Tatiyana, had to have her. She oozed sexuality, reeked of confidence, and Markos suspected she'd be a passionate lover.

"What are you up to tonight?" she asked, cocking her head to the right.

"I'm about to have dinner with my family. Care to join me?"

"Only if you agree to be my date for the R&B Summer Jam. My friends canceled on me at the last minute, so I'm on my own this weekend, and I don't want to go to Applause Nightclub alone."

"I have paperwork to do, and besides I'm too old for rap concerts."

Her eyes dimmed, but she spoke in a cheery tone. "No worries. I'll find someone else to take me. Have fun with your family, Markos."

Tatiyana stepped past him, and Markos captured her forearm, drawing her to his side. "Deal," he said. "Have dinner with me, and I'll take you to the concert tonight."

"I thought you'd come around."

"You drive a hard bargain, Ms. Washington."

All smiles, her eyes beguiling and bright, she coiled an

arm through his. *"Sono contento che ci siamo incontrati, e sarei onorato di avere la cena con la famiglia."*

I'm glad we met, and I'd be honored to have dinner with your family. Pleased by her words, he stared into her eyes, gauging whether or not she was telling the truth. Enraptured by the sound of her voice, he moved closer to her, brushing his lips against the curve of her ear. "You speak Italian. I'm impressed. What other secrets are you hiding?"

"There are a lot of things I can do. I'm a woman of extraordinaire talents—"

"I look forward to discovering them all."

"Patience," she replied with a wink. "Dinner first, *then* dessert."

"How long have you two been dating?"

Markos choked on the cocktail shrimp in his mouth. It hurt to breathe, and a burning sensation flowed through his chest. Glancing up from his plate, he shot Emilio a questioning look, hoping his expression conveyed his annoyance. Arriving at the table ten minutes earlier, he'd introduced Tatiyana to his family as a "friend" and jokingly asked them not to scare her off, so why were Emilio and Immanuel giving her the third degree? Why couldn't they be kind and welcoming like his cousins and their wives? Before Markos could respond, Tatiyana spoke up, shocking him and everyone else at their corner table.

"Not long, but the first time I saw Markos I knew he was the one..."

Tatiyana covered his hands with her own, sending heat surging through his body.

"I love sensitive, romantic men, and your brother's quite the charmer. And hot, too, right ladies?"

The women cheered, the men chuckled and Markos smiled so wide his jaw ached. He couldn't have asked for a better dinner companion. None of the women he knew could hold a candle to Tatiyana, and he was glad to have her at his side.

"Where's Dante?" Rafael asked, popping an oyster into his mouth. "I spoke to him on Sunday, and he said you guys were traveling together, so I expected to see him tonight."

Finishing his appetizer, Markos took a swig of his soda and set aside his empty plate. "He changed his mind. Jordana's parents are in town, and he wants to spend time with them."

"I'm confused. I thought Dante was single." Sharleen Nicholas, Emilio's wife, wore a puzzled expression on her face. "Who's Jordana?"

"His temporary wife," Emilio explained. "He married her in a courthouse ceremony back in June, in the hopes of winning full custody of Matteo, and it worked."

Markos shook his head. "Jordana's not his temporary wife. She's his soul mate."

A hush fell over the table as Markos spoke. He assured his family members the aspiring actress was a thoughtful, compassionate woman, not a gold digger with dollar signs in her eyes. "I had dinner with them last week, and it's obvious they're in love. They couldn't keep their hands off each other, finished each other's sentences and Jordana laughed at all of Dante's jokes, even the corny ones." Markos chuckled, recalling how much fun he'd had with the couple. "Dante quit his job at the Brokerage Group so he could be a better father and husband, and I think that's commendable."

Nicco whistled. "You're right. It is."

"I'm happy for him," Immanuel said, reaching for his water glass. "He's been interested in Jordana for months, and Matteo adores her, too."

Markos agreed. "You're right, he does, and Matteo's not the only one. Lourdes likes her a lot, and credits Jordana with helping her finally get clean. If Jordana gets her way, and I'm confident she will, they'll be one, big, happy family in no time."

"That's great," Rafael replied. "I'll call Dante later to congratulate him."

The waitstaff arrived, carrying silver trays topped with entrées, drinks and cocktails. Over dinner, they discussed the charity golf tournament that had brought them to town, and the celebrities the women were excited to meet. He wasn't interested in the conversation; he was interested in Tatiyana. She fit in well with his family, and every time she cracked up, he did, too.

"I can't believe I'm having dinner with a baseball star, a celebrated news anchor, a race car legend and the owner of my favorite Italian restaurant. What a treat! Someone pinch me!"

Everyone laughed, and Markos knew inviting her to dinner had been a wise move.

"Tatiyana, what do you do for a living?" Jariah Morretti, Nicco's wife, dabbed at her mouth with a napkin. "You must be in the entertainment industry because you're a firecracker."

"I wish! I'm not a star, but I love reality TV."

"Me, too!" Sharleen eagerly nodded. "Did you see the season finale of *Dating in the City* last night? I almost died when Nelson Hamilton dumped Penelope at her sister's wedding. Twenty-four hours later, and I'm *still* pissed…"

The men groaned, objecting loudly to the topic, but Paris silenced them with a menacing look. "Don't make fun. Dating's changed drastically in the last ten years, and if not for smart, thought-provoking reality shows like, *The Love Test*, and *Relationships 101*, my friends and I would still be in the dark about men."

Everyone spoke at once, but Rafael's voice cut through the noise.

"Baby, that's ridiculous," he argued, draping an arm around his wife's shoulders. "You don't need a television show to learn about men. Just ask me. I'm the only man you need."

Giggling, Paris cupped her husband's face in her hands and gave him a peck on the lips.

The waitstaff returned, carrying several bottles of champagne, and Tatiyana dropped her utensils on her gold plate. "Champagne? You're my kind of people!"

"What are we celebrating?" Markos asked, settling back into his arm chair.

Sharleen beamed. "Emilio's ESPN Athlete of the Year award."

"Another one? That's the third award of your career." Markos gave his brother a one-arm hug, then ruffled his hair. "I'm proud of you, little bro. Good job."

Clasping Sharleen's hand, Emilio raised it to his mouth and kissed it. "Baby, you deserve this award as much as I do, if not more," he said quietly. "If not for you, I'd still be sitting in my living room, watching home videos of Lucca, drowning in grief and despair."

"As usual, you're giving me *way* too much credit. You're the talent, baby, not me."

"Sharleen, could you be a little less supportive?" Angela wore a sheepish expression on her face. "I want my man to win that coveted award, too, but Emilio's impossible to beat."

"Keep hope alive, sister-in-law! There's always next year."

Laughing, Dionne Fontaine-Morretti, Immanuel's wife, filled each flute to the brim. The couple had eloped to Hawaii two weeks earlier, shocking their friends and family, and Tatiyana had enjoyed hearing about their wild, romantic weekend in Maui.

"To Emilio!" Nicco raised his glass in the air. "May this award catapult you to greater heights, and cement your place in Formula One history. *Saluti!*"

Cheering, everyone around the table clinked glasses.

"What do you guys want to do now?" Angela asked.

"I've had a rough week at the news station, and if anyone deserves to party tonight it's me."

"Let's go to the sports bar," Immanuel proposed, checking the time on his gold wristwatch. "The World Rugby Championship is on, and I don't want to miss it."

"Bor-ing," the women sang in unison.

"Markos, are you ready to go?" Tatiyana asked, tucking her purse under her forearm.

Dionne frowned. "Why are you whispering, and where are you guys sneaking off to?"

"Applause Nightclub," she explained. "It's old-school night, and all of my favorite acts are performing, including Divas."

Angela whooped for joy. "Count me in!"

"Me, too." Jariah slipped on her Pashmina shawl and hopped to her feet. "I'm game."

"I'm going!" Dionne said. "I love R&B music, and I'm the biggest Divas fan ever."

Immanuel kissed her forehead. "Then it's settled. We're going to the concert."

Markos was convinced his ears were deceiving him. His brother, a security specialist with a stellar résumé, who they jokingly called Sharpshooter, wouldn't be caught dead in a noisy, smoky club. Immanuel didn't dance, preferred classical music to hip-hop and often joked he'd been born in the wrong decade. Leaning toward his brother, he kept his voice low, asking, "What happened to the rugby match? I thought you wanted to cheer on the Italian team."

"It's no biggie. I'll catch the highlights when we get back tonight."

"But you hate nightclubs," Markos pointed out, confused by his brother's behavior.

"I know," Immanuel conceded with a shrug, his gaze glued to his wife, love shining in his eyes. "But what my baby wants, my baby gets, so let's bounce."

Chapter 4

"Ma'am, I'm sorry, but the club's full," the bouncer said, folding his arms rigidly across his flabby chest. "Better luck next time."

Tatiyana cringed. It was a dig, an insult meant to embarrass her in front of the chic, crowd waiting outside Applause Nightclub, located in the Ybor entertainment district. Behind her, she heard people snicker. *Ma'am?* The word annoyed her, and the sneer on the bouncer's face confirmed her suspicions. He *was* trying to humiliate her.

"I'm calling Rafael to tell him what's going on," Paris said, putting her iPhone to her ear.

Jariah protested. "No, don't. We can handle this. We're Morrettis now, remember?"

"Exactly!" Angela agreed, fervently nodding. "We've got this. We don't need the guys to rescue us. We can take care of ourselves."

At her request, the guys had dropped them off in front of the club so they could reserve a VIP room, but if Tatiyana knew the bouncer was going to give them a hard time, she would have stuck with the guys. No way he'd insult Markos and his famous family members.

Tatiyana could hear reggae music playing inside the club, a loud, infectious beat that made her want to dance, and wanted inside the hottest party in Tampa. She knew Divas were going to put on one hell of a show for their fans, and, since Tatiyana was determined to see the group perform live, she stepped forward and glared at the heavyset bouncer. "I flew thousands of miles to see—"

"Ma'am, come back tomorrow night. Women get in free until midnight."

Tatiyana gestured to the scantily dressed women sailing past the red, velvet rope. "If the club's full, then where are *they* going?"

"That's none of your business—"

"I wish I had my iPhone," Tatiyana grumbled, mad at herself for forgetting it inside the Escalade Markos had rented for the weekend. It seated seven, and on the drive to the club the group had chatted about their vacation plans, their favorite spots in Tampa and laughed at Nicco's wild, outrageous stories about his bachelor days. It was hard for Tatiyana to enjoy herself. With each passing minute, her guilt intensified. "If I had my cell with me, I'd tweet about how the bouncers at Applause Nightclub disrespect women."

Dionne stepped forward. "This is ridiculous. I want to speak to the manager."

The bouncer turned away, ignoring them, and Tatiyana jabbed an index finger in his shoulder. "We're not leaving until you get the owner."

A slim man with greasy hair and aviators emerged from the club, clutching a bottle of Cristal. Speaking to the bouncer in Spanish, he winked and nodded.

"Are you the owner?" Tatiyana asked, raising her voice to catch his attention. Spotting Markos jogging across the street with the guys, she governed her temper. Tatiyana didn't want him to think she was a hothead, didn't want to do anything to ruin their date, and swallowed the insult on the tip of her tongue. The Morretti family was respected and admired, and Tatiyana didn't want to embarrass her companions. Once again, warning bells rang in her mind. Tatiyana had doubts about seducing Markos. She couldn't quiet her fears and struggled with what to do. Maybe she shouldn't go through with it. Maybe she should come clean to Markos, tell him everything.

Tatiyana struck the idea from her mind. *My mom already did that*, she thought with a heavy heart. *And Markos didn't believe her. He called her a liar, said Jantel was an op-*

portunist trying to ruin the mayor's reputation, and kicked them out of his office. No, she had to stick to her plan. No matter what.

"Ladies," the owner said in a soothing voice. "I understand you're upset, but there's nothing I can do. It's packed inside, and if I let you in I could get fined for overpopulating the club. Come back tomorrow. You'll be my personal guests."

Tatiyana started to argue, to tell the owner his bouncers were sexist jerks who disrespected women, but a cheer went up from the crowd, seizing her attention, and she broke off speaking. Demetri appeared at her right side and Emilio at the other.

"Is there a problem here?" Rafael asked.

Whooping for joy, his eyes big and wide, the owner pumped a fist in the air. "Demetri and Emilio Morretti? Here, at Applause Nightclub? This must be my lucky day!" Standing tall, he adjusted his peacock-blue tie. "Right this way. The VIP room is available, and—"

Angela interrupted him. "You said the club was full."

"I was kidding," he said with a hearty laugh, dismissing her words with a wave of his hand. "There's plenty of room inside for my favorite baseball player and his family. Now, please follow me to the private entrance at the rear of the club."

Markos clasped Tatiyana's hand. One whiff of his cologne made her thoughts scatter and her skin tingle. He had more game than a basketball player and the lean, toned physique to match. It was no surprise other women were staring at him, too. But he was with her, had his hands draped possessively around her waist, as if staking his claim.

Tatiyana smoothed a hand over her hair and adjusted her dress. Markos caressed her skin, told her repeatedly how beautiful she looked. He spoke in a deep, manly voice, intended to seduce, and it worked. Tatiyana wanted him so bad all she could think about was kissing him.

Wearing a triumphant smirk, Tatiyana stepped past the bouncer and followed the group through the gold door at the rear of the nightclub, anxious to get Markos alone.

"I'm ready for dessert. Are you?" he whispered, sweeping his mouth over her ear.

His words gave her pause. *Hold on.* Who's *seducing who*?

A baby-faced brunette in a white jumpsuit led them to the second floor, into a glass room with mirror balls hanging from the ceiling, velvet couches and mauve walls covered with framed paintings. The savory scent in the air tickled Tatiyana's nose and stirred her appetite. Silver trays topped with fruit, bite-size chocolates and cheese covered the marble tables, and ice buckets, filled with champagne, sat on the bar. It was an intimate, comfortable setting, and Tatiyana was impressed.

"Welcome to Applause Nightclub," a server said, tipping his head in greeting. "You have the entire floor to yourselves, so relax and enjoy the Champagne Room."

Angela plucked a chocolate off one of the trays. "Thank you. We will!"

"Can I interest anyone in a drink?"

While the server took orders, Tatiyana admired the décor. From the second floor, she had an overhead view of the club, and the dazzling light show, dance cages and swings made Tatiyana think of the Malibu nightclub she'd worked at to put herself through college. It seemed like just yesterday she was waiting tables and cramming for midterms, but it had been years since she was a student, and her life had changed drastically since graduation.

"Let's grab a seat," Markos said, gesturing to the couch. "I want to hear more about—"

"Come dance with me," Tatiyana said, swaying her hips to the beat of the music. She tried to convince Markos to dance but he stayed seated, watching her instead. One dance turned into another, and by the time Divas hit the stage an hour later, Tatiyana was out of breath.

The crowd went wild, cheering, screaming, waving fluorescent glow sticks in the air. Tatiyana hadn't been out dancing in months, and it felt good to cut lose with the Morretti family.

Markos was sitting on the couch, watching her, and when he smiled, her confidence soared. It was just a matter of time before they made love, and Tatiyana couldn't wait. Was he a good lover? Generous and passionate, or a man who'd put his needs above her own?

Hoping it wasn't the latter, Tatiyana picked up her cocktail glass from the bar and sat down beside Markos on the couch. "What a night!" she said, struggling to catch her breath. "Are you having fun?"

"Of course I am. You're very entertaining, and I'm enjoying the show. So, what do you do when you're not dancing at nightclubs?"

Giggling, she playfully pushed his shoulder, marveling at how well they got along. Less than twenty-four hours after meeting, and they were laughing and joking as if they were lifelong friends. "What do *you* do when you're not charming women on airplanes?"

"I hit the gym, play golf, travel and attend sporting events. And you?"

"I enjoy cooking, dancing, and making love—"

"We're going downstairs to take pictures with the performers. Want to come?" Jariah asked.

With her eyes glued to Markos, Tatiyana answered Jariah's question. "No, I'm good." Her voice sounded airy and breathless, as if she'd just finished an aerobics class. Tatiyana wanted to take his hands and use them to stroke her body, but since she didn't want to turn him off by making the first move, she sat tight. "My horoscope was totally on point today. It said I would meet someone special, and here you are."

"I'm the lucky one," he said, gesturing around the VIP

room with his drink. "Thanks to you, my family members are having the time of their lives."

Out of the corner of her eye, she spotted Immanuel and Dionne kissing at the back of the room. They were a playful, loving couple, and it was obvious the security specialist was smitten with the life coach. Like his brother and cousins, he was completely devoted to his wife. Tatiyana was impressed, couldn't believe how affectionate the Morretti men were. They wanted the world to know they were spoken for, and didn't shy away from expressing their feelings.

Locking eyes with him, Tatiyana slowly and suggestively licked her lips, hoping to convey her need. His gaze was so intense, so powerful she forgot what they were talking about. Flirting with Markos was a turn-on, giving her a rush, and Tatiyana was dying to kiss him.

"Bro, whose team are you playing on tomorrow?" Immanuel asked. "It better be mine, or I'll disown you."

Markos waved. "Fine, Immanuel, it's been fun knowing you. Deuces!"

Everyone laughed, including the waitstaff and suit-clad bartenders.

A couple more glasses of champagne and Markos was a different person—playful, laidback, at ease. It was obvious he enjoyed spending time with his family, and listening to him crack jokes with his brothers made Tatiyana think of Jantel. They used to be best friends, incredibly close, but these days all her sister did was lay in bed staring at the walls. Since the mayor's bachelor party, Jantel had been sad and withdrawn, a shadow of her former self. Worst of all, she ignored Allie, barely gave her daughter a passing glance. Mayor Glover was to blame for her sister's depression, and Tatiyana was going to ensure he did the right thing.

"Do you want to have lunch tomorrow before the tournament starts…" Trailing off, Markos took his cell phone out of his pocket and glanced at the screen. "I have to take this call. I'll be right back."

He strode out of the room with his iPhone glued to his ear. Tatiyana wondered if he was talking to one of his girl-friends. Why else would he abruptly end their conversation and leave the room? She'd done her research and knew Markos was dating a bevy of beauties. A surgeon, an engineer, a publicist and even a drama teacher. They were all talented and accomplished, the kind of women any man would be proud to take home to mom, so why was Markos still single? Why wasn't he happily married like his brothers and cousins? His dating history was none of her business, but Tatiyana was curious about him.

"Tatiyana, join us," Paris said, waving her over to the bar.

Finishing her cocktail, she danced with the group for several songs, but her thoughts were on Markos. Staring at her watch, Tatiyana was shocked to see he'd been gone for fifteen minutes. Who was he talking to? Was he coming back?

Tatiyana exited the room in search of her date. Heading down the corridor, she spotted a security guard and nodded in greeting. Hearing Markos's voice inside the bathroom, Tatiyana sighed in relief. "I want to be alone with my boyfriend," she said, opening her purse. "Make sure no one disturbs us."

"Of course, Miss. Not a problem."

Tatiyana took out a fifty-dollar bill and stuffed it into his shirt pocket. "Thanks!"

"Take as long as you need."

I plan to, she thought, feeling a rush of excitement.

Designed with style and comfort in mind, the bathroom had soaring ceilings, antiqued mirrors and plush armchairs. Vases overflowed with colored roses and scented candles perfumed the air, putting Tatiyana in a tranquil mood.

In the anteroom, she found Markos sitting on the chaise lounge, his head bent, singing in Italian.

Twinkle, Twinkle, Little Star, Come mi chiedo che cosa sei.

What in the world? Before Tatiyana could make sense of what was going on, Markos ended his phone call. Shaking his head wistfully, as if he couldn't believe what he'd just done, he laughed to himself.

"Important call?" she asked.

Markos looked at her, surprise evident in his eyes, but his tone was full of warmth. "Yeah, it was my four-year-old nephew. Matteo calls me every night at bedtime, and if I don't answer, he won't go to sleep. He's my little buddy, and I love our evening talks."

Her heart melted. "Markos, I'm impressed. You sing beautifully," she said, meaning every word. "What other talents do you have?"

Hours earlier, outside the steak house, he'd posed the same question to her, and now it was payback. Teasing him made her feel giddy inside, like a kid on Christmas Day.

"I'm a man of extraordinaire talents," he joked, stealing her line.

"And I look forward to discovering each and every one of them."

"Why wait? Now's a good time."

Enraptured by the sound of his voice, Tatiyana couldn't think, let alone move.

"Come here," he demanded. "I want you."

"I want you, too—"

"Then why are you standing so far away?"

He seized her hand, drawing her in between his legs, and Tatiyana sank onto his lap. His touch thrilled her, making her feel alive, and his husky voice tickled and teased her ears.

"You look like you want to kiss me. Go ahead."

Before she could, his lips claimed her mouth. They were soft, felt warm against hers, and sent tingles careening down her spine. His kiss was full of hunger, longing and passion, and Tatiyana wanted more.

Boldly possessing her mouth, Markos used his tongue to excite her, to show her what she'd been missing all her life. *Wow, no one's ever kissed me like* that, Tatiyana thought, as they feasted on each other's lips. Markos licked them, and sucked them. They were in public, making out in the VIP bathroom, but Markos wasn't in a rush. He took his time kissing her, stroking her body, didn't seem to care that someone could walk in on them at any minute.

"I wish I had protection..." he said between kisses.

Grabbing her purse, she stuck a hand inside and pulled out some condoms. "What flavor do you want?" she asked, waving them under his nose. "Strawberry, mint or chocolate?"

His jaw dropped, and Tatiyana smirked. She enjoyed shocking people, got off on making men blush—especially dignified men like Markos—and kissed him hard on the lips to prove how much she desired him. "I'm glad we met," she said between kisses. "I haven't had this much fun since I went to Coachella with my girlfriends last year."

"Do you believe in love at first sight—"

"No, that's a fallacy," she argued, interrupting him. Markos was getting ahead of himself, and she had to be the voice of reason. "Love takes time, commitment and trust. It doesn't happen in the blink of an eye. I believe in lust at first sight, though. Now, that's real."

"Care to elaborate?"

Tatiyana met his gaze, challenging him to disagree with her. "The moment I saw you I *knew* I was going to have you. And I will."

Chapter 5

Mischief gleamed in Markos's deep brown eyes, and an amused expression warmed his face. Tatiyana could feel her temperature rising, the electricity pulsing between them as their stares locked. Aroused, she kissed him with every ounce of passion in her body.

Taking his hands, she guided them to her breasts, urging them to explore. Markos was every woman's dream man, and Tatiyana desired him more than she'd ever desired anyone.

"I admire your fearless attitude."

His words filled her with pride. "You do?"

"You always say exactly what's on your mind, and I find it refreshing."

"That's the only way to live."

Markos brushed his fingers against her cheek, tenderly caressing it. He wore a thoughtful expression on his face, and spoke in a whisper. "*Dannazione*," he murmured, his tone thick with desire. "You're so beautiful I can't stop staring at you…"

Her breath caught in her throat. His deep, husky voice made her skin tingle and her panties wet. At the thought of them making love, her heartbeat quickened. Tatiyana dated often, but she hadn't had sex in months, and was ready for her sexual drought to finally come to an end.

"Are you sure you want to do this?"

Tatiyana was torn between doing the right thing, and *doing* Markos but she silenced her doubts. Straddling him, she draped her hands around his neck, pulling him close. "Yes, of course, why not?"

"Because we're in a public washroom—"

"Yeah, a washroom fit for a king and queen," she quipped,

gesturing at their luxurious surroundings. "Hell, this room is nicer than my first apartment."

Tatiyana laughed, and Markos kissed her, trapping the sound inside her mouth. She closed her eyes, sealing her in the moment as he ravished her with his lips.

Running her hands over his torso, she whispered naughty words in his ears, confessing how much she wanted him. Her desire for Markos was overwhelming, an all-consuming need she couldn't control. Every nerve ending in her body stirred, throbbed and tingled as their tongues mated. She reveled in his kiss, the joy of his touch, of being in his arms. His caress was sensational, and Tatiyana wanted more, everything he had to offer.

Markos buried his face in her cleavage, making circles across her chest with his tongue, nipping at her skin with his teeth. He cupped her breasts, tweaking and rubbing her nipples. Goose bumps tickled her flesh, warming her body all over. This was what Tatiyana wanted, what she needed—Markos, the only man she wanted to make love to.

"Someone could catch us."

"Not tonight," she said with a cheeky grin. "I paid the security guard to be our lookout."

"You've thought of everything, haven't you?"

"Of course. An opportunity is a terrible thing to waste."

They kissed over and over again, until Tatiyana couldn't think straight. His tongue explored her mouth, seeking, teasing, and pleasing. He slipped a hand between her legs, pulled her panties aside and squeezed her bottom.

Heat singed her skin. Nibbling on her earlobe, he slid a finger inside her sex, swirling it around in circles. He was having his way with her, and she was weak for him. Desperate. Unzipping his pants, she freed his erection from his boxer briefs, boldly seized it in her hands. At the sight of his length, her temperature rose. Watching Markos put on a condom, she hungrily licked her lips. Tatiyana wanted to taste him, to take him inside her mouth, but there was no time. Markos thrust inside her, powerfully, urgently, stealing her breath. His length filled her, electrifying her body. She loved what he was doing with his mouth, how his hands stroked her flesh, and the sound of his voice in her ears.

"Sei una stuzzicante bellezza," he whispered between kisses.

Pride filled her heart as he showered her with compliments and praise.

"Stunning sia dentro che fuori, e ti desidero in ogni senso della parola..."

His words played in her mind, giving her a rush. *You're a tantalizing beauty. Stunning both inside and out, and I desire you in every sense of the word. More than I've ever desired anyone.* Was he telling the truth? Tatiyana told herself it didn't matter. It wasn't important. They were making love, living in the moment, and she was going to enjoy every minute of it.

They were a perfect fit, moving together as one, holding nothing back, and it was a thrilling, exhilarating ride. Panting, she hiked her legs up on the couch to deepen his penetration. Gripping his shoulders, she rocked against him, moving to an inaudible beat. *Is this actually happening? Am I having sex with Markos or is this a wonderful, erotic dream?*

"Tatiyana, stai girando me out."

I'm turning you out? More like the other way around!

Markos rubbed her bottom, squeezed and stroked it. Moans fell from her mouth, bouncing off the ceiling and ricocheting around the walls. Tatiyana clamped her lips together to smother the sound, but Markos drew his teeth along her skin, and she yelped.

"Baby, I'm sorry. I didn't mean to hurt you."

"You didn't." Tatiyana smiled to assure him everything was okay. The more they touched and teased and played, the giddier Tatiyana felt. This was a dream, the most exhilarating moment of her life, and she'd never forget her thrilling, passionate night with the sexiest attorney alive. "I liked it, Markos, and I like you, too. You're a terrific guy."

Gazing at her, he brushed her hair away from her face. "I want more than one night with you."

"All we have is tonight."

His hands explored her body, tenderly stroking her skin.

"We live on opposite ends of the country," she reminded him. "It's just not worth it."

"I have access to a private plane—"

"I hate being tied down. I'm a modern, contemporary woman who enjoys her freedom."

"I thought you were looking for Mr. Right."

"I am, but in the meantime I'm doing what I want, when I want, and who I want."

The smile slid off his face. "You routinely have one-night stands in public places?"

"No, never, but you're irresistible." Seizing his hands, Tatiyana pinned them to the wall and rubbed her body against his. "Where were we?"

Markos exploded into laughter. *"La mia famiglia aveva ragione. Sei un petardo!"*

"You're right. I *am* a firecracker, and proud of it."

He plunged his erection between her thighs, thrusting with all his might. Needing more of him—all of him— Tatiyana opened her legs wide, inviting him deeper inside. Guilt snuck up on her, overwhelming her conscience and troubling her mind. They had a strong connection, and Markos was such a kind, sensitive man Tatiyana wished they had met under different circumstances. She'd traveled to Tampa to meet him, in the hopes he'd reconsider helping her kid sister. They were having such a good time together she was developing feelings for him. Feelings that could lead to heartbreak.

"You're sexy as hell," he whispered. "How did I get so lucky?"

Tatiyana shook off her thoughts and smiled at him. Seeing his enjoyment was a turn-on. She desired him even more, wanted to do everything in her power to please him sexually.

Hearing voices outside the bathroom, Tatiyana froze. She hoped the security guard was at his post, and listened intently for several seconds. Markos pressed a finger to her mouth, silencing her, and she swallowed the moan inside her mouth.

Markos didn't stop loving her, continued kissing her and caressing her flesh. The voices faded, and Tatiyana knew the security guard had effectively handled the situation. Sighing in relief, she made a mental note to give him another tip. "That was a close call."

"You have nothing to worry about." He spoke in a quiet tone, but his confidence shone through. "If someone barges in here, I'll whisk you away to safety."

"You sound like an English gent," she joked. "How noble of you."

"That's the Morretti way. It's my duty to protect the woman I'm with."

Tatiyana arched an eyebrow. "Even someone you've only known for a few hours?"

"It doesn't matter how long we've known each other. We're together, living in the moment, doing something we both obviously love, and that's all that matters."

"You are *such* a charmer."

"It's easy to be charming when I'm with you…"

Their eyes locked.

"I know we just met this morning, but there's something about you that speaks to me," he said, brushing her hair away from her face. "It's as if some unknown force is drawing me to you. It's so powerful I can't resist it. Can't resist you."

At a loss for words, she sat there, his explosive confession playing in her mind. Markos kissed her, swirling his tongue inside her mouth and his erection between her legs.

Tatiyana couldn't stop the orgasm that rocked her body. She was melting and exploding at the same time, shaking so hard she feared she was going to slide off his lap. In a trance, she couldn't think straight. Her vision blurred, and her heart was pounding, beating loud and fast. She couldn't speak, lost all sense of time and place.

Tingling from her ears to her toes, she pressed her eyes shut, riding out the delicious wave rising inside her. Tatiyana felt light, weightless, as if she were walking on air. She'd never experienced anything like it. Never had an orgasm so powerful it stole her breath. Collapsing on his chest, Tatiyana snuggled against him, basking in the afterglow of their lovemaking.

Looking drowsy, as if he was struggling to keep his eyes open, Markos wore a lopsided grin on his face. "That was hot."

"You can say that again."

"That was hot!"

They laughed, then shared another kiss.

"We better get back to the VIP room before your family comes looking for us."

"They won't. Did you see all the dirty dancing that was going on? I'll be surprised if they even noticed we were gone." Markos reached out, drawing his fingertips over her cheeks. "Spend the night with me."

Tatiyana blinked, couldn't believe what she was seeing and hearing. By all accounts Markos was a player, a man with a bevy of beautiful women at his beck and call, so the loving expression on his face, and his gentle tone threw her for a loop. Tongue-tied, her head spinning, she searched her mind for the right words to say. "I don't do sleepovers."

"Why not?"

"Because I don't want to confuse what this was. It was a quickie. Nothing more."

Sadness flickered in his eyes, but he spoke with bravado,

as if he couldn't care less. "Cool," he said, coughing into his fist. "No worries. I just thought I'd ask. No big deal."

But it was. His jovial mood disappeared, and Tatiyana felt like the biggest jerk on the planet. She'd hurt his feelings, and if she didn't do something to make amends, he'd probably never speak to her again, and she had big plans for them tomorrow night.

Way to go! You pissed him off. Good one!

"We should head back to the party. It's late, and I'm ready to return to the resort."

His anger was evident in his narrowed gaze and stiff posture. Standing, Markos discarded the condom, and washed his hands in the sink.

To get back in his good graces, Tatiyana said, "That was amazing. *You're* amazing. I hope we hook up again before you return to LA, because that was the best sex I've ever had, and I want more."

"You do?"

"Absolutely. I'm going to have fun getting to know you better."

Playing it cool, she adjusted her dress and fixed her ponytail. Tatiyana stood, but her legs were wobbly, making it impossible to walk. Scared her knees would give way, she braced her hands against the wall and waited for her limbs to quit shaking.

"Don't worry, baby, I got you."

Markos slid his hands around her waist, holding her tight. Gazing at him, she realized he was more than just a handsome face. He was a thoughtful, generous man, and it was obvious she'd misjudged him. He wasn't the monster her mother had made him out to be—he cared about others, and it was evident in everything he said and did. Still, she couldn't lose sight of her goals, of why she'd come to Tampa. It wasn't to make a love connection with Markos, it was to help her kid sister. Her family was depending on her, and she wouldn't let them down.

Chapter 6

On Saturday morning, Markos sat at the oak desk inside his executive suite willing his eyes to focus and his brain to work. At breakfast, he'd had three cups of strong, black coffee, but the drinks didn't give him the energy boost he needed.

Markos yawned. He couldn't go five minutes without nodding off, and felt tired and out of sorts. Three hours of sleep wasn't enough. If his cell phone alarm hadn't gone off at 9:00 a.m., he'd probably still be in bed dreaming about Tatiyana—his titillating one-night stand with the wicked sense of humor and delicious curves.

At the thought of her, a grin curled his lips. After their tryst, they'd returned to the VIP room and spent the rest of the night partying with his family. They liked her, and Markos did, too. They'd returned to the resort in the wee hours of the morning, high on life and each other. Against his better judgment, he'd invited Tatiyana to his room again for a nightcap. She'd declined, given him a peck on the lips, then disappeared inside her suite. He didn't like it, wanted to spend the night with her, but had respected her decision. They were playing in the golf tournament that afternoon, but Markos wanted to see her now. She'd blown his mind last night, put it on him so bad he couldn't stop thinking about her.

Markos turned on his laptop and flipped open his monthly planner. If he didn't finish his to-do list, he'd be swamped when he returned to LA, and he didn't want to have to work late on Monday night; he wanted to attend Matteo's soccer game. He loved his nephew and was looking forward to watching him play at Lincoln Park.

Waiting for his documents to load, he stretched his neck

from side to side, flexing and cracking his muscles. Enough sitting around. He had motions to write, and he didn't want to disappoint his clients—or himself. It was a challenge, but he put all thoughts of Tatiyana out of his mind and got down to work.

Two hours later, after several more cups of coffee, Markos had answered his emails, finished drafting a divorce settlement and had a brief video conference with Kassem. Having met while studying in college, Markos had known Kassem Glover for over a decade, and was proud of what his friend had accomplished. Kassem had offered to campaign on his behalf during the next election, and Markos appreciated his support. In his ten years of practicing law, he'd been called everything from a liar to a snake in an Armani suit, but he let the insults roll off his back. His clients appreciated his hard work and dedication, had promised to support his political endeavors and that was all that mattered.

Needing a break, Markos picked up his cell phone and reclined in his leather chair, crossing his legs at the ankles. He had ten new text messages from the surgeon. What did she want now? Caroline Walsh was the type of woman his father would like him to marry—educated, successful, born into a wealthy family—but she was an opportunist who was more interested in attending movie premiers than getting to know him as a person. They saw each other a couple times a month, and that suited Markos just fine. Caroline talked endlessly about her patients, droned on and on about the latest fashion trends, and the last time they'd had dinner he'd left the restaurant with a splitting headache.

As Markos scrolled through his text messages his iPhone rang, and he put it to his ear. "Morning," he greeted, turning off his computer. "How are you?"

"Terrible. I miss you. When will you be back in LA?"

Convinced he'd misheard her, he stared down at his cell. "You miss me?"

"Baby, of course I do. It feels like you've been gone forever."

"It's been two days."

"I wish you were here," she replied. "I hate when we're apart. It's torture."

"You never missed me when you traveled to South America in March with your girlfriends," he pointed out. "You were gone for a month, but you never called. Not even once."

"We weren't a couple then."

Markos choked on his tongue. "We're a couple now?"

"Yes, silly!" She giggled as if he'd made a funny joke, but sobered quickly. "I'm just calling to remind you to get tickets for the Governor's Masquerade Ball in October. They're selling like hotcakes, and I don't want us to miss the biggest social event of the year."

"I already have tickets. The governor gave them to me the last time we played golf."

"Perfect! Now, all I need is a dress and I'm good to go."

Why? He took a swig of his lukewarm coffee. *You're not my date.*

"I have my eye on a lace Valentino gown, but I can't find it anywhere," she complained. "I think a trip to New York is in order. Three or four days should suffice."

"Have fun."

"What do you mean, 'have fun'? We're going together."

"No, we're not. I have to work, and furthermore we're not a couple. We're just friends."

"But I want to go to the Governor's Masquerade Ball with you!" she protested, shouting her words.

Of course you do. You're addicted to the limelight and you'll do anything to rub shoulders with my A-list friends and clients. "I have to go. We'll talk soon."

"Markos, wait, I love you!"

He laughed out loud, couldn't believe Caroline thought

she could fool him. "You don't love me. You love my wealth and status—"

Caroline gave a shaky laugh. "That's ridiculous. I adore you. You know that."

"Okay, humor me," he said, deciding to put her to the test. "What's my favorite drink?"

"Ahhh...water?"

"No. Rum and Coke." The phone on the end table rang, but Markos ignored it. He wanted to know if Caroline was as self-absorbed as he thought she was, and he wasn't letting her off the hook until she answered his questions. "What's my nephew's name?"

"Mason!"

"Wrong again. Matteo." Annoyed, Markos shook his head. "Where was I born?"

"I know! Somewhere in Italy."

"We've known each other for over a year, but you still know nothing about me."

"That's a lie. I do," Caroline argued, speaking in a confident tone. "You're a partner at one of the most prestigious law firms in the state, you have vacation homes in Ibiza, Saint Tropez and Palm Springs, and you have an impressive sports car collection as well."

Yeah, but none of those things matter. Material things don't mean shit to me.

"We're going to the Governor's Masquerade Ball together," she insisted. "Everyone's expecting us to be there, and as my man, you have to ensure I look my best. We're going to New York next weekend so I can get the perfect gown, shoes and jewelry."

"I can't drop everything to take you shopping out east. I'm an attorney, Caroline, not a stylist or a human ATM."

"Do you want to be my boyfriend or not?" she snapped, her tone thick with anger.

"Not." Ending the call, he tossed his cell phone into his briefcase. His stomach grumbled, reminding him he needed to eat, and he rose to his feet. Markos was starving, hankering for a steak burger from the resort sports bar, but first he needed to shower.

A sharp knock on the door drew his gaze across the room. It was probably Immanuel. His brother was an early riser, who exercised first thing in the morning, and Markos wouldn't be surprised if Dionne was at his side. These days, the couple went everywhere together and when they were apart, Immanuel looked lost, sadder than a kid who'd lost his lucky dollar.

Crossing the room, Markos noted how bright it was outside. The sun was shining, promising another gorgeous day in Cigar City, and a fragrant aroma wafted into the suite through the open windows. He opened the door, expecting to see his brother, but his gaze landed on Tatiyana. She was clad in a floral hair scarf, purple bikini top and a white, flouncy skirt, and he couldn't take his eyes off her. Her big, beautiful breasts were spilling out of her flimsy top, tempting him. Markos pictured himself burying his face in her décolletage, could almost taste her nipples inside his mouth, and swallowed hard.

"Hey, you!" she said with a radiant smile. "I brought lunch…"

At the sound of her cheery voice, Markos broke free of his explicit thoughts. Tearing his gaze away from her cleavage, he noticed the food cart in front of her. A sweet, piquant aroma tickled his nose, and Markos licked his lips. *Forget lunch*, he thought, his hungry gaze sliding down Tatiyana's mouth-watering curves. *Let's start with dessert…*

"I apologize for dropping by unannounced, but I called your room several times with no luck. I figured you were hard at work and could probably use a break."

A group of bare-chested men in swim trunks approached, talking loudly, but conversation stopped when they spotted Tatiyana. They gawked at her, drooling all over themselves, but she paid them no mind and gave him her undivided attention.

"I hate eating alone. You have to keep me company."

Images of her naked body flashed in his mind, derailing his thoughts. Seconds passed before his head cleared, and he reunited with his voice. "I'd be honored. Nothing beats having lunch with a smart, captivating woman."

"Not even winning a huge court case?"

"Not even wining a huge court case," he repeated, speaking from the heart.

Stepping aside, he watched as Tatiyana strode into his suite, switching her hips.

"I wanted to thank you for last night, so I hijacked a room-service cart and here I am." Tatiyana lifted the covers off the entrées with a flourish. "I hope you like Chinese food because I brought wonton soup, sweet and sour pork, shrimp fried rice and spring rolls."

"Everything sounds delicious. Let's eat!"

Within minutes, the coffee table was covered with plates, utensils and alcohol from the minibar. Over lunch, Tatiyana entertained him with stories about her childhood, books she'd read and loved, and her volunteer work at the Los Angeles Women's Shelter.

Opening a bottle of wine, Tatiyana asked Markos about his educational and professional background. Markos loved his job, enjoyed talking shop and was impressed with her questions. She had an opinion about everything, wasn't afraid to speak her mind, and argued her point with the skill of a seasoned attorney.

"Markos, I agree with you. The United States is one of the best, if not the best country in the world to live in, but you're wrong about the situation in the inner city."

"I am? The way I see it, everyone in this country has the same opportunity to be successful if they apply themselves."

"Some people were born with the chips stacked against

them, and for whatever reason they just don't have the mental fortitude it requires to pull themselves out of the trenches."

"You did. You were born in a rough neighborhood, but you didn't succumb to the negative things in your environment. You rose above it."

A look of sadness touched her features. "But many of my friends and family members didn't, and seeing their struggles firsthand made me want to do more for my neighborhood," she explained, her voice thick with emotion. "After I receive my business degree, I hope to work in the nonprofit sector, advocating on behalf of the less fortunate, troubled youth, single mothers and the homeless community."

"That's admirable, Tatiyana. With your tenacity and ambition, I have a feeling you're going to take the nonprofit world by storm."

"That's the plan!"

Laughing, they clinked glasses.

"Did you always want to be a lawyer?"

"No. Growing up I wanted to be an emergency-room doctor, but after watching a friend give birth my freshman year at UCLA, I knew medicine wasn't for me."

"I don't know any guys who'd venture into the delivery room," Tatiyana said, her eyebrows raised, her tone filled with awe. "Your friend must have been very special to you."

Markos coughed to alleviate the lump in his throat, and the burning sensation inside his chest, but the pain remained. "Abigail was three months pregnant when we met, but I didn't care. She was a sweet girl and I wanted her to be happy, so when she asked me to be in the delivery room for the birth of her son, I agreed."

"How long did you guys date for?"

Markos answered with a shrug. "A couple years."

"What happened?"

Picking up his glass, he took a swig of his orange juice. Tatiyana pressed him for details, but he didn't elaborate.

Markos couldn't talk about his first love without sounding bitter, and he didn't want to ruin the mood by rehashing the past. It wouldn't change anything. His ex had chosen someone else and wasn't coming back, so why bother? Besides, he was having fun with Tatiyana, and he didn't want to drive her away by bad-mouthing his first love. "You ask a lot of questions."

"And you're skilled at evading them."

"We wanted different things out of life, but we remain good friends."

A scowl twisted her lips. "I don't believe you. You're lying."

"I'm lying?"

"Your body language gave you away. You're mad at her, why?"

"Because I cared about her, and she played me for a fool. Every time her son's father resurfaced, begging for a second chance, she'd pull away from me, and it was hurtful," he confessed. "I've never had a successful relationship, and I'm starting to think love isn't in the cards for me."

"That makes two of us, Markos. I know exactly how you feel. I suck at relationships, too."

"You do?" Surprised by her honesty, Markos leaned forward in his chair, eager to hear more. "Why did your last relationship end?"

Markos expected her to lie, to sugarcoat what happened with her ex, but she was open and honest about her failed relationship. He listened intently, found himself engrossed by her story, wondering how anyone in his right mind could dump her.

"Apparently, I'm not the marrying kind." She spoke with a smile, as if she didn't have a care in the world, but her gaze was filled with sadness. "My ex-boyfriend's family didn't think I was good enough for him, so after three years of dating we parted ways."

"Would you give him another chance if he begged you to come back?"

"And deal with his uptight parents and boogie sisters? Hell, no!"

Chuckling, Markos reached for a fortune cookie from the wicker basket and cracked it open. Tatiyana was something else. Passionate, and outrageously funny, she was one of the most interesting women he'd ever met, and he was enjoying her company immensely.

Reading his fortune, he was struck by two things: his name was on it, and Tatiyana was wearing a mischievous expression on her face. *Markos, you're the best lover I've ever had* it read. He didn't know if it was true, but his chest swelled with pride.

Curious how Tatiyana had pulled off the unexpected surprise, he picked up another fortune cookie, anxious to read the message within. *A thrilling experience is in your future.*

"What does it say? Go on, read it," she urged, her smile coy, her tone seductive.

Their eyes locked.

"Why don't you *show* me what it says?"

"With pleasure. I'd like nothing more."

Tossing down her napkin, Tatiyana came around the table and sat on his lap.

"I can't stop thinking about last night," he confessed, brushing his mouth against her ear.

"Me neither, Markos. That's why I'm here."

Untying her bikini top, he took off the flimsy material and tossed it aside. Markos closed his eyes and buried his face into her cleavage. He took her erect nipples into his mouth, eagerly sucking them, licking them, teasing them with his tongue. "Baby, I can't get enough of you. I want you *bad...*"

Tatiyana kissed him hard on the mouth, as if she was consumed with passion. He tasted fruit on her lips, hints of ginger and paprika. Markos liked the sweetness, the warmth of her skin and the urgency of her kiss. He was used to dating prim-and-proper types, women who did everything by the book, but Tatiyana was spontaneous and impulsive, and he enjoyed living in the moment with her.

"I love how I feel…" Giggling, she trailed off speaking. "I mean, I love how *you* feel."

"Maybe we shouldn't do this." Doubts troubled his mind. His parents had raised him to be a perfect gentleman, and he didn't want Tatiyana to think all he cared about was sex. "You've had a lot to drink, and I don't want to take advantage of you."

"Take advantage of me? Please do!" Her eyes were wild with desire, her tone breathless from his kiss. "I want you."

"You're sure you want to do this?"

"Absolutely," she said, kissing the corners of his lips. "Make love to me."

Standing, Markos shed his clothes. She fondled him, stroking him with her soft, delicate hands, and Markos loved it, couldn't imagine anything better than having sex with her.

Tatiyana pushed him down on the couch and lowered herself to the floor. Producing a condom, she sat between his legs and rolled it onto his long, stiff erection. She sucked him into her mouth, twirling and swirling her tongue around his length. Watching her, feeling her lips against his shaft was a turn-on, and Markos feared he was going to explode right out of the gate. Groans fell from his mouth, and his eyes rolled in the back of his head. *It doesn't get any better than this!* Untying her scarf, it fell to the floor and he dug his hands in her hair, playing in her dark, lush locks. Bold and aggressive, Tatiyana did things no one had ever done to him before. She licked him all over, turned him out with her erotic words, her juicy lips and her warm hands.

"Dannazione," he grunted, his teeth clenched. "I love making love to you…"

Tatiyana froze, staring up at him with a wide-eyed expression on her face.

The moment the words left his mouth, Markos regretted them. He'd let his emotions get the best of him, but to his relief Tatiyana laughed out loud. "Of course you do," she quipped, giggling. "I brought you lunch, and now I'm treating you to dessert."

Desperate for her, he pulled her to him, kissing her passionately, mating hungrily with her tongue. Stretching out on top of her, he entered her in one, quick thrust. "You're hot, tight and intoxicating," he murmured, hiking her legs up in the air. "Everything a man could want."

Being inside Tatiyana was incredible, better than winning a six-figure settlement, heaven on earth. Warmth rippled across his skin, sensations he'd never experienced before. His body responded enthusiastically to her kiss, her touch, his erection growing, swelling inside her.

"Slower, baby," she said, her plea a soft purr against his ears. "There's no need to rush. We have all day…all night… the rest of the weekend if you want."

"I love the sound of that."

Her tongue eagerly searched his mouth, teasing and pleasing him. He wrapped her up in his arms. The couch was too small for his six-foot-six frame, but her legs were clamped so tight around his waist Markos couldn't move.

Their lovemaking was everything he wanted it to be—wild, passionate and intense—and Markos didn't want it to end. Not until he'd had his fill of her. He loved the way she cursed, cried out and moaned, couldn't get enough of it. He'd had sex before, but he'd never been intimate with such a vocal, passionate woman. Tatiyana knew what she wanted, what she needed, and she wasn't afraid to ask. Her seductive moves aroused him, and her dirty talk was music to his ears, sexier than a Maxwell song.

"That's it baby, right there." Tatiyana bucked against

him, rocking and swiveling her hips, moans falling from her mouth. "Yes, yes, yes..."

They were in sync, one, completely tuned into each other. Her tightness, the feel of her pushed him over the edge. His muscles contracted and shivers stabbed his flesh. Panting, she thrust her pelvis against his erection, and all hell broke loose. Markos flipped her onto her stomach, clutched her hips and dove into her over and over again.

Shooting him a teasing smile over her shoulder, Tatiyana poked her butt in the air. *I don't know how much more of this I can take. I'm only human.* Markos groaned and grunted, couldn't stop himself from plunging even deeper inside her. Climaxing, he collapsed beside her and drew her into his arms. Markos didn't know what to say, had no words, needed a moment to catch his breath. He drew his fingers across her flesh, loving the feel of her skin. "That was—"

"Amazing," she panted, mopping the hair away from her face.

His cell phone rang, drawing his attention to the desk. Markos noted the time on the wall clock hanging above the entertainment unit and swallowed a curse. He wanted a beer, and a nap, but he'd have to wait until after the charity golf tournament. It had started thirty minutes ago, and if he left his brothers hanging, they'd be pissed.

Markos kissed Tatiyana, couldn't resist cupping her big, beautiful breasts in his hands, got off on squeezing and tweaking her nipples. "Let's take a shower," he proposed, pressing his mouth to the curve of her ear, tickling it with his tongue. "I'll clean you up."

Her face brightened. "I like the way you think."

"Anything else you like?"

"Come into the bathroom. I'll show you." Tatiyana sprung to her feet, her naked body glistening with sweat, and strode across the suite with the confidence of a runway model. Up on his feet, Markos went after her, eager for round two.

Chapter 7

Tatiyana tossed her hair over her shoulders, caught Markos watching her and returned his smile. He was a six-foot-six distraction with dreamy eyes and dimpled cheeks, and every time he looked at her, explicit images flashed in her mind. Their afternoon tryst was all she could think about. He'd had his way with her, sexed her in the shower and the bedroom, but it wasn't enough. Tatiyana wanted more. Needed more. There was nothing better than kissing him, loving him, and her desire for Markos was so strong that her body craved him.

Breaking free of her thoughts, Tatiyana grabbed her putter and approached the ninth hole. She had to nail this shot. Had to beat Markos. His opening drive had earned him thunderous applause from onlookers, and the attention of several Hollywood actresses playing in the tournament. Women with toothy smiles and perfect bodies were ogling him, and Tatiyana didn't like it. Not one bit. She didn't like sharing, wanted Markos all to herself, and hoped he wasn't romantically interested in any of his female admirers.

Standing aside the ball, her feet shoulder-width apart, Tatiyana loosely gripped the golf club, hoping to impress Markos with her golfing skills. On weekends, she often played with Daphne, and had developed a strong game over the years. Playing with the Morretti family was intense, but fun, and she was enjoying their company. Dionne, Angela and Paris were the most competitive and listening to them tease each other made her laugh out loud.

Taking a deep breath, she inhaled the crisp, refreshing fragrance of the great outdoors. The sky was crystal blue, gleaming with sunshine, and a warm breeze whistled through the trees. Tatiyana smelled pine, cypress, the unmistakable scent of barbecue and glanced at the nearby food cart. The Rashawn Bishop Charity Golf Tournament had celebrities, an open bar, a female DJ spinning the latest music tracks and world-renowned photographer Kenyon Blake and his reporter wife, Makayla, on hand to capture all of the festivities. The grounds were filled with golf enthusiasts of all ages, and the mood was loud and lively. Spectators screamed whenever a celebrity strode by, but Tatiyana didn't care who'd just arrived on the scene. She only had eyes for Markos.

"Great form, Tatiyana."

Her club slipped from her hands, but she caught it before it fell to the ground. "Quiet," she said, pressing a finger to her lips. "I'm trying to focus."

"My bad. I won't say another word. Do your thing."

He wore an apologetic smile, but Tatiyana wasn't fooled. Markos was trying to sabotage her shot, using praise and compliments to throw her off her game, but it wasn't going to work. "Nice try, Markos, but you can't rattle me. I've got this."

"Prove it."

"I will." Meeting his gaze, she tried not to laugh when he winked at her, pretending to be unfazed by his antics. It was hard to focus when he stared at her. It took every ounce of her self-control not to kiss him.

I can do this, she chanted inwardly, visualizing the ball falling into the hole. "Markos, take notes. I'm going to nail this shot, and you're going to *wish* you had game like me."

His brothers exploded in laughter, and the women cheered her on. "Show him, girl!"

Bending her knees, Tatiyana pushed her hips back and leaned forward, her feet pressed hard into the ground. She felt her quads tighten and knew she had the proper form. Clutching the club, she raised it above her head and swung with all her might. Her body tensed as she watched the ball sail through the air. Once the ball dropped onto the grass, it rolled down the slope, picking up speed as it sailed past the other balls—including Markos's—and fell into the hole.

Whistles and applauding filled the air, and Tatiyana whooped for joy.

"I told you I had game!"

"I can't believe it. A hole in one? That's crazy."

Tatiyana danced around Markos, shaking her hips like a trained belly dancer. "Who's the man?" she jeered, cupping a hand behind her ear. "Speak up, Markos, I can't hear you. That's right. It's me! *I'm* the wo-man!"

Chuckling good-naturedly, Markos pulled her into his arms. "Nice shot," he said, giving her a one-arm hug. "Where did you learn to play golf like that?"

Her good mood fizzled, as painful memories overwhelmed her. "My ex taught me. His family loved to golf, and he thought it was important for me to learn the game."

"Do you miss him?"

"No. We broke up a year ago, and now he's happily engaged to someone else. Someone his parents approve of." Tatiyana heard the bitterness in her voice, and cleared her throat. "We weren't meant to be."

Markos squeezed her shoulder. "Give it time. Things will get easier."

"I'm fine. Never been better." Projecting confidence, she stood tall and raised her chin. "I can't move forward if I'm always looking over my shoulder at the past, so I don't."

"Well said."

He winked at her, and the tension in the air receded. Tatiyana avoided talking about her ex. She got angry every time she thought about the years she'd wasted with him, but she felt safe with Markos and had opened up to him about her ex that afternoon during lunch. Being with Markos, getting to know him and the rest of his family, made Tatiyana feel low for befriending him. Guilt plagued her conscience, and when he smiled at her, Tatiyana wondered if she was doing the right thing.

"You've hit three big shots today. You know what that means, right?"

Tatiyana didn't have a clue and shook her head. "I have no idea."

"You're buying my drinks tonight. Golf rules."

"Sure, why not? It's the least I can do. I'm going to beat you *bad* Markos."

He consulted the scorecard. "I hate to burst your bubble, but there's still lots of golf to be played, and there's no way in hell I'm losing this match. I'll come out on top. I always do."

"I was on top earlier," she whispered with a knowing smile. "And you loved it."

Lust sparked in his eyes. "You're right. I did."

A golf cart, driven by a resort employee, stopped behind them. "All aboard."

"Let's walk. I want to stretch my legs, and I could use the exercise."

He smirked and jokingly said, "I might get a little jealous with all the looks coming your way."

What looks? she thought, perplexed by his words. Did he think he had any competition? *I want you, Markos. Only you. Isn't it obvious?*

"There's my favorite family in America. Welcome back to Tampa!"

Tatiyana turned, just in time to see Rashawn "The Glove" Bishop and his wife, Yasmin Ohaji-Bishop give the Morretti family hugs and kisses. With their striking good looks, and matching golf attire, the couple made an arresting pair, drawing the attention of everyone standing nearby, including A-listers.

"Thanks for coming," Yasmin said. "This means the world to us."

Markos rested a hand on Tatiyana's back and leaned in close. "Tatiyana, this is my friend, boxing legend Rashawn 'The Glove' Bishop and his wife, Yasmin—"

"No introductions necessary, Markos. I know who they are. Rashawn and Yasmin are Tampa royalty, and I've been a fan of 'The Glove' for years."

The boxer cocked an eyebrow. "What do *you* know about boxing?"

"I know you have one of the best right hooks in the game," she said, fervently nodding. "Not to mention two Olympic gold medals and one of the greatest records of all time."

"You told me!"

Everyone chuckled, and Tatiyana felt Markos tighten his hold on her waist, saw the proud expression on his face when he looked at her. "Rashawn, when's your next match?" Tatiyana asked. "It's been years since you creamed Sawyer 'Bulldog' Kane at MSG, and your fans are anxiously awaiting your next bout."

"I haven't officially retired, but I doubt I'll ever return to the ring." He stared at his wife with love and admiration in his eyes. "Yasmin, our three kids and The Rashawn Bishop Foundation keep me busy, and I've never been more content."

A reporter appeared, requesting an on-camera interview, and the couple obliged.

"How do you do it?" Markos asked.

"Do what?"

"Charm everyone you meet regardless of age and gender?"

A smirk curled her lips. "I'll never tell."

Strolling through the course, enjoying the peach Bellini she'd swiped from a waiter's tray, Tatiyana couldn't have asked for a better day. She was getting fresh air, exercise and spending time with Markos. He flirted with her, told dirty jokes in Italian and made her laugh until tears filled her eyes.

"I haven't had this much fun in years." Markos took her hand in his, and kissed her palm. "What do you like to do besides schooling people on the inner city, and playing golf?"

"Nothing too exciting. I hang out with my friends and family, go for long walks in my community, and play peekaboo with my niece. It's the highlight of my day! Her laugh makes everything better, and I can cuddle with her for hours."

"I feel the same way about Mateo. He's a terrific kid, and better company than most of my friends."

They walked and talked, but when Markos and his brothers set off to search for a missing ball in the pine trees, the women kept her company, filling her in on all of the Morretti family drama. "How did you meet your husbands?" Tatiyana asked, sipping her fruity, ice-cold drink.

"I did a series called, *Athletes Behaving Badly*, which featured Demetri, and he showed up at the TV station to confront me," Angela said with a sheepish smile.

Jariah took a putter out of her pink golf bag and inspected it. "Nicco hired me to be his assistant, and totally seduced me."

"Rafael and I have known each other for almost a decade. We were college sweethearts, but we lost touch after graduation. We reunited in Venice at my best friend's wedding, and now we have a great marriage, three adorable children and a fantastic life. He's the best thing that's ever happened to me, and—"

"Paris, she didn't ask for your life story," Angela quipped, giving her sister-in-law a shot in the ribs with her elbow. "Jeez, once you start talking about Rafael there's no stopping you."

Sharleen smirked. "She's not the only one, *Angela*. This morning at breakfast I asked you to pass the juice, and you went on and on about your romantic weekend in Belize last month."

"I can't help it," the reporter argued. "My husband's a sweet, sensitive soul with a chiseled body, and he's mine, all mine!"

Tatiyana cracked up. "You guys are hilarious. Hands down the funniest women I know."

"Good, you're having fun, so that means you'll keep in touch with us, right?"

"Of course, she will, Jariah. We're going to be in her wedding one day," Sharleen said.

"W-w-wedding?" Tatiyana choked on the word. "What wedding?"

Smirking, her eyes bright with interest, Paris leveled a finger at her. "Oh, don't play coy. You guys are a perfect match, and it won't be long before you guys are walking down the aisle. Girl, Morretti men are irresistible…"

Who are you tellin'? Every time Markos smiles at me I want to dive into his arms!

"And the more you resist his advances the more he'll pursue you," Dionne said with a wistful smile. "Take it from someone who knows. I had zero desire to get married again, but when Immanuel proposed on my birthday I screamed 'yes,' and I was so anxious to be his wife, we eloped to Hawaii."

"Ladies, you're getting *way* ahead of yourselves. Markos and I just met, and furthermore, I'm not the only woman in his life. In case you haven't noticed, your brother-in-law loves the ladies, and they love him, too."

Glancing around, as if she was about to spill family secrets and feared getting caught, Angela spoke in a whisper. "Tatiyana, you're right," she conceded. "Markos brings a different woman to every family function, but I've never seen him like this. Trust me, girl, he's totally into you."

Tatiyana closed her gaping mouth. "You think?"

Dumbfounded, they spoke at once, their voices loud and adamant.

"Woman, open your eyes!"

"Of course he's into you! You're exactly his type. Smart, witty and gorgeous!"

"Markos can't take his eyes off you. If that isn't love, I don't know what is."

"Love?" Shaking her head, Tatiyana dismissed their

words, refusing to believe that Markos had true feelings for her after spending only one day together. "That's impossible. Like I said, we hardly know each other, and he's dating more women than an NBA star!"

"That highfalutin surgeon doesn't stand a chance," Angela said.

Sharleen spoke up. "None of his former flames do. My brother-in-law has his sights set on you, Tatiyana, and what Markos wants Markos gets."

Three hours after tee off, Nicco was crowned the winner of the fifth annual Rashawn Bishop Charity Golf Tournament. Spectators and participants exploded into cheers and applause as the famed restaurateur stood on the podium, posing with his shiny, gold trophy.

"Thanks to each and every one of you, and our generous corporate and private sponsors, we raised a million dollars for impoverished children," Rashawn shouted, his voice echoing around the course. "I couldn't have done this without you, so thank you from the bottom of my heart. And now that the tournament's officially over, let's party..."

Sinking onto the nearest chair outside Seminole Café, the upscale restaurant overlooking the eighteenth hole, Tatiyana sipped a mango margarita. The oversize, white umbrella above the table shielded her face from the searing sun, but the air was humid and all Tatiyana could think about was taking an ice-cold shower.

At the table to her right, a group of silver-haired ladies were enjoying a steak dinner, and hearing them gush about their children made Tatiyana miss her mom. She decided to call Lena to check in with her, but when she spotted the Morretti family headed her way, she dropped her cell inside her purse and waved in greeting. Her eyes scanned the grounds for Markos, but she couldn't find him anywhere. Disappointed, she forced a smile on her lips as his relatives gathered around her table, discussing Nicco's impossible, come-from-behind win.

"Congratulations," she said, setting down her empty glass. "Great win."

"Thanks, Tatiyana." Grinning, he sat and pulled Jariah onto his lap. "It feels good to finally beat my brothers and cousins. They've had it coming to them for years!"

The women laughed, and the men groaned in despair.

"You were amazing," Jariah shrieked, lobbing her arms around her husband's neck.

Kenyon appeared, camera in hand, poised to shoot. "How about a group shot?"

He snapped away, taking a half-dozen photos, then moved to the next table.

"Where's Markos?" Tatiyana asked. "He went inside to take a call but never returned."

"There he is!" Dionne pointed at the golf course, her eyes narrowed, her lips pursed in disapproval. "Some women have no shame. Look at them. Throwing themselves at your man."

Peering around the waiter who obscured her view, she found Markos at the bar, and he wasn't alone. Her stomach lurched. He was laughing, obviously having the time of his life with the voluptuous brunettes in neon bikinis. Jealousy consumed her, but Tatiyana played it cool. "It's no biggie," she said with a shrug. "He knows where to find me."

"Tatiyana, I'm sure it's nothing." Emilio spoke in a soft, soothing tone. "Markos is always on the clock, always trying to drum up business for his law firm, but I know my brother. He wouldn't disrespect you by hooking up with someone else. He's not that guy."

"It's cool. We're not married. He does his thing, and I do mine."

The men exchanged a worried look, then surged to their feet.

"Ladies, we'll be right back." Rafael kissed his wife on

the cheek and squeezed her shoulders. "I know you're hungry, so go ahead and order. You don't have to wait for us."

Paris picked up a menu and flipped it open. "Don't worry. I won't! I'm starving!"

Everyone laughed, except Tatiyana.

The men left, strolling purposely across the course, ignoring the females who smiled, whistled and waved at them. They sidled up to Markos, surrounding him like a SWAT team, and pulled him away from the bar. Tatiyana grabbed her purse. It was time to go. Markos had completely forgotten about her, and she refused to sit around waiting for him. Sure, she hadn't achieved her goal, but there was always tomorrow.

Tatiyana dropped the menu on the table and pushed back her chair. "Ladies, it's been fun, but I've had enough sun for one day."

"Girl, you better go over there and get your man," Dionne drawled, raising an eyebrow.

Everyone nodded, insisting the successful businesswoman was right.

"That's not my style."

"Tatiyana, that's not my style, either, but when other women pursue my man, I let them know in no uncertain terms that I'll fight for what's mine."

"Preach!" Angela shouted. "So do I!"

The women agreed with the reporter, sharing their own personal stories, but Tatiyana saw the situation differently. In her experience, men loved female attention, got off on hooking up with different women every night of the week, and that would never change, so why fight it?

Smiling to prove there were no hard feelings, she rose to her feet and waved at the group. "It's been fun. Hopefully, I'll see you guys tomorrow."

Leaving the patio, Tatiyana heard her cell phone chime and took it out of her purse. She had three new text messages from Everly, and laughed as she read them. Her cousin was threatening to disown her if she didn't call her, but the nail technician was having man trouble again, and Tatiyana didn't feel like listening to her talk about her bad-boy boyfriend.

Head bent, typing furiously, she walked past the bar.

"There you are."

Tatiyana glanced up from her cell just in time to see Markos standing in front of her, and slammed into his chest. He caught her before she fell and cradled her in his arms, as if it were her permanent resting place. Straightening, Tatiyana stepped back and adjusted her clothes.

"Where do you think you're going?"

"Back to my room."

"But you agreed to have dinner with us."

"I changed my mind…"

Hearing a commotion in the lobby, Tatiyana trailed off speaking and glanced over her shoulder. Children raced around, bumping into guests and each other, and wide-eyed tourists used their cell phones to capture the picturesque surroundings. The scent of garlic was so heavy in the air Tatiyana's mouth watered at the enticing aromas drifting out of the restaurant, and she gazed longing at the couples reclining in wicker chairs feeding each other ice cream.

"Talk to me," Markos urged. "Did something happen? Did someone upset you?"

"No, of course, not. Your family's incredible."

"Are you mad because I've been busy networking?"

Networking? she scoffed, swallowing a laugh. *Is that what you call flirting?* Tatiyana wrangled her thoughts back in and spoke in a cheery voice to hide her true feelings. "Markos, don't be silly. I'm fine. Don't sweat it."

"Are you going to the pool party tonight?"

"No. It's not my scene."

Her cell phone lit up with her mother's number, but Tatiyana let the call go to voice mail. First, she'd speak to Markos, then she'd check in with her family.

"A lot of celebrities will be there—"

"Is that supposed to impress me? Well, it doesn't."

A smile covered his face. "This is my last night here, and I want to spend it with you."

"Your last night? I thought you were leaving on Monday."

"No, tomorrow," he said, moving closer to her, swallowing the space between them. "I fly out at 5:00 a.m. I have an emergency meeting in Santa Barbara that I can't miss."

"But it's Sunday."

"Tell that to the sixth richest man in LA. He wants to meet, and I can't refuse him."

"This is goodbye, then."

Markos touched her cheek, caressing it with his fingertips, his gaze full of tenderness and warmth. "No way. You're mine for the rest of the night."

"I love the sound of that—" Tatiyana pressed her lips together, to trap the truth inside her mouth, but it was too late. Markos knew what she was thinking, how she was feeling, and the broad I'm-the-man grin on his face proved it. *What's the matter with me?* Tatiyana thought, strangling a sigh. *Why didn't I keep my big mouth shut?*

"We'll eat in the private dining room, then return to my suite."

"No, *my* suite," she insisted, reclaiming her voice. "We need a change of scenery."

"Sure, Tatiyana. Whatever you want."

Markos clasped her hand, holding it tight. Their eyes met, zeroing in on each other, and desire warmed her skin.

"This is our last night together. We should make the most of it."

"I couldn't agree more." Smiling, she fell into step with Markos as he strode toward the restaurant entrance. Tatiyana was excited, anxious to get him inside her plush, third-floor suite, but she couldn't shake the feeling that she was making the biggest mistake of her life.

Chapter 8

Markos stood beside the queen-size bed, watching Tatiyana sleep, contemplating what to do. *Should I stay, or should I go?* Hearing the question echo in his mind, he realized there was nothing to deliberate. He was going home. Back to work. They'd had their fun, played and partied for days, and now it was time to return to LA. He had an important meeting that afternoon, and if he stayed in Tampa, the other senior partners would be pissed.

His thoughts returned to yesterday, and his body tensed. While replenishing his scotch at the bar, he'd checked his email and noticed several messages from the HR Department. His secretary, Blanche Sutherland, was out sick with pneumonia and would be off work for three weeks. Truth be told, Markos wasn't going to miss her. She spent most of her day gossiping with Izzy and flirted shamelessly with his male clients. For the time being, Markos was on his own, and he wasn't looking forward to it.

Driven by need, he reached out and caressed Tatiyana's smooth, brown skin. She was clad in a short, silk nightie, her curvaceous body on full display. Markos felt his mouth dry and his temperature soar.

His hands lingered on her hips, stroking her fine, womanly shape. Markos wanted to wake Tatiyana up and thank her for a great weekend, but stopped himself. Last night, after making love, he'd asked her for her cell number again, but she'd skillfully changed the subject. Why did she have to reside on the east coast? Why couldn't she live closer, instead of thousands of miles away? And why was she against seeing him again? What was that about?

Feeling his cell phone vibrate inside his pocket, Markos took it out and turned off the alarm. He didn't want to miss his flight, knew there'd be hell to pay if he did, but something Tatiyana said last night was gnawing at him, preventing him from leaving her suite. Her words played in his mind, troubling him afresh.

"When it comes to the opposite sex, I keep my expectations low," she'd said matter-of-factly. "That way, when he screws up, which he inevitably will, I won't be heartbroken."

He'd filed the information to the back of his mind. Markos wanted to see Tatiyana again, was open to meeting up with her the next time she was in LA, and had tried to debunk her views about the male species. "Not all men are dogs."

"I never said they were, but most guys would rather play the field than settle down, and since I'm nobody's fool, I keep my heart under lock and key, *especially* around suave, charismatic Italians who can have any woman they want."

He'd scoffed, shook his head to ward off the bitter memories of his college days. "If we'd met ten years ago, you wouldn't have given me the time of day. No one did."

"Liar! You're attractive, intelligent and debonair. Who wouldn't want you?"

"In university, I was nobody's first choice. I was skinny, my ears stuck out of my head like Dumbo, and I had a horrible stuttering problem."

Eyes bright with desire, she'd licked her lips and gave him the once-over. "And look at you today. You're a sexy attorney with a dreamy smile and a killer bod!"

Markos had chuckled heartily. He'd felt energized, as if he'd just finished a session with his personal trainer. Tatiyana was hilarious, spontaneous and fun, and her naughty ways were a turn-on. She had great energy, told it like it was, and they shared common interests.

"I have learned that success is to be measured not so much by the things a person owns, or the position that one has reached in life but by the obstacles which he has overcome while trying to succeed."

Tatiyana had touched his cheek, and caressed his face with tender care. "I love that quote, and whenever I get down on myself, I remember how far I've come. That usually does the trick, and when it doesn't, I drink Merlot."

Surfacing from his thoughts, he continued to admire her. Markos wanted to see Tatiyana again, but he wasn't going to ask for her number. *Don't sweat her. She'll think you're weak*, he told himself, tearing his gaze away from her face. *There'll be others. There always are.*

Then why are you still here? And why did you leave that note?

Markos rubbed the back of his neck. He thought of grabbing the note off the pillow and ripping it up, but he wanted Tatiyana to call him, and if he threw out the note, he'd probably never see her again. The thought made his heart ache, filling him with sadness, and the urge to kiss her was so strong he couldn't stop himself. Lowering his face to hers, he inhaled her fragrant scent, and whispered, "Bye, beautiful. Until we meet again."

Markos kissed her lips, then abruptly turned away from the bed. Using the light from his iPhone, he marched through the darkened suite, careful not to wake her, and out the door.

Tatiyana cracked open one eye, searching the room for Markos. His cologne lingered in the air, mingling with the perfume of their lovemaking, the sweet, intoxicating scent tickling her nose. She'd had fun with the Italian stallion last night, a raucous good time in the bedroom, but Tatiyana was so anxious to check the tape recorder she hadn't slept a wink.

Hearing the door close, Tatiyana tossed aside her blanket and leaped from the bed. Her heart was pounding, drumming in her ears, and butterflies danced in her stomach. This was it. The moment of truth. Flipping on the potted lights, her limbs shook uncontrollably as she picked up the tape recorder she'd discreetly concealed with her pillow. Thankfully Markos hadn't noticed. Pressing the Rewind button, Tatiyana reflected on their romantic night together.

Tatiyana clutched it to her chest, hoping everything she needed was on the device.

Last night, after a scrumptious dinner in the private dining room, they'd returned to her suite and shared a bottle of Cabernet Sauvignon. Sitting on the balcony, stretched out in chaise longues, stargazing, had been the perfect way to end their date. They'd talked for hours, opened up to each other about past relationships, their families, even some of the problems Markos was having with his staff, and several of his high-profile celebrity clients. Had she made a mistake? Should she delete the recording? Was her plan going to backfire in her face?

Holding her breath, her hands shaking uncontrollably, she hit Play on the tape recorder. Markos's strong, masculine voice filled the room, and her heart skipped a beat. Thoughts of him made her smile, and Tatiyana longed to see him again. Everything she needed was on the tape, but listening to it made her feel guilty for betraying his trust. He'd been reluctant to talk about specific clients, but she'd encouraged him to vent his frustrations.

"I love being an attorney, and I enjoy working with my celebrity clients, but some of them make me feel like pulling out my hair," he'd said with a laugh.

Tatiyana had made her eyes wide. "Really? Who's your most difficult client and why?"

"Don't get me started. Once I start talking about work it's hard for me to stop!"

Markos didn't mention anyone by name, but he didn't need to. If Tatiyana leaked this recording to the media it would embarrass Markos, and his clients would place a dark cloud over his entire firm.

Filled with shame, Tatiyana turned off the tape recorder. Her gaze wandered around the suite. Tatiyana frowned.

There was a blue paper taped on the Sony TV. Curious, she stood, walked across the room, and ripped it off the screen. Unfolding the paper, a gold card fell onto the carpet. Picking it up, she admired the tasteful design. The elegant, custom-made business card listed Markos's personal information, including his email. Now, she wouldn't have to spend hours searching for it online. The note had two, simple sentences, and reading the handwritten message brought mixed emotions—happiness, regret and guilt.

Call me the next time you're in LA. You're an incredible woman, as smart as you are beautiful, and I'd love to see you again.

Touched by his words, Tatiyana hugged her arms to her chest. She reflected on their time in Tampa, on how they'd talked and laughed nonstop, and he'd always have a special place in her heart. They were polar opposites, who couldn't be more different, but she'd cherished every minute they'd spent together. Markos was a class act, in a league of his own, and she'd never forget their romantic weekend in Tampa.

Dropping the note inside her purse, Tatiyana marched into the bathroom and turned on the shower. She had shopping to do, gifts and souvenirs to buy for her family, and if she didn't hurry, she'd miss her 10:00 a.m. flight to LA.

Her thoughts returned to Thursday morning, to the exact moment she first laid eyes on Markos. This time around, he wouldn't be on the flight, and she'd be sitting in coach, not first class. Tatiyana didn't care. She'd achieved her goal, successfully seduced the hotshot attorney with the successful law practice, and she had the recording to prove it. As hard as it was, she had to put aside her feelings and forget the passionate nights they'd shared, because she was going to help her sister, by any means necessary.

Chapter 9

"Princess, is that you?" Lena Washington asked.

Entering the foyer of her three-bedroom bungalow in Sherman Oaks, Tatiyana dropped her keys on the marble table and took off her sunglasses. "Yeah, Mom, it's me," she said, kicking off her bejeweled ballet flats. The air smelled of okra and shrimp, tantalizing and delicious, and Tatiyana suspected Lena was making her famous seafood gumbo for dinner.

Starving, her mouth watered in anticipation. It was good to be home. Her flight had been uneventful, boring without Markos around to keep her company, so to pass the time she'd looked at the pictures and videos they'd taken in Tampa. Thankfully, she was sitting alone, because it would have been impossible for her to hide her guilt, and the tears that filled her eyes as she reflected on her weekend with Markos and his family. Daphne had called as she was leaving LAX, inviting her over for drinks, but Tatiyana was tired. She had promised her friend they'd have dinner tomorrow night after they volunteered at the shelter.

Tatiyana dumped her purse on the wooden bench and set off down the hall in search of her family. She'd only been gone for a few days, but it felt like weeks since she'd seen Allie, and Tatiyana was looking forward to spending time with her niece.

Hearing pots clanging and 70s music playing, Tatiyana headed for the kitchen. Bright and sunny with large windows, it had peach wallpaper and potted plants, and the cozy nook overlooking the backyard had comfortable furniture and vibrant pillow cushions. The kitchen was Tatiyana's favorite room in the house, where she spent most of her free time, and when she wasn't experimenting with recipes she was baking brownies for the volunteers at the women's shelter. As expected, her mom was standing at the breakfast bar, chopping vegetables, and singing along with the radio. Her mother's full name was Cornelia, but she thought it was old-fashioned and insisted her friends and family call her Lena, like the iconic singer and actress.

Full-figured, with toffee brown skin, Lena had a youthful, fun-loving vibe. A self-proclaimed cougar, she told male suitors her daughters were her younger sisters and lied about her age. Tatiyana didn't like it, wished her mom was proud of being fifty-five-years-old, but there was nothing she could do about it. Lena changed her appearance on a daily basis, and her thick bangs, dramatic eye makeup and gold belted sundress made her resemble Cleopatra.

"Welcome home," Lena said, kissing her cheek. "How was your trip?"

"Uneventful. What's up with the outfit? Hot date tonight?"

"You know it! I met a stockbroker at the bank yesterday, and he's taking me out for dinner, so I need you to watch Allie tonight."

Hearing her stomach groan, she grabbed a handful of chopped carrots and tossed some into her mouth. "Sure. Not a problem. I'd love to."

"How did things go in Tampa?" Her eyes were bright with interest, and her voice was full of excitement. "Did you get close to Markos Morretti?"

"Mom, let's talk about something else."

"What?" Inclining her head to the right, an incredulous expression on her face, she stuck a hand on her broad hip. "Don't play coy with me. It was *my* idea for you to befriend him, remember? Now, spill it. I'm dying to know what happened."

Tatiyana balked, vehemently shaking her head. No way. She couldn't do it. They were close, but she wasn't going to tell Lena about the intimate things she'd done with

Markos. They were private, treasured memories, experiences so special they were locked away in her heart. "Mom, I'm not going to discuss my personal life with you—"

"What personal life?" she quipped. "Hell, I go on more dates than you, and I'll be fifty-six on my next birthday!"

That's because you're always on the prowl for a new boy toy. Lena loved men, the younger the better, and spent hours online flirting with other lonely singles in LA. For as long as Tatiyana could remember, her mother had always been man-crazy, and her behavior baffled her.

Painful memories darkened her thoughts. Growing up, she'd seen men come and go from their shabby, inner-city apartment on a daily basis. It had saddened her how they'd disrespected her mom. They took her money and used her car without permission, but were nowhere to be found when Lena needed them. Tatiyana didn't know who her father was, had never met him, but her mom's older brother had raised her as his own. Byron was a marine stationed in North Carolina, and she'd seen him only a handful of times since graduating from high school, but Tatiyana knew if she ever needed her uncle he'd be on the first flight to LA. "Where's Jantel?"

"You have to ask? In bed as usual."

"How long has Allie been sleeping?"

Glancing at the wall clock, Lena tossed a handful of chopped celery into the bubbling pot. "About an hour, but she should be up soon for her bottle."

"I'm going to go talk to Jantel."

"Okay, but hurry back. I want to hear all about your weekend with that smug attorney."

Dodging her mother's gaze, she pretended to inspect her gel nails. Her first thought was to lie, her second to flee, but if she did, Lena would be hot on her trail, so Tatiyana shrugged and said, "There's nothing to tell. He did his thing at the charity golf tournament, and I did mine."

"We'll at least you tried," she said with a sad smile. "I'm

not giving up. Mayor Glover took advantage of my baby girl, and I'm going to make sure he does right by Jantel and Allie, even if it means making daily visits to his office."

"Mom, we agreed I'd handle it—"

"Fine, but if you don't arrange a meeting soon, the ball's back in my court."

Groaning inwardly, Tatiyana fled the kitchen. Her mom had a temper, and Tatiyana feared what would happen when Lena came face-to-face with the mayor. She walked down the hall, munching on her snack, thoughts of Markos on her mind. What was he doing? Was he with one of his girl-friends? Tatiyana couldn't stop thinking about him and wondered if he was thinking about her, too. As if! He's a Morretti. Females threw themselves at him 24/7, and hang-ing out with him at the golf tournament had proved it—he loved the attention, and would never be content with one woman.

Tatiyana stopped at the end of the hall and peeked into her sister's room. The TV was on, but Jantel wasn't watch-ing it. She was curled up in bed, staring out the window.

Entering the room, Tatiyana stepped over dirty clothes, ripped magazines and discarded candy wrappers. The air smelled of garbage, but she resisted the urge to plug her nose and sat on the edge of the bed. "Hey, you," she said in a cheery voice. "Do you want to go for a walk? It's gor-geous outside, and it would be a waste to spend the entire day in bed."

"Maybe another time."

Her voice was small, so quiet Tatiyana strained to hear her. Months ago, Jantel's psychiatrist had prescribed anti-depressants, but her sister refused to take them. These days, her mood was dark, and negative.

"You have group therapy this week," she reminded her. "Is it okay if I come? I missed your last session because I had a job interview, but I have no plans on Thursday."

"I'm not going."

"Why not?"

Jantel pulled the blanket up to her chin and closed her eyes.

"Sis, talk to me. Why don't you want to go to group?"

"Because…" She trailed off speaking.

"Because what?"

"Hearing other people's stories makes me feel worse about my situation."

"Would you like to meet with Dr. Chopra alone?"

"I don't know."

The silence was deafening, the air thick with sadness and despair.

"Jantel, hang in there. I know it's been a rough year for you, but things will get better—"

"How?" she shouted. "I'm a screwup!"

"No, you're not. You're being too hard on yourself."

"I slept with a man who doesn't want me, got pregnant and now I have a sick child to take care of. I have no job, and medical bills I can't afford to pay." Wiping at her eyes, she spoke in a whisper. "Life sucks, and it won't get better."

Tatiyana sighed deeply. Her sister's words echoed in her mind, conjuring up images she couldn't escape. Her mother had worked two, sometimes three jobs, and as a tween Tatiyana was left in charge of the house. She'd been taking care of Jantel since they were young, and it broke her heart to see her sister in pain. Two years ago, her sister was a popular bartender at an exclusive gentleman's club. Jantel, and four exotic dancers had been hired for the Mayor's bachelor party and even though Jantel loved flirting with her customers, she didn't seduce Mayor Glover. He'd willingly hooked up with her, and he needed to do the right thing for Allie.

"It's me against the world," she continued. "I have no one."

"That's not true. You have me, Mom, Everly and Uncle Byron. We'll always be here for you." They'd had this conversation numerous times, but the more Tatiyana tried to reason with Jantel, the more bitter she seemed. Still, she pressed on, reminding her about all the people who were in her corner. "Jantel, you're not alone. You have the support of your family, and everyone at the women's center. We're here for you whenever you need us. And for Allie, too."

"How am I supposed to take care of her? I have no job, no hope, no future."

"Don't say things like that." Tatiyana took her sister's hand and held it tight. It was cold and clammy, and trembling uncontrollably. "We're family. I have your back."

"But Allie's sick. I can't take care of myself, let alone a sick child. How am I going to pay her medical bills? And what if something happens to me? Who will raise her?"

A searing pain stabbed her heart. Tatiyana's eyes watered, but she willed herself to be strong. Two weeks ago, after Allie had trouble breathing and was rushed to the emergency room, they'd learned her niece had Ventricular Septal Defect, a genetic abnormality in her heart, and needed surgery. Doctors were confident the procedure would be a success, but Jantel had been stressing about all the things that could go wrong since they'd left the clinic.

"Jantel, be positive. The medical staff at the hospital have high hopes for Allie, and so do I. She'll pull through. I know it."

"And if she doesn't?"

Tatiyana refused to entertain the thought, couldn't imagine anything happening to her niece. Allie was a vibrant, energetic baby who was achieving all of her developmental milestones, and the surgery would be a success. It had to be. Her niece was the pride and joy of their family, and Tatiyana was going to make sure she received the best medical care. "The surgery has an 83 percent success rate if performed within three months of diagnosis—"

"What if Allie's part of the 17 percent who don't make it?" she asked quietly.

Stumped, Tatiyana couldn't think of a response. Researching her niece's condition at the hospital library had alleviated her fears, but Jantel was convinced the diagnosis was a death sentence. The surgery was thousands of dollars, money their family didn't have, but if Tatiyana had to remortgage her home to pay for Allie's procedure, so be it. That was the least of her problems. Tatiyana was worried sick about Jantel. These days, her mood was hopeless, and Tatiyana feared her depression was getting worse. She hardly ate, refused to take her antidepressant medication and spent hours in bed staring at the ceiling. They were going to meet with Dr. Chopra next week, even if she had to drag Jantel to the clinic. Her sister was drowning in despair, spiraling out of control, and Tatiyana had to do something to help her.

"Jantel, nothing's going to happen to Allie, and nothing's going to happen to you," she said in a firm voice. "You'll get through this. You're a Washington, and Washingtons are fighters. Never forget that."

"I'm tired of fighting."

Panic swelled inside Tatiyana's chest. Every breath was a struggle, harder than the last.

Jantel raised her head, meeting her gaze, and Tatiyana froze. She saw the hurt, the pain in her sister's eyes, and gathered her in her arms.

"I'm going to make this right."

"How?" she croaked. "There's nothing anyone can do."

"We're going to meet with the mayor, and if he refuses to take a paternity test, we'll get a court order," Tatiyana explained, stroking her sister's short, matted hair.

"People will say that I'm lying. That I'm a gold digger with ulterior motives who seduced a powerful, wealthy man." Her voice was resigned, sad, as she tugged at the sleeve of her gray sweatshirt.

"Screw them. It doesn't matter what they think."

"The Mayor has power, money and connections. I can't win."

"You can and you will. It doesn't matter who he is, or what he has. DNA tests don't lie."

Her frown deepened.

"Jantel, I'm going to take care of things on my end, but you have to do your part, too."

"My part?" she repeated, wiping at her eyes. "What do you want me to do?"

"Take your medication, and attend group therapy."

"I can't. I'm not strong enough to do it on my own."

"Munchkin, you don't have to. You have me, and mom, and Allie. We'll do it together."

Jantel nodded, but her shoulders sagged.

To make her laugh, she gave Jantel a wet, sloppy kiss on the cheek. "I love you, Munchkin, and I always will, even when we're old, senile chicks playing dominoes at the nursing home!"

For the first time in months, Jantel laughed, and Tatiyana smiled through her tears.

Chapter 10

"Sir, are you ready to review the day's schedule, or should I return in an hour?"

Markos blinked, turned away from the window in his office overlooking downtown LA and regarded his paralegal. *Dannazione!* he thought, strangling a groan. *How long have I been standing here daydreaming about Tatiyana?*

Glancing at his gold wristwatch, his eyes widened in alarm. Instead of working on his cases, or answering his emails, he'd wasted an hour fantasizing about a woman he needed to forget. A woman who wanted nothing to do with him. It was an impossible feat, damn hard to do. Not only had Tatiyana given him the best sex of his life, she'd made him feel young again, cool even, and five days after their sexual encounter in Tampa, he was craving her bad.

A scowl twisted his lips. He had to move on. Had to stop thinking about her. Since returning to LA, he hadn't let his cell phone out of his sight for fear he'd miss her call, but she never did. Markos was pissed, couldn't figure out why she was giving him the cold shoulder. Women like Tatiyana—sensual, effervescent beings—were hard to find, only came along once in a man's lifetime, and Markos wondered if they had what it took to have a lasting, committed relationship. He hadn't been this excited about anyone in years and wanted to see her again. More than anything. His family liked her, and he did, too. His feelings for her were real, and he was going to track her down—

"Sir?" Izzy prompted, clutching her notebook to her chest. "You seem preoccupied. I'll come back later. When you're less busy—"

"No, no, it's fine. Come in."

The brunette tottered into his office and sat on one

of the padded chairs. To impress his clients, Markos had spared no expense decorating his office. Attractive, modern and spacious, it had everything an attorney could want. Shelves lined with law books, Ralph Lauren furniture, a mini fridge stocked with wine coolers, brownies and Cuban sandwiches, powder-blue walls adorned with photographs of his celebrity clients, and a private bathroom.

"The phones have been ringing off the hook all morning, and I can't keep up…"

Sitting behind his desk, Markos opened his side drawer and grabbed one of the round, yellow balls. He clutched it in his palm, squeezing it in the hopes of relieving his stress. It didn't help. His muscles still felt tense, stiff and sore, and all he could think about was Tatiyana, rubbing and squeezing her beautiful—

"Add to that," Izzy continued, wearing a sad face, "I'm falling behind on my paperwork."

Markos broke free of his thoughts and cleared his throat. "Did you call Staffing Unlimited and ask them to send over an experienced secretary?"

"Yes, but they didn't have anyone available, so I'm doing double duty today."

"Thanks for going the extra mile, Izzy. I appreciate it."

Stars twinkled in her eyes. "Anything for you, boss! Just call me Superwoman!"

Chuckling, Markos turned to his computer and consulted his online schedule.

"Mrs. Zapata called again. She's having doubts about the divorce, but I reminded her why she filed in the first place, and she reluctantly agreed it's for the best."

Markos had a unique knack for calming people when they were upset, but his techniques didn't work on the temperamental pop star. Emotional and flighty, she was impossible to please, and by far his most difficult client. Yesterday, he'd met with the psychologist and social worker involved with Mrs. Zapata's case, then drafted motions regarding custody of her toddler son, child support and occupancy of the marital home. "Good work, Izzy. I like your initiative."

"Divorce is big business, and our objective at LA Family Law is to win every case, especially the high-profile ones. Our job isn't to coddle clients, or babysit them. It's to tell them the truth, no matter how painful it is."

Impressed, Markos nodded in appreciation. "Sounds familiar."

"I learned from the best," she quipped. "See, you're wrong, I *do* listen to you."

"Did you confirm my one o'clock appointment with Mayor Glover?"

"The mayor had to cancel. He's attending the Asian Business Summit in Tokyo, and he won't be back in LA for several weeks," Izzy explained, consulting her agenda. "His secretary penciled you in for October 1, but that's subject to change."

"Okay, not a problem. I'll use that vacant time slot to prepare for court."

"Speaking of court, do you need me this afternoon, or can you manage without me?"

"What do you think?"

Shrugging, a sheepish expression on her face, she tapped her ballpoint pen on her notebook. "I don't know. That's why I asked."

"Izzy, you're my paralegal. Of course I need you there."

"But if I miss my appointment at LA Cosmetic Therapy, I won't get my deposit back."

Convinced she was pulling his leg, Markos said, "You're funny. What's next on the—"

"Please?" she whined. "This is the last favor I'll ever ask. I swear."

"Are you kidding me?" Struggling to control his temper, he spoke through clenched teeth. "On Monday you called in sick, on Tuesday you left early and yesterday you took a two-hour lunch. If I didn't call to inquire about your whereabouts, you'd probably still be at The Ivy with your girlfriends."

Izzy gave him a blank look, staring at him as if she didn't know what the problem was.

"I expect you at the courthouse at 2:30 sharp. Understood?"

"But I…"

Narrowing his gaze, he silenced her with a dark, menacing look.

"*Don't* make personal appointments during business hours," he warned, his voice stern.

"Sorry, Sir. I won't let it happen again."

"Good. I expect you to work hard just like everybody else at this firm. No excuses."

Ignoring the crestfallen expression on her face, he consulted his desk calendar. "Remember to type up the notes from the Nunez case conference. It's been almost a week since the meeting, and I'd like to review them *before* I retire."

"Yes, Sir, I'll have it to you within the hour. Is there anything else?"

"That's all for now—"

The door burst open, drawing Markos's attention across the room, and his eyes widened. Time screeched to a stop, and the room flipped upside down, spinning out of control. He opened his mouth to speak but choked on his tongue. Tatiyana? Here in LA? At his office? Markos shook the cobwebs from his mind and rubbed at his eyes, but Tatiyana remained in the doorway, wowing him with her beauty. On Saturday, she'd looked like a sex kitten in her short, black negligee, but today her hair bun, ivory pantsuit and multicolored scarf gave her a mature, sophisticated appearance. Diamond stud earrings adorned her ears, her gold necklace held a cross at the end and her makeup was tastefully done.

"Good morning, Mr. Morretti. It's great to see you again…"

Markos cocked an eyebrow. Why was she addressing him in such formal terms? In Tampa, they'd had sex all over his executive suite, and when their eyes met, Markos knew she was reliving their sexual escapades in her mind, too. He was excited to see her, couldn't believe his good fortune and was eager to get her alone. Back in his arms where she belonged. Markos wanted to stand, to go to her, but his back was glued to his leather swivel chair.

"I know you're busy, but I'd like to discuss a very important matter with you."

"Can I help you?" Izzy asked, standing up.

Tatiyana captured his gaze, holding it in her seductive grip, but she spoke to his paralegal in an authoritative voice. "I'm here to speak to Mr. Morretti."

"Sir, do you want me to call security?"

"No, that won't be necessary," he said calmly, reclaiming his voice.

"If you need me, just shout and I'll come running."

Amused, Markos swallowed a laugh. "Thanks, Izzy."

She left, closing the door behind her, and Markos sighed in relief. Crisis averted, though he knew she'd gossip about Tatiyana to the entire office. He didn't care. Markos wanted to be alone with her, and he didn't care who knew.

His gaze returned to Tatiyana, landing on her lush, red lips, and desire engulfed his body. *Have mercy.* She looked just as he remembered—tempting, tantalizing and hot— and she smelled divine. Markos inhaled her fragrant scent, could feel himself falling under her spell. Did she bathe in champagne that morning? Is that why she smelled rich and intoxicating?

"This is a pleasant surprise," he said, smoothing a hand over his three-button suit. "Why didn't you tell me you were coming to LA? I would have picked you up from the airport."

"There was no need. I live here, Markos. Born and raised, in fact."

"You told me you were from Bridgeport."

"I told you a lot of things, and most of them weren't true. I feel horrible for lying to you, Markos, but I had no choice. I have to help my sister…"

Her words confused him, sounding like garble in his ears.

"Three weeks ago, my mom and sister, Lena and Jantel Washington, met with you to discuss an incident at Mayor Glover's private residence two years ago," she said in a calm, composed voice. "Jantel attended the mayor's bachelor party, got drunk and slept with him."

A lump formed in his throat and fear welled up inside him. Markos gripped the armrest so hard his hands throbbed in pain. This couldn't be real. It had to be a sick joke. His brothers had put her up to this, right? What else could it be? They had a connection, something special right, isn't that why she was here? To rekindle their sizzling romance?

"Three months later, Jantel discovered she was pregnant and contacted Mayor Glover, but he's been dodging her ever since. His chief of staff, Christopher Nelson, threatened to have her charged with harassment if she comes to city hall again, but she's done nothing wrong."

As he shot to his feet, his chair flew back against the window and fell on its side. "What?" The word exploded out of his mouth. "You knew who I was all along? You tricked me?"

Guilt covered her face, but she met his gaze. "Yes. I knew who you were when we met."

"Is that why you slept with me? Because you thought it would help your cause?"

"No, I slept with you because I'm attracted to you, Markos. You're a sexy, desirable man, and I wanted you the moment I laid eyes on you."

Her words embarrassed him, making his face flush with heat, and for some strange reason he wanted to kiss her, to taste her lips one more time. "What do you want?"

"A meeting with the mayor. My sister is telling the truth, and I can prove it."

"I don't care about you or your sister—"

Her speech was smooth, polished, obviously something she'd rehearsed, and listening to her made a bitter taste fill his mouth. Naked images of her—kissing him, straddling him, thrusting her breasts in his face—flashed in his mind. Markos pressed his eyes shut, blocking all memories of their sexual encounter. Tatiyana was the enemy, and if he was going to defeat her, he needed a clear head.

"You're messing with the wrong person."

"Markos, it's nothing personal. I sought you out because you're good friends with the mayor, not because I have a personal vendetta against you. I think you're a great guy, and an incredible lover, as well."

"Is that supposed to make me feel better?" Markos pointed at the door. "Leave or I'll call security to escort you out. It's your choice."

"You have until Monday to decide."

Sneering at her, he barked a laugh. "Decide what? I'm not doing shit."

"Very well. You leave me no choice." Tatiyana opened her purse, took out a tape recorder and raised it in the air, as if it were a lethal weapon. "I didn't want to do this, but—"

"I can't believe this," he raged, voicing his anger. "I thought you were a good woman, someone I could actually settle down with, but I was wrong. You're a liar and a con artist."

Her face fell, and her hand dropped to her side. Her eyes looked glossy, as if they were filled with tears. Made him think of the heartbroken mourners at his nephew's funeral years earlier. Hanging her head, she shifted and shuffled her feet.

"That's not true," she said quietly, shoving the tape recorder back into her purse. "I'm none of those things. I just want to help my sister. I'm not trying to hurt you."

Adrenaline shot through his veins. For the first time since Tatiyana barged into his office, Markos knew he had the upper hand and launched a counterattack. To capitalize on the moment, he picked up his office phone and spoke in a stern voice. "You don't scare me, and furthermore I don't respond to threats. You can negotiate with the authorities. How's that?"

"Fine, suit yourself, but don't say I didn't warn you when my sister goes public with her story, and the paparazzi camp outside your office, hounding you day and night."

Tatiyana marched off, switching her hips in such a provocative way Markos couldn't stop staring at her backside. Remembering all the times they'd made love made his temperature rise and his heartbeat speed up. Lust infected his body, and an erection rose inside his boxer briefs. Damn her! Her story was pure fiction. Nothing but a desperate attempt to exhort money from the mayor, and Markos wanted nothing to do with it. He was a human lie detector, as astute as a police chief, and suspected Tatiyana was lying. Could feel it. Sense it. Knew it in his gut. Markos needed to talk, to vent, and knew just who to call. He dialed Immanuel's cell number and waited impatiently for him to answer. His brother's voice filled the line, and Markos sighed in relief. Immanuel would know what to do, he always did.

"Bro, what's up? How's life treating you in La La Land?"

"We need to talk."

"Go ahead. I'm all ears."

Markos shook his head. "Not on the phone. In person."

"Can it wait until next week? I'll be in LA on business, so we can talk then."

"Fine, but in the meantime I need a huge favor."

"Sure, bro, anything for you. What is it?"

"I need you to do a background check on Tatiyana ASAP."

"Why?" He sounded amused, as if he was trying hard not to laugh. "What happened? Did her ex-boyfriend rough you up and order you to stay away from her? I told you Tatiyana was too much woman for you to handle, but you just wouldn't listen!"

"Sharpshooter, knock it off. This is serious."

Sobering, he adopted a serious, no-nonsense tone of voice. "Okay, chill, don't get your tighty-whities in a bunch. Text me the necessary information, and I'll get right on it."

Line two lit up, signaling he had another call, but Markos ignored it. This was important, and he didn't have time to waste. "What do you need?"

"The usual. Her birthdate, home address and social insurance number if you have it."

"I don't. All I know is her name."

Immanuel scoffed, ribbing him good-naturedly. "And you've been dating for how long?"

Markos thought hard, trying to remember everything Tatiyana had told him about herself in Tampa, and snapped his fingers. "Her full name is Tatiyana Washington, and she's a twenty-seven-year-old executive secretary for Pinnacle Microsystems. Or, at least that's what she told me. I don't know what to believe anymore."

"Damn, bro, what happened? You guys were all over each other in Tampa…"

I know. Don't remind me. My ego's taken enough of a beating today. Markos coughed to clear the lump in his throat, then spoke in a confident voice, one that masked his profound disappointment. "Nothing. I'm good. Life couldn't be better."

"You're lying. Something's wrong. I can tell. What is it?"

Markos scooped his stress ball off the desk and squeezed it so hard his hands turned bone white. He wanted to open up to Immanuel, but he couldn't risk someone in the office overhearing their conversation. "How long will the background check take?"

"A couple days," he said.

"I need it in by the end of the day, bro. Make it happen."

"I'm on it. I'll see what I can do."

"Thanks, Immanuel. You're a lifesaver."

"No worries, man. Hang tight. I'll call you tonight with an update."

Markos dropped the phone in the cradle. To become partner, he'd taken his father's advice and revitalized his image. He'd pretended to be a player, dating a different woman every week, joined his colleagues for drinks during happy hour instead of hanging out with his golf buddies, and attended Hollywood parties and events, but it was all for show. A facade. His brothers teased him for being a softie, for wearing his heart on his sleeve, but he'd rather have one special woman in his life than twenty. Markos wanted what his cousins, Nicco and Rafael had—love, stability and support. They had wives, children, a future, and for some insane reason, he'd actually thought Tatiyana could be the one.

Sadness pierced his heart, but he pushed his feelings aside, refusing to think about her or their romantic weekend in Tampa. She'd used him, played him for a fool, and he'd never forgive her. Seething with anger, he picked up his coffee mug and hurled it across the room.

Sweating profusely, he blew out a breath and plucked at his navy-blue dress shirt. Markos faced the window, replaying his conversation with Tatiyana in his mind. How could this happen? How could she do this to him? Didn't she know he had feelings for her? Markos thought they had a connection, something special, a strong bond, but he'd been kidding himself. It didn't matter. This wasn't over. He was going to get even, discover everything there was to know about her and use it to his advantage, and by the time he was done with Tatiyana, she'd be begging for mercy.

Chapter 11

Markos strode into his darkened media room, clutching a bottle of Appleton rum, and flopped down on his favorite armchair. To keep his mind off his troubles, he turned on the eighty-inch TV and jacked up the volume. ESPN was showing soccer highlights, but Markos didn't care who'd won the European championships. He'd had the day from hell, one problem after another since Tatiyana's unexpected visit that morning, and he couldn't stomach any more bad news.

Flipping channels, he decided on the local news and dropped the remote on the side table. Markos took a swig from the bottle, savoring the taste of his drink as it hit the back of his throat. Normally, he didn't drink alcohol on workdays, but he needed a pick-me-up, something to help him relax after a long, stressful day at the office, and Jamaican rum always did the trick.

He pressed the On button on his chair, which started to vibrate, relieving the aches and pains in his joints. Heat flooded his body, relaxing him, and Markos closed his eyes. His thoughts returned to that afternoon. Court had been a disaster. A living nightmare. He couldn't concentrate, had spilled coffee on his documents and had snapped at Izzy twice. To his surprise, his billionaire client was pleased with his performance, even praising him for a job well done after his blistering cross-examination of the CEO's estranged wife. Pissed at Tatiyana, he'd taken his anger out on the mother of five and cringed every time he remembered their heated exchange in court. He owed her an apology, but since he didn't want to compromise his case, he'd call his favorite florist shop tomorrow and send her an anonymous floral arrangement. Problem solved.

Markos stared at his iPhone, sitting in the cup holder, willing it to ring. It was eight o'clock, but Immanuel still hadn't called him with an update. What was up with that? Didn't his brother realize how important this was to him? Didn't he care? Or was he too busy romancing his wife to help? Tatiyana's warning rang in his thoughts, piercing his eardrums.

"Fine, suit yourself, but don't say I didn't warn you when my sister goes public with her story, and the paparazzi camp outside your office, hounding you day and night."

What am I going to do? Should I call her bluff and hope things blow over, or talk to Mayor Glover? Neither option appealed to him. He'd rather fight a Siberian tiger than grill his friend about his sex life. For the second time in minutes, his gaze landed on his cell phone. Markos needed to talk to someone and considered calling his grandfather in Venice. Pride prevented him from dialing the number. They didn't talk often, only a few times a year, and Markos didn't want to burden his grandfather with his problems. He had enough on his plate. Because of his poor health, his grandfather hadn't been to the office in months, and spent most of his days in bed at his villa. Tomorrow, he'd call Demetri. His cousin would know what to do. Over the course of his twelve-year career, the baseball legend had experienced it all—deception, betrayal and blackmail— and if anyone could give him sound advice, it was his superstar cousin from Chicago.

"In other news, Mayor Glover arrived in Tokyo today for the Asian Business Summit, and caused a frenzy at Narita International Airport when he took a picture with a group of geishas," the news anchor reported. "The mayor's critics say he should be ashamed of himself for socializing with glorified prostitutes, but Mayor Glover defended his actions, saying…"

Listening to the news report, Markos considered his conversation weeks earlier with Lena and Jantel Washington, dissecting every aspect of their ten-minute meeting. The frail, twentysomething woman had spoken in a small, meek voice, as if she were afraid of her own shadow, but Markos didn't believe her story. Knew in his gut she was lying. It was an act. Had to be. He knew Mayor Glover well, knew he was madly in love with his then fiancée. No way she'd been a guest at the Mayor's bachelor party, let alone slept with her. Unless...

Markos bolted upright in his chair, spilling rum onto the carpet. Was Jantel an exotic dancer? Had she been paid to perform at the mayor's party? Now, everything made sense. How Jantel knew about the location, the layout of the Bel Air mansion and the cell phone ban. The bachelor party, an upscale event planned by the mayor's chief of staff, was an exclusive, invite-only party held at the mayor's private residence. Dozens of male celebrities had attended the event, and the only women at the party were strippers.

Markos took a swig of rum, then another. His theory was crazy, but the more he thought about it the more the pieces of the puzzles fit. Interestingly enough, Jantel never told him she was a stripper. Not that it mattered. She was lying, trying to ruin the mayor's reputation, but Markos wasn't going to let it happen.

At forty-three, Kassem Glover was the suave and charming African-American mayor of Los Angeles, and he had superstar appeal. The UCLA graduate had won voters over by being open and honest about his political agenda, and won the election by a landslide. Maroon 5 had performed at the mayor's inauguration, and there were so many celebrities in attendance Markos thought he was at the Oscars. Mayor Glover spoke in a calm, personable way that voters found endearing, and had boosted the struggling economy by pouring money into city projects, offering tax breaks to business owners and strengthening connections to global firms. The mayor had promised to back him during the next election in two years' time, and Markos wasn't going to let

Jantel Washington—or anyone else—ruin his chances of being the next mayor of Los Angeles.

The lights came on, blinding him, and Markos squinted.

"I hope you're not in here drowning your sorrows in Jack and Coke."

Speechless, his mouth agape, Markos stared at his younger brothers in disbelief.

"Damn, bro, it's worse than we thought. He's drinking Jamaican rum." Dante ripped the bottle out of Markos's hands. "Trust me, you'll thank me in the morning."

"What are you guys doing here?"

"Sharpshooter called, told me about the bizarre conversation you had with him this morning, and I told him to get down here pronto, because it's obvious you need us."

"Dante picked me up from the airport, and here we are. Surprised?" Immanuel asked.

"But you weren't due in LA until next week."

"Nothing matters more to me than family. You know that," he said, clapping Markos on the back. "I wasn't going to leave my favorite brother hanging."

Dante gave Immanuel a shot in the arm, but he spoke in an amused voice. "Hey! What's up with that? In the car you said *I* was your favorite!"

The men chuckled, their voices carrying around the room, filling it with cheer.

"Did you do the background check on Tatiyana? Find anything useful?"

"Dinner first, then business." Immanuel rubbed his stomach. "I'm starving. All I had on the plane was a turkey sandwich, and now my stomach's growling. Should we eat in, or head out?"

Markos wasn't hungry, had lost his appetite the moment Tatiyana told him about her troublesome sister, but he turned off the TV and rose from his chair. Glad for the company, he headed for the kitchen with his brothers in tow. Minutes later, they were seated around the table, eating the food his personal chef had prepared for him that evening. Over prime rib, the men talked about business, sports and the Rashawn Bishop Charity Golf Tournament in Tampa.

"I'm sorry I missed it, but I couldn't leave Jordana behind. Her parents were in town for the weekend, and I wanted to spend time with them."

"How is Jordana doing?" Markos picked up the gravy boat and poured the thick brown liquid over his food, drenching everything on his plate. "I'm surprised you're not still joined at the hip. She's become a regular fixture in your life ever since your fake wedding at city hall, and it's nice to see. Jordana's good people."

Love shone in Dante's eyes, brightening his face. "I found the girl of my dreams, and I couldn't be happier," he confessed. "When you find a woman who sticks by you during hard times you hold on to her, and that's what I'm going to do."

"What's going on with you and Tatiyana?" Immanuel picked up his beer bottle. "Why are you checking up on her? Did something happen?"

Markos felt ashamed, stupid for being duped by the twenty-seven-year-old beauty, but he confided in his brothers about his troubles. He told them about meeting Tatiyana on the flight, their romantic weekend in Tampa and their showdown that morning in his office. "I feel like a jackass. I'm an attorney. I should have seen this coming."

Frowning, Dante shook his head. "You're a lawyer, Markos. Not a psychic. How were you supposed to know her true identity?"

"I can't believe you met Tatiyana on your way to Tampa. You certainly fooled me. Hell, you fooled us all. You acted like she was 'the one,' so we all welcomed her with open arms."

"No, I didn't. Immanuel, you're exaggerating."

"Yes, you did. You couldn't keep your hands off her,

and you introduced her to everyone at the tournament as your lady," he argued, pointing his fork at Markos's face. "You ditched us for Tatiyana."

"I wasn't the problem," he shot back. "If you guys would've left your wives at home like you were *supposed* to, I never would have hooked up with Tatiyana."

"Bullshit! Don't pin this on us. You wanted her the moment you saw her."

Markos wanted to argue, but he didn't. It was true. The first time he saw Tatiyana he knew he had to have her. And he had. All over his executive suite. In every imaginable position.

"Hooking up with Tatiyana had nothing to do with the guys, so don't blame us because you got bamboozled. I told you she was out of your league, but you wouldn't listen."

"I don't need a lecture. I need your help."

"Don't sweat it," Dante said with a sympathetic smile, his tone filled with understanding. "Quit beating yourself up. We've all been there—"

Immanuel scoffed. "No, we haven't."

"*Yes*, we have. Nicco's best friend stole from Dolce Vita and set him up to take the fall, you caught Emilio in bed with your ex-fiancée, and Lourdes left me for my business rival."

"I guess you're right," Immanuel said with a nod. "We've all been burned by love."

"Markos, all you can do is learn from this experience and move on. What doesn't kill you can only make you stronger, right?"

Immanuel groaned. "I hate your pep talks. Do you have to quote pop songs?"

Chuckling, the men bumped elbows and beer bottles. Joking around with his brothers had improved Markos's mood. Still, he wanted to know if Immanuel had uncovered anything incriminating about Tatiyana. Excitement shot through his veins at the thought of getting even with her.

And he would, even if he had to be sneaky. No one messed with him and got away with it—not even a woman he had strong feelings for. Images of her filled his thoughts, but he struck them from his mind. Tatiyana was the enemy, and they'd never be lovers again.

"What did the background check reveal?" He spoke in a calm voice, but he was dying to know the truth, could feel his heart racing and his palms sweating. "Is she a criminal? Does she have a history of scheming people? Are there other victims?"

"No, quite the contrary. Tatiyana has a terrific credit score, an impeccable résumé and a long history of volunteering at charity organizations. She's never gotten as much as a parking ticket, or paid her cable bill late. By all accounts she's a model citizen."

"Right!" Markos barked a laugh. "Model citizen my ass."

"You don't believe me? Here, I'll show you."

Putting down his fork, he reached into his jacket pocket, which was draped behind his chair, and took out a piece of paper. "Here. Read it for yourself," he said, handing it over.

Markos scanned the document, committing the information about Tatiyana to memory—her birthdate, her address, her former employers. His eyes narrowed, zeroing in on an interesting fact his brother had failed to mention. "Tatiyana was fired from Pinnacle three weeks ago?"

"Yeah, I called and spoke to someone in their HR department this evening to get the inside scoop." Immanuel forked a baby potato into his mouth and chewed slowly, as if he was savoring every bite. "Apparently, they eliminated her position."

"Bullshit. Tatiyana was an executive secretary. They're always in high demand."

Immanuel nodded. "I agree. It's obvious they wanted her gone, but why?"

Leaning back in his chair, Markos stroked his jaw, considering his brother's question. His interest piqued, he decided to call his accountant friend at Pinnacle Micro-systems for answers. He didn't know what to do with the information, how to use it to his advantage, but knowing Tatiyana's secrets made him feel confident, as if he was finally back in control, and he relished the feeling.

"I'm going to play devil's advocate for a minute."

Cranking his head to the left, his hands gripping the neck of his beer bottle, Markos wore a disgusted look. "Don't," he warned. "I don't want to hear it, Dante. I'm not in the mood."

"Hear me out. I know you and the mayor are good friends, and you think highly of him, but a lot of famous people feel they're above the law. They think the rules don't apply to them, and they'll do everything in their power to destroy the truth *and* their accusers."

"Since the mayor took office it's been one problem after another," he explained, frustrated that his brothers were giving him grief. "This isn't the first woman who's made accusations, or claimed to have had an affair with him, and it probably won't be the last."

"I hear you, bro, but that doesn't mean Tatiyana and her sister are lying. I don't know her well, but my impression is that she's someone who loves and supports her family. Just like you."

Markos scoffed. His brothers knew about his disastrous dating history, about all the times he'd met a woman only to discover she was more interested in his wealth and status, than getting to know him as a person. And Tatiyana was no different. "Now that you guys are happily married, and living the American dream, you forgot what it's like to be a bachelor," he argued. "A lot of women are scheming and conniving—"

"And a lot of women aren't. At the very least, look into her sister's case, and see if her story has merit."

"You think I should investigate her claims? Why? She's screwing me over!"

"No, she's supporting her sister. *You*, of all people, should understand that." Dante wore a knowing smile. "You spoil Francesca silly, and she can do no wrong in your eyes."

Markos hid a grin, couldn't refute his brother's claim. He adored his sister and would do anything to make her happy. When Francesca visited LA, he gave her money, treated her to shopping sprees on Rodeo Drive and introduced her to his celebrity clients. Francesca had lost her child, and as her older brother, it was his job to support her, to help her heal, and he wasn't going to shirk his responsibilities. "That's because she's smart, beautiful and perfect."

"Yeah, a *perfect* pain in the ass!"

The brothers laughed.

"Sometimes people do the wrong thing for the right reasons," Dante continued, wearing a sympathetic expression on his face. "It doesn't make them evil, Markos. It makes them human."

Markos drummed his fingers on the table. Considering his brother's advice, he decided Dante was wrong about Tatiyana and dismissed his words. Markos wanted nothing to do with her.

Sure you don't, said his conscience. *That's why you're obsessing about her!*

Consulting the background check once more, he shook his head in disbelief, shocked by Tatiyana's long list of accomplishments. She had a bachelor's degree in Communications, a stellar résumé filled with years of charity work and a perfect credit score. Thanks to his brother's report, he knew Tatiyana had lost her job at Pinnacle Microsystems last month, and was working at a staffing agency. His father had always advised him to befriend his enemies—then destroy them—and that's what Markos was going to do.

"Be smart," Immanuel advised, rising to his feet. He opened the fridge, searched around for several seconds, then took out the ricotta pie on the bottom shelf. "Go to the authorities. They'll know what to do. They're the experts, so let them handle it."

"And have my business end up in the papers? No thanks, Immanuel. I've got this," he said confidently. "Tatiyana messed with the wrong person."

"Don't keep us in the dark." Dante straightened in his seat. "What are you going to do?"

A sly grin curled his lips. "Fight fire with fire, of course. That's the Morretti way."

Chapter 12

Van Nuys Park, Tatiyana's favorite hangout spot in Sherman Oaks, had a colorful jungle gym, wooden benches, tennis courts, a field overrun with pint-size soccer players. Pushing the stroller along the walkway, soaking up the sunshine, Tatiyana noticed the park was noisy and crowded. Joggers ran along the trail, cyclists sped through the park, children flew homemade kites, and couples lazed under palm trees, listening to music on electronic devices.

Smelling barbecue, delicious aromas tickling and teasing her nose, Tatiyana licked her lips. The park was filled with families, couples and sports enthusiasts. Their animated voices floated on the evening breeze. Tatiyana nodded in greeting at everyone she passed, couldn't stop smiling. Yesterday, after returning home from her shift at the medical clinic, she'd persuaded Jantel to attend a group therapy session at the women's shelter, and afterward they'd gone to a nearby coffee shop. Her sister didn't say much, had seemed perfectly content sipping her black currant tea, and admiring the mosaic paintings hanging on the pale blue walls. Today had been an even better day. For the first time in months, Jantel had eaten dinner with their family and had even given Allie a bath. Her sister still wasn't her old self, but it was a step in the right direction, and Tatiyana was so happy she felt as if her heart would burst with happiness.

Thoughts of Markos—her dreamy crush with the piercing gaze, rock-hard body and sex-me voice—consumed her mind. On Thursday, Tatiyana had gone to his office, thinking he'd be sympathetic to her story, but no such luck. He'd insulted her, accused her of trying to destroy the mayor, riling her anger. She'd stood in his office, clutching her tape recorder, prepared to play the incriminating tape for him, but thankfully she'd come to her senses. Markos was a good man, and she didn't want to hurt him or his family. Not even to save her own.

"Hi, Tatiyana! Give your mom my love!" shouted a male voice with a Spanish accent.

Laughing, she waved at the gregarious widower with the toothy smile.

Every night, Tatiyana and Lena took Allie for a walk, but since her mom had a date with a firefighter, Tatiyana was on her own. She didn't mind. Needing time to think, she appreciated being alone with her thoughts. That afternoon, she'd taken Jantel to see Dr. Chopra, and her therapy session had been an eye-opener. Her sister had spoken about her feelings, and hearing about her struggles made Tatiyana more determined than ever to help her.

Sitting at a picnic table, she unbuckled Allie and picked her up. Cradling her to her chest, Tatiyana marveled at how big her niece was. It seemed like just yesterday Jantel had brought her home from the hospital. *God, I love this little girl.* Before her family came to live with her, her life had consisted of work, university and dates with a variety of successful, accomplished men. Tatiyana thought she was happy, often bragged to her girlfriends that she had a perfect life, but she'd been deluding herself. Spending quality time with her family, and taking care of her niece, had given her life meaning, and Tatiyana was thrilled they were all living under the same roof.

Bouncing Allie on her lap, she beamed as the nine-month-old cooed and giggled. It was a sweet, joyous sound, music to her ears, and Allie's gummy smile warmed her heart. "Who's the smartest baby in the world?" she said, making her eyes wide. "That's right, Allie, *you* are!"

Brushing her nose against Allie's cheeks, she inhaled her clean, sweet scent. It was moments like this that Tatiyana lived for. She didn't have a husband, or children of her own, but she had a loving family, and they were her greatest gifts.

"You have a daughter?"

Startled by the voice, Tatiyana glanced over her shoulder. "Markos?" she said, convinced her eyes were deceiving her. Her head was spinning, and she felt woozy, but she masked her features and spoke in a casual, relaxed tone. "What are you doing here?"

"*I'm* the one asking the questions, not you."

His tone was sharp, and his eyes were dark with anger. "Why didn't you tell me you had a daughter? Do you have a husband, too?"

"No, Matlock, this is my niece, not my daughter."

A frown wrinkled his smooth brow. "And that's the truth?"

"If Allie was my daughter, I'd want the world to know." Staring longingly at her niece, she stroked her tight, black curls. "She's a sweet baby, and I'd be honored to be her mom…"

A commotion on the basketball court startled her, and she trailed off speaking. Players from opposing teams, in oversize jerseys and sneakers, were pushing and shoving, but a burly security guard with dreadlocks arrived on the scene and the fighting stopped.

"We need to talk."

Her body was tingling, desperate for him, and she couldn't stop staring at his broad, sensuous mouth. Markos looked sharp in his fitted, T-shirt, knee-length shorts, and leather sandals, but his eyes were his best feature, and when his gaze zeroed in on her, goose bumps flooded her skin. Tatiyana wanted Markos to leave her alone, but since she didn't want him to know he was making her nervous, she said, "Go ahead. I'm not stopping you. It's a free world."

Exhaling deeply, as if he had the weight of the world on his shoulders, Markos sat across from her, took off his sunglasses and clasped his hands. Hands he'd used to please her. Tatiyana tried to wipe the naked images of Markos from her mind, but they remained, reminding her of their weekend tryst.

"You told me you were an executive secretary at Pinnacle."

His statement surprised her, catching her off guard. Thinking about her former job and her colleagues saddened her. They were more than just her coworkers, they were friends, and she missed them dearly, especially the interns she'd taken under her wing last summer. "Markos, what do you want? I don't have time for games—"

"You lied," he said, cutting her off. "You were fired three weeks ago."

"So? People get axed every day. Big deal."

"Everything you told me about yourself was a lie."

Dread churned in the pit of her stomach. "Have you been spying on me?"

"It's only fair. I need to know who you are, and what I'm up against."

For some reason, the smug I'm-the-man expression on his face tickled her funny bone, but since there was nothing funny about Markos showing up at her neighborhood park, Tatiyana swallowed her laughter. "Why are you here? What do you want?"

"I don't get it. How could you smile in my face, share meals with me and sleep in my bed, all the while plotting against me and my family?" he demanded. "Who does that?"

"Someone who's desperate to save her sister!" Tatiyana shouted. "You don't know what it's like to watch someone you love waste away. I do. My sister's in a dark place right now, and I'll do anything to help her. I can't lose her. She's my world. My best friend."

His expression softened, and Tatiyana knew her words had hit home.

"Tell me everything, from the beginning, so I know exactly what happened."

"My family did that already, but it got them nowhere.

You called Jantel a liar, kicked her out of your office and gave her a three-hundred dollar bill she can't afford to pay—"

Hearing someone shriek, Tatiyana broke off speaking.

"Oh, my goodness, what a precious baby!" exclaimed an elderly woman with stringy hair and a leather fanny pack. "Your daughter is beautiful. What a precious family!"

Markos erupted in laughter, startling them both, and the senior rushed off.

"What's so funny?" Tatiyana asked, puzzled by his outburst.

"The idea of us having a child. You hate me."

His words pierced her heart. "Markos, I don't hate you."

"Then why deceive me? Why didn't you tell me who you were from the beginning?"

"Because I knew if I told you the truth you wouldn't give me the time of day. Jantel wants to meet with the mayor face-to-face, and you're the only one who can help us."

"Why me?"

"You've been friends with Kassem Glover for years, and from what I've read, he has a great deal of respect and admiration for you. If anyone can convince him to talk to us, it's you."

"You didn't have to lie to me, Tatiyana. You could have just asked."

"That got my sister nowhere, so I decided to take matters into my own hands."

"Did you deceive your former boss, too? Is that why you got sacked?"

The question was an insult, a slap in the face, and Tatiyana was so shocked by it that she couldn't think of a comeback. "I'm out of here." Jumping to her feet, she grabbed the stroller and set off down the path. To her surprise and dismay, Markos fell in step with her, matching her stride for stride. Damn! Was he going to follow her home? No. No. No. Tatiyana didn't want him to know where she lived.

Not because she was ashamed of her neighborhood, it was because she didn't want Markos showing up unannounced at her house, giving her grief about her deception.

"Where are we going?"

"We're not going anywhere," she shot back, speed walking past the basketball court. "Don't you have plans with one of your girlfriends tonight?"

"Nope. No plans. I'm chillin' with you."

Tatiyana smirked. "Chillin' with me, huh? When did you start using slang?"

"What's that supposed to mean? Don't let the Rolex fool you. I get around—"

"No, you don't. You're an acclaimed attorney at a prestigious law firm, *not* a boy in the hood, so drop the act. You came from money, were educated at the best schools and this is probably the first time you've set foot in this middle-class neighborhood."

"Wrong again. I've spoken at several of the elementary schools in the area for career day," he explained, sliding his hands into the pockets of his shorts. "Don't be so quick to judge, Tatiyana. My family's wealthy, but that doesn't mean I think I'm better than the people in this neighborhood, or anywhere else. I don't."

Shame burned her cheeks. Damn. Markos was right. She was judging him because of his last name, because of his lucrative career, and it was wrong, but Tatiyana couldn't bring herself to apologize. He'd picked apart her sister's story line by line, then insinuated Jantel was a liar. Asking for his forgiveness was out of the question.

Exiting the park, Tatiyana turned left, in the opposite direction of her house. Deciding to do some window-shopping, she headed toward the nearby plaza on Wilmington Avenue, hoping to shake Markos once they reached the busy shopping complex. Checking on Allie, she noticed her niece was sleeping and pulled down the plastic visor to shield her from the hot, searing sun.

"Tatiyana, I'm going to be straight with you. I don't be-lieve your sister. She's lying."

Her hands gripped the stroller handle, but she imagined it was his neck. "No, she's not."

"She never told me she's a stripper, and her story had huge gaping holes in it," he continued, putting on his black, Ray-Ban sunglasses. "Jantel couldn't answer any of my questions, and she burst into tears whenever I pushed her for details."

"That's because she doesn't remember. She was drunk. The party's a blur—"

Markos scoffed. "How convenient."

"You can't expect her to remember every minute detail. She has a lot on her plate right now, and she's stressed out."

"Mayor Glover didn't hook up with your sister or any-one else that night. I've known him since law school, and he'd never do the things you're accusing him of. He loves his wife, his job, this fine city and he'd never do anything to embarrass himself or his family."

"Good, then he won't mind taking a DNA test."

Markos barked a laugh, but Tatiyana didn't let the noise rattle her. "We didn't grow up with money like you," she said, glaring at him. "Jantel and I had to fight for every-thing we have, and we'll do whatever it takes to ensure Allie receives everything she's entitled to."

"Yes, of course."

His tone was so cold and sarcastic, Tatiyana wanted to push him off the sidewalk.

"I have nothing against exotic dancers. I have a problem with people who lie and try to deceive me."

"My sister isn't an exotic dancer. She was a bartender who made an honest living to pay her bills."

Markos paled and scratched at his cheek.

"Jantel has a learning disability, and never got the help she needed in school," she explained. "She dropped out in tenth grade, but she was in the process of getting her

GED when she slept with the mayor and got pregnant with his child."

"Stop saying that. It isn't true."

"Yes, it is," she argued, ready to go toe-to-toe with him. "My sister's telling the truth."

"Mayor Glover is a man of morals and integrity, and I can assure you nothing nefarious happened at his bachelor party. A few of the guests got rowdy, but security handled it swiftly and discreetly."

Her feet slowed. "Oh, so you were there that night?"

"No, I was out of town on business, but several of my business associates attended the party, and they said a wonderful evening was had by all."

"So?" she shot back, annoyed by his comments. "They don't know what happened behind closed doors, and neither do you, so quit bad-mouthing my sister."

The mood was terse, strained, and tension polluted the air.

"You're right," he conceded. "I wasn't there. I don't know what happened."

Feeling bad for shouting at him, she joked, "Of course I am. I'm a smart, perceptive Capricorn who can out-argue anyone, even a famed attorney with a winning record."

He cracked a smile, and Tatiyana did, too, sensed it was the right time to apologize.

"Markos, I feel horrible about lying to you, but I didn't know what else to do. I was desperate, and I let fear cloud my judgment," she confessed. "I'm sorry for deceiving you, and I hope one day you'll find it in your heart to forgive me, because I meant everything I said in Tampa. I think you're a great guy, and I enjoyed spending time with you and your family."

"Thank you, Tatiyana. I appreciate that. And I accept your apology."

They stood in silence, staring at each other for a long moment.

His eyes bore into her, piercing her flesh, and Tatiyana gulped. Images of him—on top of her, inside her—flashed in her mind. Their romance was over, a thing of the past, but she wanted him, longed for his touch. They had a connection, incredible chemistry, and he'd always have a special place in her heart. *I wish we were still in Tampa*—

"If your sister agrees not to speak to the media, I'll help her."

Breaking free of her thoughts, she stared at him in disbelief. "What did you say?"

"I said I'll do it. I'll arrange a meeting with the mayor."

Tatiyana felt her jaw drop. His words knocked the wind out of her, leaving her speechless, and when Markos took her hand in his, her heart stopped.

Chapter 13

Tatiyana wanted to do cartwheels along Lennox Avenue and shout for joy. The unthinkable had happened, a miracle in Sherman Oaks, and she couldn't wait to get home and share the good news with her family. After two years of frustrations and disappointments, Jantel would finally have the opportunity to introduce Allie to her father, and Tatiyana knew her sister would be thrilled.

"People think I'm a heartless jerk, but I'm not. I grew up in a large, loving Italian family, and we were raised to not only look out for each other, but our community as well…"

Listening intently as Markos spoke, her respect and admiration for him grew—so did her desire. Men who cared about others, who had a heart for women and children, were damn sexy in her book, and it was obvious the divorce attorney had a big heart. Speaking with feeling, and emotion, he confessed he was nothing without his family and would do anything to help them. Drawn to him, she moved in closer. It was a fight to keep her hands to herself, but she remembered they were in LA, not in Tampa at the Oasis Spa and Resort, and gripped the handle of the stroller to prevent herself from touching him.

"Money doesn't solve problems, it creates new ones, and contrary to what you think, my life isn't perfect," he said in a solemn tone. "I know what it's like to watch someone you love suffer. It's a sad, hopeless feeling, and I wouldn't wish it on anyone."

"It sounds like you've experienced some hard times."

He resumed walking, and Tatiyana did, too, but his words consumed her thoughts.

"Three years ago, my five-year-old nephew died in a pool accident at Emilio's estate."

"Oh, my goodness, how tragic. I am so sorry for your loss." Her gaze strayed to the stroller, zeroing in on Allie, and love filled her heart. "I don't know what I'd do if anything ever happened to Allie. She's a very special child."

"Lucca was, too." His expression was grim, and his tone was somber. "Francesca and Emilio were inconsolable after Lucca's death, hell, my entire family was, but we supported each other, and we're a stronger, tighter unit because of it. Nothing can ever tear us apart."

"You have a terrific family," she said, remembering all the fun she'd had with the loud, spirited group in Tampa. "It's just me and Jantel, and growing up I always wished I had a big, boisterous family. Still do."

He smiled, but his sadness was evident.

"Would you like to have a child of your own?"

They stopped at the intersection, and Tatiyana grabbed her water bottle from the cup holder. "One thing at a time, Markos. First, I have to find a husband."

His grin was deadly sexy. "Look no further."

"As if! You're married to your career and anti-relationships."

Sipping her drink, Tatiyana eyed him over her bottle, noting his wrinkled brow.

"Damn. What is it? Dump on Markos day?"

"I'm sorry. That was a bit harsh, wasn't it?"

"Very." Sniffing, he hung his head and dabbed at his eyes. "I'm going to need intense therapy for the rest of my life."

Tatiyana burst out laughing. It felt good to laugh with him, to joke around like in Tampa. They'd had fun in Cigar City, plenty of romantic moments and spirited discussions, and Tatiyana thought he was a great guy. Markos was a perfect gentleman, someone she enjoyed being with, and she hoped they could be friends.

Liar! shrieked her inner voice. *You don't want him to be your friend. You want him to be your man. Just admit it!*

She thought of making love with Markos again, and heat flooded her body, her nipples hardening under her sundress. Her skin was tingling, but she kept her hands to herself and maintained her composure despite the needs of her flesh. It was a struggle, but she wasn't going to cross the line.

Arriving at the plaza, Markos rested a hand on her lower back. His touch, though innocent, caused her body to sweat. He made her nervous, gave her butterflies and goose bumps, and Tatiyana noticed she wasn't the only one at the plaza making eyes at him. Females winked and waved, trying desperately to catch his attention, but Markos ignored them.

"Are you hungry? I'm starving." Taking off his sunglasses, he gestured to a popular burger joint. "Let's head inside and grab a bite to eat."

"I made ribs for dinner, and I'm still full."

"You made my favorite meal and didn't invite me over?"

Tatiyana knew she shouldn't tease Markos again, especially in light of her earlier joke, but she couldn't resist poking fun at the most eligible bachelor in the city. "My bad," she said, wearing an innocent expression on her face. "I thought you were out with the surgeon, and I didn't want to disturb you. Next time I promise."

"She's not my girlfriend. I don't have one."

"I know. According to the celebrity blogs, you have *several.*"

"Didn't your mother ever tell you not to believe everything you read?"

"No, but she *did* tell me to stay away from handsome attorneys with roving eyes."

Markos lowered his face to hers, and Tatiyana willed him to kiss her.

"I haven't met Ms. Right yet, but when I do, I'll have no problem committing to her."

For some reason, his words hurt. Tatiyana wanted to be *that* woman, the one Markos committed to, but she knew it would never be. She'd deceived him about who she was, blown her only chance with him, and he didn't trust her.

"I could use a coffee," he said, stopping in front of a quaint café and reading the menu on the chalkboard. "Why don't you grab us a table, while I go inside and get us a snack?"

Tatiyana found seats on the patio, under an oversize umbrella, and checked on Allie. Her eyes were closed, but she was wiggling around in her stroller, murmuring in her sleep. She'd have a drink with Markos, then go home. She was working at California Family Care in the morning, and if she wanted to wow her new employer, she needed a good night's sleep. It was a temporary placement, only expected to last three weeks, but she wanted to make Daphne proud.

"Your niece is a good sleeper." Markos appeared, holding a tray filled with drinks, sandwiches and desserts, and set it on the round, glass table. "Matteo never slept. Every time I went to visit Dante, he was screaming down the house."

"How is Matteo doing?" she asked, helping herself to one of the drinks. "Did his team win its big soccer game on Monday?"

Markos raised an eyebrow. "You remembered?"

"Of course I did! You talked about your nephew non-stop when we were in Tampa."

"He's great. I saw him yesterday. He loves swimming, so I took him to the water park."

As they ate, Markos educated her about the exciting new projects happening in the neighborhood and the robust real-estate market. Captivated by the sound of his voice, Tatiyana found herself hanging on to every word that came out of his mouth. He was a great conversationalist, oozing with charm and charisma, and she enjoyed his stories.

"How's your mini cream pie?" Markos asked, dusting bread crumbs off his designer shirt. In less than five minutes, he'd devoured two BLT sandwiches and a plate of chocolate chip cookies, but he was still eying her dessert. "It looks delicious. Is it any good?"

"Oh, my goodness. You have *no* idea. My mouth is rejoicing right now." Tatiyana took another bite of her dessert and moaned in appreciation. The strawberries were plump, the cake moist and the ice-cream cold and refreshing. It was the perfect snack for a hot, summer day, and Tatiyana loved everything about the sweet, decadent treat. "Markos, I owe you one—"

Allie whimpered, seizing her attention and Tatiyana dropped her fork on her plate.

"Allow me. Finish your dessert, and I'll keep Allie company until you're done."

"Sure. Knock yourself out."

Markos grabbed a wet nap off the table, cleaned his hands and tossed it on his empty plate. Reaching inside the stroller, he unbuckled Allie's safety belt and picked her up. "You're as light as a cloud!" he joked. "Hello, Allie. I'm Markos. It's nice to meet you."

He spoke in a low, soothing voice and held Allie comfortably in his arms. If Tatiyana's eyes weren't open, she'd swear she was dreaming. *Talk about a dramatic turn of events. An hour ago, we were arguing, and now he's holding my niece!* Tatiyana knew she was beaming, wearing a wide-eyed expression on her face, but she couldn't stop smiling at Markos. "You're a natural."

"I know," he said, winking good-naturedly. "Just call me the Baby Whisperer."

They laughed together, and Tatiyana hoped it was a sign of things to come.

His cell chimed, and Markos glanced down at his iPhone.

"I'll take Allie." Tatiyana took her niece from his arms and kissed the tip of her nose. Opening the pink baby bag, she retrieved Allie's bottle and put it into her mouth. "Good girl."

"You've got to be kidding me!" Scowling, his fingers

moving rapidly across the screen, he mumbled under his breath in Italian. "Sorry, it's work, and if I don't respond immediately to this text, my client will throw a hissy fit."

"Clients can be difficult sometimes, can't they?" she joked, batting her eyelashes.

Markos raised his cell in the air. "It's a wealthy oil tycoon, and when he doesn't get his way, he can be really mean and vindictive."

Her eyes zeroed in on his face. Consumed with desire, she felt the overwhelming urge to touch him, yearned to reunite with his lips, but since Tatiyana knew nothing good could come from them hooking up again, she stared down at her niece. "When will you contact the mayor? How soon do you think we can meet?"

"Not until the end of September. Mayor Glover's out of town on business."

"But that's four weeks away. That's crazy! How can he run the city if he isn't here?"

"There's a lot more to being mayor than just attending council meetings and passing bylaws. To make progress, Mayor Glover travels extensively, promoting the city. Los Angeles is a great place to do business, and a vital part of the mayor's role is creating positive relationships with world leaders, executives, investors and successful businessmen around the globe."

"And you're sure he's overseas until the end of September?"

"Don't believe me? Google him."

His tone gave her pause. Tatiyana heard the edge in Markos's voice, knew he was annoyed with her, but decided not to argue with him. "What's the mayor doing in Asia?"

"He's attending the Asian Business Summit in Tokyo this week, then heading to London for the International Leadership conference. Mayor Glover's the keynote speaker, and if I didn't have to be in court every day this week, I'd attend the event."

Tatiyana didn't believe him, sensed he was playing her. She thought of taking out her cell phone to check his story, but decided to hold off. Later, after she put Allie to bed, she'd do her research, and if it turned out Markos was lying about the mayor's whereabouts, she'd know he was a fraud and convince Jantel to go to the media with her story.

You're a fine one to judge! You lied to him, secretly taped one of your conversations and planned to blackmail him with the recording, remember, Miss Perfect?

"I guess we have no choice but to wait." Tatiyana felt defeated, as if she'd taken two steps forward, then ten steps back. "This meeting is long overdue, so contact me as soon as the mayor's back in town. I'll be waiting for your call."

"I will. Don't worry. You have my word."

"Thanks, Markos. I really appreciate it. You have no idea how much this means to me."

"So, we're cool?" he said smoothly, leaning forward in his chair. "You still think I'm the sexiest attorney in LA, right?"

A smile tickled her lips. "Yeah, we're cool."

"Good, because I need a favor. My secretary is out sick with pneumonia, and I want you to fill in for her until she returns to work on the thirtieth."

Tatiyana laughed. "I can't work for you. We'd probably kill each other my first day."

"Please?" he begged, clasping his hands together. "The temp agency sent someone over on Friday, but the guy was so lazy I sent him home after lunch. His grammar was atrocious, he couldn't spell to save his life, and he smelled like an ashtray."

Though she'd never admit it to him, Tatiyana loved the idea of working at his law firm. It would look great on her résumé, could open a lot of doors for her in the business world, and best of all she could help Jantel pay for Allie's upcoming surgery.

And you'd be working side-by-side with Markos every day.

It was a challenge, harder than climbing Mount Kilimanjaro in stilettos, but she tore her gaze away from his face and wrangled her thoughts back in. "I wish I could, but I can't. I work full-time at my friend's staffing agency, and if I bail on her, she'll never forgive me."

"I admire your loyalty."

What was *that* about? Was he making fun of her? Tatiyana couldn't tell. She opened her mouth to question him, but his cell phone rang, and he promptly answered it. Tatiyana burped Allie, then put her back in her stroller. As she changed her niece's diaper, she listened closely to Markos's telephone conversation. His voice grew deeper, huskier, and Tatiyana suspected he was talking to a woman. Why else would he sound so dreamy?

"You can't call off the divorce." Drumming his fingers on the table, he released a deep breath. "I'm on my way. Stay put, and whatever you do, don't make any hasty decisions."

Ending his call, he swiped his wallet off the table and put back on his sunglasses.

"Is everything okay?"

"No, but it will be," he said with a confident smile. "I have to run. My client needs me."

"Do you always go running when your clients call?"

Markos chuckled. "Every good attorney does."

"Then in that case you better get going."

"I will after I walk you home," he said, putting several bills on the table.

Standing, Markos came around the table and pulled out her chair.

"But I'm not ready to leave yet. I need to grab some groceries."

"Tatiyana, I'm really pressed for time."

"Go ahead. I'll be fine. I don't live far from here."

Markos checked his watch, then glanced around the plaza. "You're sure you'll be okay? It's getting dark, and I don't feel comfortable leaving you and Allie here."

"Don't be silly. I grew up in this neighborhood. I'm perfectly safe." To reassure him, she smiled and patted his cheek softly. Touching him felt good, better than she remembered, and her body longed for more. "Thanks for dessert. I loved it."

"Let's have dinner tomorrow night. I know how much you love Chinese food, so we'll eat at Shanghai Palace. The food is exceptional, and the service is second to none."

"I don't think it's a good idea we see each other."

Lines wrinkled his forehead. "Why not? We had a great time together in Tampa, we have lots of things in common and you spent the last three hours talking my ear off."

"Things could get complicated. Furthermore, I need to support Jantel."

"What does your sister have to do with us?"

It was a good question, and since Tatiyana didn't have an answer, she kept quiet.

"I better go. Take good care of yourself and baby Allie."

Leaning over, he kissed her cheek. Her eyes fluttered closed, sealing her in the moment. His cologne washed over her, and Tatiyana shivered involuntarily. She couldn't speak, had no words, couldn't think of anything to say. His words rang in her ears, exciting her. Suddenly, she had a change of heart. Eager to accept his dinner offer, she parted her lips and opened her eyes. But it was too late. Markos was gone.

Chapter 14

"You want me to do *what*?" Tatiyana shouted, shock reverberating through her body. Gripping the steering wheel of her Jeep, she took a deep breath to calm her rattled nerves. Her head was spinning, but she focused her gaze on the road, carefully driving along the congested, tree-lined street. *Daphne can't be serious! She's joking, right?*

"Our company slogan is, Matching Outstanding Employees with Successful Businesses, and you and LA Family Law are a perfect match," Daphne explained.

Needing to think, Tatiyana turned off the radio. Five minutes earlier, she'd been in good spirits, singing along with the Britney Spears song playing on the radio, but now she wanted to rip out her earpiece, chuck it out the window and reverse over it for good measure. On the drive to the medical center, she'd been surprised to receive a call from Daphne, and knew from the sound of her friend's voice that she was over the moon. Little did Tatiyana know that Markos was the reason why. "I can't work at LA Family Law," she argued. "They're expecting me at California Family Care in twenty minutes, and I don't want to let them down."

"No worries. I'll call the clinic, explain the situation to Dr. Voth and send Kyung-Soon in your place. See? Problem solved."

"No! Don't! I like working at the clinic." Staring out the windshield, Tatiyana thought for a moment, racking her brain for a solution. A thick layer of smog obscured the sky, the air was humid and a pungent scent drifted through the car windows. "Why can't you send Kyung-Soon to the firm? Why are you insisting that I go?"

"Because Markos Morretti called this morning and personally requested you," she explained. "And what the client wants, the client gets. Understood?"

"Not this time. I can't work for him."

"You can, and you will. Markos thinks you'd be an asset to his firm, and so do I. Furthermore, he agreed to pay *double* the daily rate for your services, and promised to send more business my way in the near future. I'm not going to refuse him, and neither will you."

"Daphne, you don't understand. I know him. We've butted heads a few times."

You've done a lot more than just *butt heads* quipped her inner voice. *You sexed him in Tampa, and you're dying to do it again.*

"This is a win-win situation for everyone, especially you. A thousand-dollar bonus is nothing to laugh at," she pointed out. "You could use the money to pay bills, or do something nice for your mom. You're always talking about how great Lena is with Allie, so treat her to a spa day."

"Forget it. I'm not going. Send someone else."

"What about the bonus?"

"What about it? It's just money. I can always make more."

A silver Bentley with personalized license plates cut Tatiyana off on Wilshire Boulevard, and she smacked her horn. It felt good, relieved some of her frustration, so she did it again. Stopping at the intersection, she dragged a hand through her lush, loose waves. Wanting to look professional, she'd selected a purple, A-line dress, tasteful accessories and high-heel sandals. Cross-shaped earrings dangled from her ears, and a gold necklace adorned her neck. She'd worked at the clinic for only four days, but Tatiyana enjoyed being at the office and admired the hardworking team of nurses and doctors.

"Daphne, sorry, but I'm not going. Not today, not tomorrow, not ever."

"Very well." Her voice was stiff, cold, her disappointment evident in her tone. "I'll call Markos back, tell him you're no longer employed at Staffing Unlimited and refund his money."

Swerving to the left, she narrowly avoided hitting the curb, and pulled her Jeep onto the shoulder. "W-w-wait. Hold on a sec," she stammered, pressing her Bluetooth closer to her ear. "You're firing me because I don't want to work for Markos Morretti?"

An awkward silence followed. Tatiyana heard a door slam, papers ruffle and knew Daphne was in her office doing paperwork.

"It's nothing personal. It's business."

Tatiyana shouted her words. "I thought we were friends!"

"So did I, but if you were my friend, you wouldn't screw me over."

"Daphne, don't say things like that. It's not true. I'd never do that."

"Yes, it is. If you don't go to LA Family Law, it will make me look bad, unprofessional and you of all people know how hard I've worked to build my business."

"You don't understand."

"No, *you* don't understand," Daphne shot back. "Everything isn't always about you, Tatiyana. Sometimes you have to put your feelings aside to help someone else."

A cold chill stabbed her flesh. Tatiyana started to argue, but swallowed her retort. She wanted to tell Daphne about Jantel's baby-daddy drama, the real reason why she'd traveled to Tampa, and her hot, weekend fling with Markos, but she couldn't risk her friend blabbing to the other women in the office. Daphne loved gossip more than chocolate, and Tatiyana didn't want the world to know her business.

Rubbing her throbbing temples, Tatiyana considered her options. She wanted to see Markos again, but feared what would happen if they were alone. She desired him and had to restrain herself from diving into his arms whenever he was around. Pressing her eyes shut, she dismissed the thought. Her focus was supposed to be on helping Jantel, not on Markos—

"Please, Tatiyana? This is the last favor I'll ever ask you. I swear on my Jimmy Choos."

"Fine, fine, I'll go. Quit twisting my arm."

Daphne cheered. "I knew you'd come around!"

"Just make sure you mail my bonus today," she said with a laugh.

"I'll do it this afternoon. I promise. Thanks, girl. I really appreciate this."

Tatiyana checked her rearview mirror, pulled into the left lane and punched the gas. "When does Markos want me to start?"

"Now. He's expecting you at LA Family Law by nine, so step on it!"

LA Family Law, one of the most prestigious firms in the state, resembled a high-end art gallery, and as Tatiyana stepped off the elevator and entered the lobby, she was struck by the tranquil ambience. The air smelled of peppermint, pendant lamps lit up the space, and Bach was playing softly in the background. Sculptures were displayed on raised, glass tables, framed paintings of world monuments beautified the ivory walls and the all-white furniture made the office look chic, as if it belonged in an issue of an architectural design magazine. Men in designer suits, clutching coffee mugs and cell phones, breezed by, and a group of middle-aged women stood in front of the water cooler, speaking in hushed tones.

Catching sight of her reflection in the wall mirror, Tatiyana raked a hand through her hair, and adjusted her dress. During the twenty-minute drive to LA Family Law, she'd fretted about working at the firm, and couldn't shake the feeling she was making a mistake.

"What can I help you with?"

Tatiyana regarded the petite brunette in the black pantsuit glaring at her. Her makeup was flawless, her hair was piled on top of her head in a bun and her turquoise accessories complemented her outfit. Tatiyana recalled meeting the paralegal last week, when she'd surprised Markos in his office, but couldn't recall her name. "Good morning. I'm Tatiyana," she said, wearing her best smile. "Staffing Unlimited sent me over. I'm the new secretary."

The other woman offered her hand in greeting. "I'm Izzy Braunstein. Markos's kick-ass paralegal and personal assistant. Welcome to LA Family Law, Tatiyana. You're going to love it here."

Smiling, the women shook hands.

"So," she drawled, raising an eyebrow. "Tell me more about you and Markos."

"There's nothing to tell."

Unfazed, Izzy pumped her for information, asking personal, intimate questions about Markos, but Tatiyana raised her hand in the air, putting an end to her game of twenty questions.

"We're not dating. He's helping me with a legal matter. That's it."

"I figured as much." Izzy shrugged. "You're not his type."

Not his type? What did *that* mean? What kind of women *did* he like? Tatiyana didn't know if it was a dig or not, but she refrained from asking the questions on the tip of her tongue. They were at work, after all, not at the local pub during happy hour, and she didn't want Izzy to think she was romantically interested in Markos.

Izzy gave her a tour of the office, showing her how to answer the phones, and sign into the computer. "Now that you know the ropes, let's have lunch."

"Lunch? But I haven't done anything yet."

"I know, isn't it great?" Giggling, she opened her handbag, retrieved her oval-shaped sunglasses and put them on. "Markos is in San Diego, meeting with a disgruntled trophy wife, so we can have a nice, long lunch at The Polo Lounge."

"I'm not hungry yet, so I'm going to stay here and familiarize myself with the office." Tatiyana picked up the policy-and-procedures binder beside the phone and flipped it open. "I don't want to look like a ditz when I'm talking to clients, so I'm going to read up about the company and review the minutes from last month's staff meeting, as well."

"Suit yourself. See you later!"

Waving, Tatiyana watched Izzy sail through the open doors and into the waiting elevator. Curious about the firm, she sat at her desk and began reading. Jotting down questions as they came to her, she made note of the policies Markos had written, and noticed they were interesting and engaging—just like the man himself.

The phone rang, startling her, and Tatiyana put on the headset. Taking a deep breath, she pressed Line 1 and spoke with confidence, as if this were her hundredth day on the job rather than her first. "LA Family Law. Markos Morretti's office. How may I help you?"

"You made it."

A girlish smile exploded onto her mouth. Tatiyana hadn't seen Markos since he'd surprised her at the park five days earlier, and hearing his voice made her pulse race and her temperature soar. "Hello, Mr. Moretti. What can I do for you today?"

"I'm calling to check up on you."

His smooth, oh-so-sexy voice tickled and teased her ears.

"How is your first day going?" he asked.

"So far so good. To be honest, I'm a little restless. I haven't done much yet."

"Have you had lunch?"

"No. It's only eleven o'clock."

"That didn't stop Izzy from leaving thirty minutes ago, did it?"

Convinced he was hiding somewhere, Tatiyana glanced

frantically around the office in search of him. "Where are you? How did you know that?"

Tatiyana heard the sounds of traffic in the background and knew Markos was calling from his car. Was he on his way to the office? The thought made her heart sing.

"I know Izzy like the back of my hand. She thinks I don't know about her long lunches and marathon phone conversations with her boyfriend, but I do."

Surprised, and confused, she asked, "If Izzy's not doing her job, why keep her around? Why not find someone else? Someone you can trust to stay on top of things in your absence?"

"Because I promised her mother I'd look out for her, and I want to keep my word. Izzy was devastated when her parents split up and blames her mom for her dad moving out…"

Moved by his kindness and compassion, Tatiyana nodded in understanding.

"Izzy's a good kid," he continued. "I have faith in her. She'll get her act together."

"And if she doesn't?"

"I'm going back to Venice. I don't need this grief. I'm only thirty-six!"

Laughing, Tatiyana closed the policy-and-procedures binder and pushed it aside. She'd done enough reading for one day. She wanted to talk to Markos, not review more company memos.

"I'm on my way to the office but wanted to know what you'd like for lunch."

"Don't worry about me. I'm fine. I brought a salad."

"A salad? I've seen you eat. That's not going to be enough food for you."

"I hope you're not implying that I'm an eating machine," she joked, feigning anger. "I'm not. I'm just a girl who enjoys a good, hearty meal and the occasional glass of Chardonnay."

"Among other things…" He deliberately allowed his words to hang in the air, leaving no doubt in her mind that he was talking about sex. "I've never met anyone like you, Tatiyana. You're one of a kind."

"Is that a good thing or a bad thing?"

"It's a *great* thing."

His deep husky voice tickled her flesh. Her mind flashed back to the night they made love at Applause Nightclub, and her skin flushed with heat.

"I'll be there in twenty minutes. See you then."

Wanting to freshen up before his arrival, Tatiyana whipped off her headset and grabbed her purse from underneath the mahogany desk. Standing, she was shocked to see Ashley Zapata pacing in the lobby. Known for her big voice, voluptuous shape and trend-setting style, the Colombian pop star and acclaimed actress was loved worldwide by her adorning fans.

Approaching her, Tatiyana said, "Hello. May I help you?"

"Is Markos around?" She gestured wildly with her hands, her ponytail swishing back and forth. "I need to talk to him. It's an emergency."

The desk phone rang, but it was obvious Mrs. Zapata was upset, and Tatiyana didn't want to leave her. "He'll be here soon," she said, nodding in assurance. "Why don't you come inside and wait for him in the conference room? I'll bring you a cup of coffee and—"

"No coffee. Too much caffeine. It's bad for the heart. Do you have wine?"

Minutes later, Tatiyana sat inside the conference room, watching the beloved pop star guzzle her third glass of Merlot, wondering where Markos was. She'd called him and left an urgent message on his voice mail when it clicked on, but he hadn't responded yet.

"Can I have some more?" Mrs. Zapata licked her plump lips. "I'm really thirsty."

"Yes, of course." Tatiyana picked up the bottle and filled her empty glass to the brim. The mini fridge at the rear of the room had a wide assortment of snacks, so she offered the pop star something to eat. "We have fruit, cheese, sushi and—"

"Sushi?" Water filled her eyes, her bottom lip trembled and she burst into tears.

Tatiyana reached out and rubbed her back. Tears streamed down the pop star's cheeks, splashing onto her jumpsuit, and her shoulders shook.

"I'm sorry. I'm not a crier, but today's my birthday, and I want to spend it with my husband." She sniffed, hanging her head. "We're separated. Have been for almost two years."

Tatiyana wore a sympathetic smile. Sadly, she understood what the pop star was going through. Over the years, she'd suffered her fair share of heartbreak, too. Knew what it was like to lose someone you loved, to feel alone and abandoned. Her ex was a mama's boy who needed to grow up, and Tatiyana didn't respect him. Markos, on the other hand, was his own man, a gentleman through and through, and if they'd met under different circumstances, she'd date him. Clearing the thought from her mind, Tatiyana gave the weeping pop star her full attention.

"Every year Yoshiro makes me homemade sushi to celebrate. He's such a good cook. Better than a celebrity chef!" Using the back of her hand, she dabbed at her eyes and mascara-stained cheeks. "I don't want to have dinner with my staff tonight. I want to be with my husband and son. Yoshiro means everything to me."

"You should call him."

"Markos said I shouldn't. He said if I do, I could ruin everything."

"What do *you* want?" Tatiyana asked.

"I want my husband to come home. I want us to be a family again."

Mrs. Zapata opened her purse, took out a pink, silk handkerchief and blew her nose. For several seconds, she fiddled with the pear-shaped diamond ring on her left hand.

"Do you still love him?"

"With all my heart. I never stopped. If anything, being apart has only made me love and appreciate him even more. I'm miserable without Yoshiro, and I want him back."

"Then go get your man."

"But Markos said—"

"But nothing," she argued, unable to hold her tongue any longer. Tatiyana knew it was none of her business, but it broke her heart to see the woman cry. The pop star was hurting, and Tatiyana wanted to help her. "A good man is hard to find, and if I found someone who cooked for me, and took care of me I'd never let him go. I'd worship the ground he walks on!"

"I don't know what to do. I'm so confused."

Tatiyana patted her hand. "Follow your heart. It will never lead you astray."

"I want to, but Markos said it's too late to call off the divorce."

"If I found my soul mate, I wouldn't let anyone keep us apart."

"You wouldn't?"

"Hell, no! I'd do anything to be with him—"

Someone cleared their throat, seizing her attention, and Tatiyana broke off speaking. Glancing over her shoulder, her body tensed, and her tongue froze inside her mouth. Markos stared at her, his gaze dark and narrowed, and Tatiyana knew she was in a world of trouble.

Chapter 15

"What did you do?" Markos slammed his office door so hard the windows rattled and the floor shook. Folding his arms, he hit Tatiyana with a cold, dark stare. Finding the women inside the conference room, speaking in hushed tones he'd sensed something was terribly wrong—and there was. His worst nightmare had come true, and his chatty new secretary was to blame. "Mrs. Zapata said she no longer needs my services."

Tatiyana didn't answer, wore a blank expression on her face, as if she didn't understand why he'd buzzed the front desk after walking Mrs. Zapata to her car and ordered her into his office. That morning, as he was driving to San Diego, he'd called Staffing Unlimited, asked to speak to the manager and persuaded her to send Tatiyana to his firm. But now, Markos wondered if he'd made a mistake.

To regain control of his emotions, Markos took a deep breath. He didn't need this shit. Not today. Not after the stress of the past twenty-four hours. Thinking about yesterday, he felt a headache forming and pinched the bridge of his nose. One of his clients, a former beauty queen, had propositioned him inside her kitchen. Shedding her satin robe, she'd chased him around the breakfast bar, desperately pawing at his clothes. Sprinting out the front door wasn't his finest moment, but he wasn't going to ruin his reputation by hooking up with a client.

As Markos was speeding away from the Hidden Hills estate, Romeo had phoned, ranting and raving about his on-again, off-again model girlfriend, but when Markos suggested his brother dump the fiery Norwegian once and for all, he'd turned on *him*. He had accused him of being jealous, then abruptly ended the call. Pulling into his driveway, he'd spotted Caroline sitting on his doorstep, and cursed in Italian. Inviting her inside was his first mistake, allowing her to stay for dinner was his second. She'd droned on and on about work, demanded he take her to the governor's ball and grilled him about his love life. Bored out of his mind, he'd sent on her home midway through dessert, then lifted weights in his home gym to alleviate his stress.

"I don't understand why you're upset," Tatiyana said. "I did nothing wrong."

"What did you say to her?"

"Nothing. Mrs. Zapata talked, and I listened."

Markos heard his cell phone ring, felt it vibrating in his back pocket, but he didn't answer it. He had unfinished business with Tatiyana, and wanted to get to the bottom of things before the situation spiraled out of control. "And you're sure that's all that happened?"

"Mrs. Zapata loves her husband, and she doesn't want a divorce, so I encouraged her to have an open and honest talk with him. Is that a problem?"

Staring at the ceiling, he threw his hands up in the air. "Are you trying to ruin me?"

"No. I was trying to help."

"You have a funny way of showing it."

"Markos, I'm sorry. I didn't mean to upset you…"

Studying her, he stroked the length of his jaw. Tatiyana sounded contrite, looked it, too, but he couldn't shake the feeling that she was playing him again. Was this another trick? A ploy designed to screw him over? He'd never lost a case, or a client, and wondered what the other senior partners would think when they heard the news. Would they be disappointed? Angry? Would they blame him for losing one of the firm's richest clients?

"This is messed up. A total nightmare." Pinching two fingers together, he spoke through clenched teeth. "I was this close to a settlement, and now everything's ruined.

Eighteen months' worth of hard work just went down the drain!"

"A good attorney does what's best for his client, not his bank account."

Markos glared at her, didn't hide his contempt. "What's *that* supposed to mean?"

"It's not about you. It's about your clients," she said calmly, looking him straight in the eye. "You work for Mrs. Zapata, not the other way around…"

Her tone was quiet, but her words were powerful.

"You need to listen to her, and most importantly take her cares and concerns into consideration. Divorce is a life-altering decision that affects everyone involved, and clients have the right to change their minds without fear of being belittled or bullied."

His jaw hit his chest with a thud. Markos was frustrated about the Zapata case, wished he'd been there to talk to the temperamental pop star instead of buying lunch, but she'd given him something to think about. Tatiyana had a mind of her own and wasn't afraid to disagree with him, which made him respect her even more. Markos had feelings for her, and deep down he liked the idea of them being a couple, but he feared Tatiyana would double cross him again, and if she did it would hurt like hell.

"I didn't persuade Mrs. Zapata to call off the divorce. I didn't have to. She had her mind made up before she got here. I had nothing to do with it."

For a moment, they sat in silence, alone with their thoughts.

"I love what I do," he said, feeling the need to defend himself and the choices he'd made. "I don't want to do anything else. This is it for me."

"No one's disputing that, Markos. It's obvious you love being an attorney, and from what I've read you're a skilled negotiator with a keen legal mind, but there's more to being a lawyer than just winning cases and posing for the cameras."

A skilled negotiator with a keen legal mind? Pride filled

his heart. *Tatiyana read my interview in* GQ *magazine! Yeah, baby!* Leaning up against his desk, Markos crossed his legs at the ankles. Amused, he watched his new secretary with growing interest. She had an aura about her, a presence that drew her to him. It was more than just her beauty. It was her spirit, her personality, how she carried herself that appealed to him, and Markos was looking forward to getting to know her better outside the bedroom. *Though, I wouldn't mind if she wanted to pick up where we left off in Tampa.*

"Do what's best for your client, regardless of how you feel about their case, and listen to them. Support them. Let them know you're their biggest supporter."

"I'm an attorney. Not a therapist."

"Markos, you're wrong," she argued, shaking her head. "A good attorney *is* a therapist. He's also a friend, a confidant and a teacher…"

Consumed with guilt, Markos stared down at his black leather dress shoes. Listening to her, he realized he was wrong for yelling at her earlier. It wasn't Tatiyana's fault he was having a bad week, and he shouldn't take his frustrations out on her. She'd done nothing wrong, and deep down he'd always known Mrs. Zapata wouldn't go through with the divorce.

"If you can't support your clients wholeheartedly, and put their needs first, you shouldn't be practicing law," she said, her tone matter-of-fact. "Maybe it's time for a career change."

His tongue fell limp in his open mouth. Her words hurt, were more painful than a dagger to the heart. Damn. He hated to admit it, wished it wasn't true, but Tatiyana was right. All he cared about was winning. Crushing the competition. Keeping his winning streak intact. That was all that mattered. It was what he lived for, why he woke up every morning and worked fourteen-hour days. It was the driving force behind every decision he made, but for the first time in his life, Markos questioned his methods. "I'm a Morretti," he said with shrug and a sheepish smile. "Winning is all that matters."

"Not in my book. Helping others and making a positive impact in their lives means more to me than anything else."

Her speech convicted him, challenged him, made him want to do better, be better. For some strange reason, he wanted to impress her, to prove to Tatiyana that he wasn't a cutthroat attorney driven by the almighty dollar. In Tampa, they'd had great conversations about life, spent hours talking and laughing in bed, and he didn't want his negative attitude to turn her off. Markos tried to smooth things over with her, but she interrupted him.

"Do you want me to leave?"

Hell no! You just got here! Straightening to his full height, he stepped forward, closing the gap between them. The air was thick, the mood more hostile than a child custody hearing, but Markos wasn't letting Tatiyana walk out the door. "No. Of course not."

"Are you sure? It's *your* office, your clients, and I don't want to piss you off again."

"I'm positive. You're staying, and that's final. I'm the boss, remember?"

Tatiyana nodded, but he sensed her inner turmoil, and feared she wouldn't return tomorrow.

"How did you become so wise?" he asked, considering her earlier comments.

"Like they say, experience is the best teacher."

"Did you learn a lot about life from your relationship with your ex?" he asked. "Is that why you're so insightful?"

Pain flickered in her eyes, and Markos knew his question had hit a nerve. Gesturing to the couch, he offered Tatiyana a seat, but she declined. His thoughts ran wild, but instead of grilling her, he waited patiently for her response.

"My ex-boyfriend's mother was the former district attorney of Santa Clara County, and I was her assistant for years," she explained, with a sad smile. "That's how I met Seth. He came into the office one day, invited me out for lunch and the rest is history."

"Was it love at first sight?"

Tatiyana scoffed. "He said it was, but his actions suggested otherwise."

Engrossed in her story, Markos moved closer, eager to learn more about her.

"I was good enough to date for three years, but I wasn't good enough to marry. Doesn't sound like love to me."

To comfort her, he gave her arm a light squeeze. "Don't sweat it. It's his loss."

"Then why do *I* feel like such a loser?"

Hot, sweat clinging to his skin, Markos plucked at his dress shirt. Tatiyana was the one who'd opened up about her past, so why did *he* feel exposed? As if *she* could see into his soul?

"Can I take my lunch break now, or should I wait for Izzy to get back from her break?"

"No, please, go ahead."

"Thank you, Markos."

He wanted to hug her, to take her into his arms, but stayed put. Didn't want to upset her. She was smiling, speaking in her usual bright, bubbly voice, but he sensed her sadness, her hurt, and wanted to comfort her. "I brought Thai food. It's in the staff room," he explained, hoping to make up for snapping at her earlier. "Let's eat together."

"I better not. The last time we had lunch, we ended up having sex on the table, and I don't want to get fired on my first day. Daphne will kill me."

Markos stood, frozen like a slab of ice, as images of that fateful day overwhelmed his mind. His head spun like the overhead ceiling fan, and it felt like his lips were glued together. He had vivid memories of their lovemaking. Could recall every sound, every scent, every delicious moan that fell from her mouth. Spreading her legs wide, he'd entered her, thrusting with all his might, pleasing her body with his tongue, and hands—

"If you need me, I'll be eating outside in the courtyard."

Watching every switch of her hips as she sashayed out the door made his mouth dry and his palms wet. Markos wanted to go after her but knew it was a bad idea. She'd think he was desperate, and that would ruin everything. He was a Morretti, and if his brothers and cousins found out he was nipping at Tatiyana's heels, they'd give him a beat down.

Noting the time on the antique clock above the door, Markos sat in his leather chair and scooped up his gold fountain pen. All wasn't lost. This wasn't over. The thought heartened him, giving him an adrenaline rush, and Markos knew it was just a matter of time before he had the upper hand.

At six o'clock that evening, Markos parked on the cobblestone driveway of Dante's Bel Air mansion and hopped out of his midnight-blue Ferrari FF. Grand, with stone archways and gigantic windows, the Italian-style estate had more amenities than a five-star hotel. It was set on ten acres of manicured grounds, with a sprawling lawn, towering palm trees and a man-made lake filled with colorful, exotic fish.

Entering the vestibule through the unlocked front door, Markos cupped his hands around his mouth and yelled, "Honey, I'm home!" Hearing the distant sound of voices, music and laughter, he strode through the main floor, expecting to find Dante in the living room watching soccer, Matteo playing video games on his beloved iPad and Jordana reading a movie script in her favorite chair. To his surprise, he found the trio in the kitchen, goofing off. Kids' music was playing on the sound system, that annoying song about Old MacDonald, and Jordana and Matteo were dancing around the table, imitating farm animals.

"Uncle Markos!" Matteo shouted, launching himself

across the room into Markos's open arms. "Did you bring me something?"

"Of course I did. I always bring something cool for my main man." Markos snapped his fingers, reached behind Matteo's ear and produced a miniature chocolate egg. "Want one?"

Matteo plucked the candy from Markos's outstretched hand, unwrapped it and tossed it into his mouth. "Do it again, Uncle, but this time make a race car appear! I want to be a Formula One driver like Uncle Emilio, so I need a superfast car."

"A race car driver?" he repeated, faking a frown. "What's up with that? I thought you wanted to be a big-shot attorney like your Uncle Markos."

"I did, but the kids at school said race car drivers are *way* cooler than lawyers."

Everyone laughed.

"Uncle Markos, stay right there. I want to show you something. Be right back!"

Wiggling out of his arms, Matteo sprinted through the kitchen and down the hallway. Taking off his sunglasses, Markos gave Dante a fist bump and kissed Jordana on each cheek. "Congratulations on the music video," he said, giving her a one-arm hug. "The song's a hit, and I can't go anywhere in the city without hearing, 'On Fleek.' Way to go, sister-in-law."

Her eyes lit up, shimmering with pride, and her lush, deep brown curls tumbled around her face when she laughed. "Thanks, Markos."

"Everywhere I go I hear people are talking about the striking Bohemian goddess in the video. How does it feel being an overnight sensation?"

"Honestly, the past few weeks have been a blur, what with my parents' visit, the album release party and countless auditions, but I couldn't be happier."

"Hey!" Dante hollered, pointing at his chest. "What about me? What am I? Chopped liver?"

Jordana winked. "No, baby, you're the icing on the cake."

"That's right, wifey, you tell 'em! You're a happily married woman, with a husband who loves and adores you," he said, showering her face with kisses.

Markos rolled his eyes to the ceiling. He knew his brother had fallen hard for Jordana since their "fake" marriage, but all the touching, and kissing, was ridiculous. "Enough already!"

"You're just jealous." Wrapping his arm around his wife, he wore a broad grin. "You *wish* you had a woman like Jordana to come home to at the end of the day, but all you have is your prized car collection, your awards and a big ole empty house."

And that's just the way I like it. No problems, no stress, no fears of getting hurt again.

Markos opened his mouth to rebuke his brother's claim, but he broke off speaking when Matteo resurfaced in the kitchen, chatting excitedly about the new Batman-themed bike Jordana had bought him yesterday. Climbing onto the bike, he gripped the handlebars.

"Cool bike, lil' man. I bet it rides like a dream."

"Uncle Markos, can you take me for a spin? Please?" he begged. "Dad promised to take me, but I've been waiting forever!"

Markos ruffled his short, brown curls. "Sure, lil' man. I'd love to."

Dante helped Matteo put on his helmet. "I'll come, too. I could use some fresh air."

Reaching into his back pocket, Markos took out his wallet and placed it on the marble counter. He'd left the office early, with the intention of exercising in his home gym, but he didn't feel like being alone tonight. He could call Catherine, or one of the other women in his Contact list to keep him company, but knew he'd live to regret it. He wasn't looking for a serious relationship, just someone fun and interesting to hang out with after dark.

An image of Tatiyana flashed into his mind.

Thinking about his new secretary with the quick wit, infectious laugh and bodacious body, made a grin curl his mouth. With Tatiyana, things were easy, effortless. She told great stories, asked smart questions and fascinated him. Like that afternoon. He was in his office, deep in conversation with the other senior partners when she'd slipped in, set a tray of coffee on the table and left. It was only her first day at the firm, but she'd made an indelible impression on him, and Markos was curious what tomorrow would bring. He was so anxious to see Tatiyana again he knew he wouldn't be able to sleep a wink tonight.

"Markos, are you staying for dinner? There's plenty, and we'd love to have you."

"That depends. What are you making?" His brothers were always teasing Jordana about her cooking, cracked jokes about vegan food being tasteless, but the air smelled of garlic, and his mouth watered at the scent. "Is that curry I smell?"

"It sure is. I'm making curried, red lentil soup, butternut squash linguine and veggie meatballs." Opening the oven, Jordana picked up the glass casserole dish and set it down on the stove. "And for dessert, I made cinnamon coffee cake and homemade ice cream."

Licking his lips, he rubbed his empty stomach. "Count me in. I'm definitely staying."

Minutes later, they were on their bikes, cruising along Bel Air Road. Inhaling the crisp air, Markos allowed the beauty of the great outdoors to soothe his mind. Landscapers trimmed shrubs and mowed lawns, tween girls played hopscotch on the sidewalk, and trophy wives, decked out in diamonds and sundresses, pushed baby strollers. A full-figured brunette, in a white tube top and Daisy Dukes waved at him, but Markos pretended not to notice her. She reminded him of his ex. They both had silky straight hair, dimples and olive skin. His last serious relationship had ended years ago, shortly after he'd been hired at LA Family Law, and although his scars had healed, he was nervous about getting serious with someone else. It was better to date around, to play the field. He could call the shots and didn't have to worry about losing his heart to the wrong woman.

What about falling for the right *woman?* asked his inner voice. *Someone strong and independent who challenges you? Someone you share an insatiable chemistry with?*

Again, his thoughts turned to Tatiyana. He had to admit that he liked having her at the firm, had enjoyed seeing her flittering around the office throughout the day, answering phones, chatting with his clients, watering the plants and flowers. She'd bent over, giving him a perfect view of her taut backside, and watching her on the sly from the comfort of his desk had been the highlight of his day. He couldn't look at Tatiyana without thinking about the weekend they'd spent together in Tampa, and wondered how long it would take to get her back in his bed. A week? Two? Markos gulped. A month? *I hope not. I can't wait that long.* He blew out a deep breath. *A man can only take so many cold showers.*

"Dad, I'm going to the park!" Matteo took off down the block, pedaling so fast his short, brown curls whipped around his face.

"Bro, are you okay? You look pissed. What's on your mind?"

"Nothing. I'm straight." To get Dante off his back, he changed the subject. "You and Jordana seem blissfully in love. How are things going?"

"Great! Marrying her was the smartest decision I've ever made."

"Are you guys thinking about having more kids?"

"I sure hope so, because Matteo needs a playmate. He's hogging my beautiful new bride, and I'm starting to get a little jealous. He gets more cuddle time than I do."

The brothers laughed.

"Enough about me and my incredible wife. What's going on with you and Tatiyana?" Dante asked, giving Markos a sideways glance. "Did you get rid of her?"

"No. I hired her."

Dante chuckled. "Right, and I actually like vegan food."

"I'm serious. Tatiyana started at the firm this morning—"

"I'm going to play with my friends." Matteo stopped at the end of the street, jumped off his bike and raced across the field to the park. Giggling, he tossed his helmet to the ground, and jumped headfirst into the sandbox.

Keeping an eye on Matteo, the brothers talked, as they circled the park on their bikes.

"Bro, I know Tatiyana lied to you about who she was when you first met her, but don't hold it against her. She made a mistake. We all do."

"Thanks, Socrates. I'll try to remember that."

"I hope you do. I screwed up big-time with Jordana, but once I realized the error of my ways, I was ready and willing to do whatever it took to bring my baby back home. And I did."

Staring at the sky, he considered his brother's words. He had the worst luck with women, hadn't met anyone who excited him in years, but Tatiyana appealed to him. She'd caught his eye the moment she boarded Flight 74, and if everything went according to plan, she'd be back in his bed by the end of the week. By the time Mayor Glover returned from his trip, he'd have the situation with Tatiyana and her sister under control.

"We all mess up sometimes, even you," Dante said with a knowing smile.

"Man, get out of here. I'm damn near perfect."

"Prove it." Releasing his handlebars, he pumped his

arms vigorously in the air. "Let's race around the park one more time. The loser washes the winner's car after dinner."

"Deal," Markos shouted, peddling faster. "Prepare to bust some suds, little brother!"

Chapter 16

Yawning, Markos exited the elevator on Friday morning with his iPhone in one hand and his leather briefcase in the other. He felt battered, more banged up than a stunt double on a Hollywood movie set, and wanted to kick himself for overdoing it that morning in his home gym. His trainer had advised him to quit after their kickboxing session, but he'd grabbed his dumbbells and pushed himself to the point of exhaustion. He'd had another X-rated dream about Tatiyana, had tossed and turned all night thinking about all of the wicked things he wanted to do to her in bed, and needed an outlet for his pent-up energy. Thoughts of her consumed him, making it impossible for him to think of anything *but* her.

Reflecting on the past three weeks made Markos grin. Tatiyana was a light, the sun, a vibrant, vivacious beauty who dazzled him with her smile, and he liked having her at LA Family Law. She had great social skills, an infectious personality, and Markos couldn't go anywhere in the firm without his male colleagues asking about her. How was Tatiyana? Would she be at happy hour? Was she seeing anyone special? Did she have a boyfriend? The questions were endless, annoying as hell, and the more he talked about her the more he desired her. Every time she sashayed past his office he did a double take. Couldn't help it. Tatiyana was that appealing, that captivating, and these days all he could think about was making love to her. On his desk. Against the bookshelf. In his private bathroom. In every position known to man—

Pressing his eyes shut, Markos cleared his mind. Enough. He didn't have time to fantasize about Tatiyana. He had work to do, and lots of it. Back in control, he gave his head a shake. Markos checked his email and groaned when he saw fifty new messages in his in-box.

Marching down the hallway, he reviewed the day's schedule. Court at nine o'clock. Lunch with the other senior partners. Meetings back-to-back. A round of golf with a potential client at the country club. His thoughts returned to Tampa, and he remembered the first time he'd played golf with Tatiyana. *It feels like I've known her for years, but it's only been a month.* He wondered if she had plans tonight. Every day after work, he asked her out for dinner, and her excuses were endless. She had to babysit her niece. Her mom needed her. She had an exam to study for. Or the worst of all—she had a date. It pissed him off that he'd made zero progress with Tatiyana since she'd started at the firm, but Markos wasn't giving up. Morrettis never did.

Markos heard voices, guessed the cleaning crew was hard at work and strode through the open door, anxious to get to his office. The air smelled of roses, instantly putting him in a calm mood, and he made a mental note to send flowers to his *nonna*. She'd brag to her friends about her grandson in LA, and thinking about his kindly grandmother made him smile.

"Morning, boss! You're looking dapper this morning."

Startled, Markos staring wordlessly at Tatiyana. He was shocked to see her in the office, dusting shelves, fluffing the chair cushions and polishing the framed certificates hanging on the walls. Tracking her around the reception area with his eyes, he admired her look. Her makeup was simple, and her straight, silky hair hung loosely down her back, but she dazzled in an orange ruffled blouse, slim-fitting skirt and leopard-print sandals.

"Nice suit," she said. "And you smell great, too. Like confidence and success."

He opened his mouth, realized he had no words and slammed it shut. *What's the matter with me? Why do I freeze up every time she smiles at me?* His behavior baffled him, left him scratching his head. In court, he could outtalk anyone, took great pride in leaving the opposing counsel speechless, but when Tatiyana was around, he clammed up. No one had ever had this effect on him before, and he didn't like it. Not one bit.

You're a Morretti, dammit! shouted his inner voice. *Get it together, man!*

"Your coffee's on your desk, as well as an updated copy of today's agenda, and the notes from Wednesday's case conference. I took the liberty of highlighting Ms. Van den Berg's concerns, specifically her fears for her three school-age children. I don't know if you noticed, but she teared up every time you said their names."

"What are you here so early?" he asked, consulting his watch. "It's six forty-five. You don't start until nine o'clock."

"I couldn't sleep, so I decided to get an early start on the day. I hope that's okay."

Desire surged through his veins. Markos told himself to look away, to quit staring at her, but his eyes didn't obey. He wanted to take Tatiyana in his arms and crush his mouth to hers, but he knew if he kissed her, he wouldn't be able to stop.

"I need a break from the computer, so I decided to clean," she continued, glancing around the reception area, her expression one of pride. "Looks good, huh?"

That's not the only thing that looks good. I'm dazzled by your inner and outer beauty. In less than a month, his life had changed for the better, and Tatiyana was the reason why. A perfectionist, with an eye for detail, she ensured everything ran smoothly at the office, and went above and beyond her job description. Everything about Tatiyana was impressive. Her maturity, how well she related to others, her positive outlook about life. It was impossible not to like her, and her bright, effervescent personality brought out the best in everyone—even Izzy. These days, his paralegal was working harder, being more professional. Tatiyana had captured the attention of everyone at the firm, and when the other senior partners joked about stealing her away from him, Markos beamed with pride. "You're incredible, you know that?"

Raising her eyebrows, she wore a skeptical expression on her face.

"Tatiyana, I'm serious. You're the best employee I've ever had, and I'm grateful to have you here at LA Family Law," he said, speaking from the heart. "It's hard to believe you've only been here a few weeks. You won the respect of your colleagues, and the hearts of the clients, as well, even the sad ones."

"I learned from the best," she said, fervently nodding. "It's been an honor to work here, and I can't thank you enough for this opportunity."

Markos felt himself moving, marching toward her, adrenaline surging through his veins.

"Is the mayor finally back from his trip or is he still hot-footing it around the globe?"

His feet slowed. *Talk about a mood killer.* Markos coughed into his fist, and took a moment to consider his words. The mayor would be back in LA tonight, but he wanted to keep the information to himself. He was having lunch with Mayor Glover next week, but he didn't want Tatiyana to know. She'd insist on joining them, and Markos wanted to talk to his friend man-to-man first. His gut feeling was that Jantel was lying, and he didn't want Mayor Glover to think he believed her. He didn't. Markos knew all too well how conniving the opposite sex could be. Over the years, people had used him and his family for one reason or another, and he wasn't going to stand by and let Jantel drag the mayor's name through the mud. "Don't worry, Tatiyana. I haven't forgotten my promise. Be patient. It will happen soon," he said. "How's baby Allie?"

Her eyes lit up. "As cute as ever, and smarter than Einstein. She's only ten months old, but she's already walking like a pro. And she can even say a few words."

"I'm not surprised your niece is excelling. It's in her blood. After all, you *are* her aunt…"

His cell lit up with his brother's name and number, and Markos trailed off. Romeo never called him during the day, so he knew his brother wanted to talk about something important. "Romeo, what's up? How's Milan treating you?"

"You're not going to believe this shit," he grumbled.

"Bro, what's wrong? You sound pissed."

"You'd be pissed, too, if you found out your girl screwed you over for a million dollars!"

"What happened?"

Tatiyana touched his shoulder. Smiling sympathetically, she took his briefcase and motioned for him to sit on the couch. Her expression was filled with concern, and thoughts of their last night in Tampa came to mind. He remembered how they'd stayed up late, cuddling and talking for hours, and wished they were still in his executive suite pleasing each other.

"Markos, sit down and relax. I'll put this away for you," she whispered.

Spinning, she marched down the hallway, humming to herself. Through the door, Markos watched her open his briefcase, take out his files and notepads and stack them on his desk in a neat, organized manner. Just the way he liked it.

"Bro, are you listening? Did you hear what I just said?"

Feeling guilty, he tore his gaze away from Tatiyana and gave his brother his full attention. "My bad. I was thinking about something else. Go ahead. I'm listening now."

"Let's FaceTime. It's easier. Fewer distractions."

Markos looked at his phone, pressed the green app and retrieved his earpieces from the pocket of his suit jacket. He liked Tatiyana, knew she wasn't the office gossip, but he didn't want her to overhear his conversation with his brother. Romeo's image filled the screen, and Markos felt his jaw droop open. His brother looked like hell, as if he hadn't slept in months, and his melancholy disposition matched the weary expression on his face. Photogenic and charismatic, Romeo's carefully cultivated bad-boy image not only added to his insane popularity in Italy, it attracted women like a sales sign in a boutique window. A favorite of gossip bloggers, he enjoyed the spotlight, and the more brazen Romeo was, the more the public loved him.

"Last weekend, I took Lizabeth to my island in Sicily to reconnect," he explained, raking a hand through his hair. "But all we did was argue. She called off our engagement."

Markos cursed in Italian. "I'm sorry to hear that. How are you doing?"

"Bad. I really wanted us to work, and it hurts like hell that she's gone," he confessed. "She's coming over tomorrow to grab the rest of her stuff, and I plan to be long gone by the time she gets here."

"Where are you going?"

"Torino. There's a business opportunity I want to check out, and I need to get out of town for a while."

"Romeo, don't sweat it. You'll be good as new in no time."

"I have a question. Is Lizabeth entitled to any sort of financial compensation? I heard from her lawyer today, and she's threatening to file a lawsuit, and write a tell-all book about our family if I don't give her a million-dollar settlement," he explained, his tone bitter. "Can you believe this? I gave Lizabeth the world, and this is how she repays me."

"Sorry, bro. I know how much you love her—"

"Loved her," he corrected, speaking through clenched teeth. "I have to do something."

"Romeo, forget her. She's not worth it."

"What are my legal rights? I don't want her writing that stupid book about our family. It will ruin us. She knows too much…"

In lawyer mode now, Markos rose to his feet and stalked into his office. Sitting, he propped his cell up against the glass candy dish and turned on his computer. Years ago, he'd argued a similar case, and accessed the file on his hard drive to review it. Romeo vented about his ex-girlfriend's betrayal, expressing his outrage and disgust. Markos could hear the pain in his voice, his hurt, and cracked jokes to make his brother feel better. "Don't worry, bro. I'll take care of everything."

"That's a relief. I have enough on my plate as it is."

"Yes, of course, I know how stressful it is to plan a birthday party."

Romeo wore a sad smile. "I don't want to do anything this year. I'm not in the mood to party."

"Of course you are, and you're going to celebrate the big day with your brothers and cousins in Monte Carlo. I could use a good Cuban cigar, some authentic Italian cuisine and a nice, relaxing weekend on your fancy yacht."

"Deal, now let's get down to work. I want to take care of this issue with Lizabeth before things spiral out of control and turn ugly."

"Not on my watch. We're Morettis. No one messes with us and gets away with it."

Nodding, Romeo wore a broad grin. "That's why I called you. When it comes to outwitting the competition, no one does it better."

Markos glanced up from the document he was proofreading at his office desk, spotted Tatiyana standing in the doorway holding a brown paper bag and dropped his gold fountain pen. Sunshine splashed through the windows, casting an angelic glow around her, and Markos decided she'd never looked more beautiful. Dumbstruck, he couldn't think or speak. Her lips were moving, but he couldn't hear her. Remembering he still wore his earpieces, he took them off, and dropped them on the file folder.

"Break time," she said. "I brought you dinner, so come eat."

Tatiyana marched over to the mahogany table, set down the oversize bag and unloaded the containers inside. A delicious aroma filled the air, tickling his nose, but Markos remained in his chair. "I don't have time to eat. I have documents to draft, motions to proof and a settlement agreement to finish before I can call it quits for the day."

"Markos, don't be ridiculous. You need a break. You've been holed up in your office since you returned from the country club five hours ago."

"Is that a problem?"

Cocking her head to the right, she narrowed her gaze and hitched a hand to her hip. "It *will* be if you don't come over here and try some of this food."

"Fine, I'll eat while I work."

"No way! You're going to sit at the table and eat like a civilized person."

"I've been eating at my desk for years. It's no big deal—"

"Well, there's a new sheriff in town, and *she* says you need a break so get up, come over here and check out what I ordered from The California Bar & Grill."

Tatiyana waved him over, insisting it was time for dinner, but Markos didn't budge.

"Fine, you leave me no choice."

Wearing a stern face, she stalked over to his desk, grabbed his forearm and pulled him to his feet. Electricity surged through his body when their hands touched, and the hairs on the back of his neck shot up. He'd taken off his suit jacket hours earlier and rolled up his shirtsleeves, so why was he sweating profusely? And why was he suddenly short of breath?

"Man, you're heavier than you look!" Tatiyana joked.

"I like when you manhandle me," he said, gazing down at her. "Reminds me of our weekend in Tampa and all the fun we had in my suite with that bottle of maple syrup."

Her nose twitched, and Markos didn't know if she wanted to sneeze or laugh. Stepping back, she slid behind one of the wooden chairs. "I bought your favorites. Samosas, tahini eggplant, honey-glazed ribs, balsamic rice and sweet-potato fries."

"Honey-glazed ribs?" he repeated. "What are we waiting for? Let's eat!"

Markos pulled out a chair for her, but Tatiyana shook her head.

"I can't. I have paperwork to do, and if I take a break now, I won't finish by six."

"You have *another* date?" he said, unable to hide his surprise. "Are you going for the Guinness World Record for the most dates in one month or something?"

Tatiyana laughed, and the melodious sound filled the office. Markos loved seeing her eyes lit up, and hearing her girlish giggles always made him grin from ear to ear.

"No. I have a quiz to study for and a paper to write for my business administration class, and since it isn't going to write itself, I have to buckle down and get it done this weekend."

"Stay and keep me company. It's been a long day, and I could use some of your positive energy right now." Markos knew he shouldn't touch her, knew he was breaking the rules, but he squeezed her shoulders. "I'll eat, but only if you join me."

"What about my job responsibilities?" she asked, biting her bottom lip. Her voice was apprehensive, and her expression was wary. "You get upset when things aren't done in a timely manner, and I don't want to get on your bad side."

You could never *get on my bad side. You're the best secretary I've ever had.*

"You make me sound like a tyrant. I'm not that bad, am I?"

Tatiyana shook her head, then eagerly nodded, and Markos laughed.

"Something smells *good*!" Izzy sailed through the door, and headed straight for the table. "I hope you bought enough for three because I'm hungrier than an actress in a too-tight dress on Oscar night."

Sitting down, Tatiyana patted the seat beside her. "Come sit. There's plenty."

Coughing into his fist, Markos tried to catch her attention, but Tatiyana was too busy chatting with his paralegal to pay him any mind. "Izzy, what are you still doing here?" he asked, noting the time on the wall clock. "It's five thirty. You never work this late."

"I know, but I wanted to clean my desk and organize the case files before I left for the day. You know me. I always give a 100 percent to this firm."

Markos cracked up, but when Izzy frowned and folded her arms across her chest, he realized she was serious and swallowed his laughter. Tatiyana brought out the best in everyone, including Izzy, and he was pleased about the positive impact she'd had on his paralegal.

Thirsty, Markos opened the mini fridge in the corner of the room, grabbed several bottles of mineral water and put them on the table. "Thanks for dinner, Tatiyana. That was very thoughtful of you."

"Yeah," Izzy agreed, licking sauce from her fingertips. "Thanks! I haven't had ribs this good since I was in the Big Easy three years ago."

"I love New Orleans. I was there last summer for the jazz festival, and I danced right out of my sandals." Her eyes twinkled with happiness, and a fond expression warmed her face. "The music was on point, the crowd was lively and energetic, the food was incredible and..."

Loud and animated, the women spoke about their favorite vacation spots, the hottest nightclubs in LA, reality TV and the upcoming Renegade concert. None of the topics appealed to him, but Markos learned several interesting facts about Tatiyana. She loved living in LA, she was deathly afraid of spiders and a die-hard *Star Wars* fan.

"Do you have any plans this weekend?"

Finally, a good question. Markos wanted to give Izzy a high five for asking the question on the tip of his tongue, but he contained his excitement and finished eating his food.

"I'm going to finish my schoolwork, get a massage and hang out with—"

"Khalid Hassan," Izzy said with a smirk. "Don't deny it. One of the cleaners overheard you two talking yesterday, so fess up. Where is he taking you on Saturday night?"

Confused, Markos glanced from Izzy to Tatiyana. What the hell? Why were they talking about his newest client? The silver-haired entrepreneur had recently separated from his third wife, and Markos had agreed to represent him in his divorce. Convinced he'd misunderstood what Izzy said, he asked, "What did you say?"

"Mr. Hassan has a *huge* crush on Tatiyana."

Scoffing, she rolled her eyes to the ceiling. "No, he doesn't."

"Yes, he does," Izzy insisted, snapping her fingers and swiveling her neck. "He invited her to go sailing on Tuesday, and he sent her a massive flower arrangement yesterday."

Intrigued, Markos leaned forward in his chair, desperate to hear more. He stared at Tatiyana, trying to read the expression on her face, but she gave him a blank look. He gripped his utensils. How could this happen? Why didn't he know what was going on? It was *his* office! The businessman was putting the moves on his secretary right under his nose, but he'd been too busy with his other clients to see it. The thought of Tatiyana with another man—a skirt-chasing executive twice her age no less—sickened him, and when she dropped her gaze to her lap, Markos knew she was hiding something.

"Izzy, go ahead. I want to hear more. What else has been going on?"

"Oh, wow, look at the time. I have to go. My, ah, mom and I are going to the movies, and she'll kill me if I'm late."

Izzy hopped to her feet, swiped her cell phone off the table and marched toward the door. "Bye. See you on Monday."

Then she turned and fled the office as if the Devil were in hot pursuit.

Chapter 17

Tatiyana coughed to clear her throat and wiped her cold, clammy palms along the sides of her pencil skirt. She wanted to throttle Izzy for blabbing to Markos about Mr. Hassan, but she smiled and waved as the gossip-loving paralegal dashed out the door. Thinking about what her colleague had said made Tatiyana want to bust a gut. As if she'd ever date a client! Moreover, Mr. Hassan was still legally married, and that was reason enough to stay far away from him. Add to that, he was a chauvinistic pig, and if he wasn't the firm's richest client, Tatiyana wouldn't give him the time of day. But since she wanted to make Markos proud she treated the businessman with respect.

"What's going on with you and Mr. Hassan? Tell me the truth, and tell me now."

Irked by his tone, and his narrowed gaze, Tatiyana glared back at him. "I've done nothing wrong, so don't yell at me," she said, struggling to keep the lid on her anger.

Markos gripped his glass so hard, his knuckles turned white. "I'm going to ask you one more time. Are you dating Mr. Hassan?"

"Fine, quit twisting my arm! It's true. He's my one true love, and I want to spend the rest of my life with him, his ex-wives, his adult children, his entourage *and* his massive ego."

He cracked a small smile, and Tatiyana knew he was trying hard not to laugh. "Markos, I'm disappointed in you. I can't believe you think I'd date a married man."

"Over the years, I've seen the good, the bad and the ugly at LA Family Law, but I'm glad you're not romantically interested in Mr. Hassan. He's a client and not the right man for you."

"He asked me out, but I declined. End of story." Meeting his gaze, she spoke in a strong, confident voice. "I'd never do anything to embarrass you, this firm or Staffing Unlimited, so mixing business with pleasure is out of the question."

Releasing an audible sigh, he sat back comfortably in his chair. "It's good to know I'm not the only one around here getting the cold shoulder."

"Don't worry," she said with a playful wink. "You're not."

Markos stared at her, and heat flooded her body. Goose bumps tickled her forearms, and it took everything in her not to dive into his lap and smother his face with kisses.

"Do you ever think about our weekend in Tampa?"

Are you kidding me? All. The. Time. For as long as I live, I'll never forget the wonderful, magical time we had. Parting her dry lips, she pushed the truth out of her mouth. "Yes, of course. I had a great time with you and your family."

He looked proud, as if he'd hit a hole in one on a championship golf course. "What did you enjoy the most?"

Tatiyana hesitated, didn't know how much to share, but she saw the earnest expression on his face, sensed he wanted her to open up to him, and did. "Making love to you at the R&B Summer Jam concert," she confessed. "You?"

"Our last night together. You blew me away, Tatiyana."

Explicit images bombarded her mind, warming her all over. He'd licked maple syrup off her breasts, drank Merlot from her navel, played between her legs until she'd exploded in ecstasy, and even now, weeks later, her body tingled at the memory of his touch.

"I wish you'd been honest with me about who you were, and what you wanted."

"I wanted to tell you the truth, but I knew if I did you wouldn't give me the time of day."

Markos shook his head. "You don't know that."

Yes, I do! Tatiyana opened her mouth to argue, to remind

him how he'd treated her mom and sister when they met with him in July, but he took her hand in his, gently stroking her fingers, and she lost her train of thought.

The desk phone buzzed, but Markos didn't move. His eyes were on her, watching her, assessing her, giving her hot flashes and heart palpitations. Tatiyana wanted him to touch her everywhere—her breasts, yearned to feel his hands under her dress, palming and squeezing her ass— but she knew hooking up with Markos would be a mistake. Tatiyana didn't want to do anything to jeopardize Jantel's meeting with the mayor, and feared if she slept with Markos again she'd be weak for him—

Ha! barked her inner voice. *Too late! You've been weak for him since the moment you met, and your body quivers every time he looks at you.*

Masking her emotions, Tatiyana pretended his touch didn't faze her, but it did. Her mouth was dry, thirsty for his kiss, and desire scorched her flesh. Moving closer, he flashed a sweet, boyish smile, and her heart melted like an ice-cream cone in the sun. Tatiyana liked that Markos wasn't a player, that he was a perfect gentleman who honored and respected women. He was too busy racking up wins in divorce court to chase Hollywood starlets, and when he wasn't pulling all-nighters at the firm, he was taking his nephew to the zoo, teaching him how to fish, or playing soccer with him at Discovery Park. Once a week, Matteo and Jordana stopped by the office to visit with Markos, and Tatiyana enjoyed spending time with his sister-in-law and his adorable nephew.

"Do you have any plans this weekend?" Her voice wobbled, sounded foreign to her ears, and her hands were shaking so hard she couldn't pick up her water glass. "Are you coming into the office again, or finally taking a well-deserved break?"

"My brothers were supposed to take me to Palm Springs for my birthday, but Immanuel has a business meeting in

Washington he can't get out of, and Dante's home sick with the flu—"

"Tomorrow's your birthday? No way! Why didn't you say anything?"

A grin brightened his eyes. "I just did."

"I wish I'd known earlier. I would've bought you a gift," she said with an apologetic smile. "It's not too late. What do you want? A watch? Personalized cuff links? Golf clubs?"

"None of the above. Just you."

Tatiyana laughed, but when Markos took her hand, she froze. He kissed her palm, brushing his lips ever so softly against her flesh, and a moan rose inside her throat. She wanted him, but Tatiyana steeled herself against his touch.

"Come with me to Palm Springs."

"Markos, that's crazy. I work for you."

"Who cares? I don't give a damn, and neither should you. We're adults. We can do what we want, when we want."

His me-against-the-world attitude was a turn-on. Adrenaline filled her, giving her a rush, but Tatiyana squelched her excitement. It was hard to keep her body in check, to stay strong when Markos was caressing her hands and gazing at her with those dreamy, bedroom eyes, but she had to resist his advances. She didn't want her female colleagues to hate her, and if word got out that she'd slept with Markos, they'd turn on her like a pack of angry wolves. No, she had to keep her hands to herself. No matter what.

"We can drive down tonight," he proposed.

Leaning in close, he draped an arm around the back of her chair. His gentle caress along her shoulders was as intimate as a French kiss.

"What do you say? I'm game if you are."

"But I don't have any clothes or toiletries—"

"I'll buy you everything you need when we get there. Problem solved."

Tatiyana clamped her lips together to trap the word *yes* inside her mouth, and deleted it from her thoughts. "I can't."

Markos cocked an eyebrow. "Why not? You're always preaching at me to slow down, to live in the moment, so I'm taking your advice. You should, too."

"I wish I could, but I have a paper to write and a quiz to study for. They're both worth 25 percent of my grade, and if I do poorly my 4.0. GPA will suffer."

"I was on the honor roll in university. I can quiz you in the car, and we can work on your paper together tomorrow."

Tatiyana considered her options. She'd never been one to play by the rules, so why start now? Watching him, she felt something she'd never experienced before—raw, primal hunger—and wanted to act on her feelings. His caress aroused her, and when he brushed his mouth against her cheek, her body tingled. Markos was a hottie with a heart, and Tatiyana desired him more than anything. *One weekend*, she thought, excitement rising up inside her. *No one will ever know.*

And if they did? So what? It was her last week at LA Family Law, and Tatiyana couldn't think of a better parting gift than spending the weekend in Palm Springs with her favorite attorney. She wanted Markos, and she was tired of ignoring her attraction.

"Help me celebrate my birthday in Palm Springs. I promise you won't regret it." Cocking his head to the right, he flashed a bad-boy grin. "You know you want to. Just admit it."

Hiding a smirk, she cocked an eyebrow. "When did you get so cocky?"

"When you had your way with me at Applause Nightclub."

"You loved it and you know it."

"Of course I did. There's nothing better than making love to a passionate, sensual woman who's comfortable in her own skin, but I'm not inviting you to Palm Springs to hook up. I enjoy your company, and there's no one else I'd rather spend my birthday with than you."

I wish he wasn't tall, dark and handsome, she thought,

her resolve crumbling. *It would be so much easier to resist him if he wasn't so good-looking.* Deep down, Tatiyana sensed she was making a mistake, that she'd live to regret sneaking off with Markos to Palm Springs, but she wanted to celebrate his birthday with him, and refused to feel guilty about throwing caution to the wind. "I'll come, but you need to help me with my schoolwork, okay, Mr. Honor Roll?"

Markos nodded and saluted. "Scout's honor. You have my word."

"Then let's get out of here. Palm Springs, here we come!" she said, linking arms with him. "Markos, this is going to be the best birthday you've ever had."

"I know. I'm spending it with you, and there's no greater gift."

Chapter 18

The mansions on Southridge Drive, an exclusive area in Palm Springs known for its well-heeled residents, were impressive, but Markos's estate was the largest one on the block. Decorative lights lit up the exterior of the ten-bedroom mansion, giving it a warm and welcoming feel, and potted plants, tropical flowers and marble statues beautified the grounds.

Staring out the windshield of Markos's SUV, Tatiyana gawked at her opulent surroundings. They'd spent the past hour talking and flirting as they drove along the interstate, but as he parked on the cobblestone driveway, Tatiyana wanted to pinch herself. She was with Markos at his swank Palm Springs estate, and it was more beautiful than a resort. The mansion had a modern design, the lawn was immaculately groomed, fruit trees perfumed the night air with their savory scent, and when Tatiyana stepped out of the car and saw the mansion up close, her eyes widened. "This is some house."

"You think the exterior is impressive? Wait until you see inside." Markos opened the trunk, took out their shopping bags and activated the alarm. Ninety minutes after leaving LA, they'd arrived in Palm Springs and made a pit stop at a local department store. There, they'd purchased everything they needed for the weekend. "Are you okay? You look shell-shocked."

Embarrassed, she wore a sheepish smile. "To be honest, I am. I've never seen a mansion up close before, let alone been inside one, and I'm dying for a tour."

"As you wish. You won't get far in your Louboutins, though, so let's grab a golf cart."

"What do *you* know about Louboutins? You're a workaholic who has no time to eat, let alone shop, so I'm shocked you know who the French designer is."

"I spoil my sister when she's in LA, so we're always on Rodeo Drive."

Spotting a two-wheeled electric board, adjacent to the triple garage, Tatiyana eyed it with interest. "Whose Segway?" she asked, touching the handle.

"I bought them for my teenage cousins when they visited from Venice last summer, but my landscapers use them from time to time."

"Can I?"

"You're wearing heels. It's not safe. You could hurt yourself."

"I won't. I'm a pro!" Kicking off her shoes, Tatiyana shrugged off her blazer and tossed it on the hood of the SUV. "Problem solved. I'm good to go."

Seconds later, they were rolling along the lush, green grass, side by side. Markos pointed out the guest quarters, the swim spa and the tennis courts, and when Tatiyana challenged him to a game, he laughed. "You should quit while you're ahead. I beat you at darts, and golf, as well."

"It's not my fault I lost. You distracted me."

Markos stopped his Segway, stepped down and took her hand. "How?"

"You know what you did," she said with a knowing look. "Your charming ways and effusive praise threw me off my game."

"Is it my fault that you're the most beautiful woman in LA, and I like to compliment you?"

"Just LA?" Tatiyana gave him a shot in the arm. "Jerk!"

Laughing, he hugged her to his side and kissed her forehead.

"What is that?" she asked, gesturing to the dimly lit building behind the bronze fountain. Made of brick, it had arched windows and wooden lion statues on each side of the door.

"My man cave."

"A man cave? You don't need one. You live alone."

"Yes, I do. When my relatives visit, I hand over the keys to the main house, grab my briefcase and make a beeline for my home away from home," he said with a laugh.

His caress along her shoulders and hips was as distracting as hell. Being in Markos's arms, snuggled against him, was amazing, better than a chocolate sundae with a cherry on top, and she reveled in the moment. *We're not in Tampa, but it sure feels like it.*

"I love when my family's around, but they're a handful, especially my kid sister."

"What do you do in your man cave?"

"Smoke Cuban cigars, eat junk food and watch old mobster movies."

Tatiyana snapped her fingers. "I knew it!" she joked, pointing at his face. "You're a buttoned-up attorney with a wild streak, aren't you?"

"I'm a Morretti. It's in my blood."

Taking her hand, he led her across the yard. As they walked, Markos talked about the history of the property, the female architect who'd spearheaded the project and his favorite features of his custom-made home. He opened the door, flipped on the lights and stepped aside to let her enter. "Welcome."

Surprised by the plush décor, Oriental area rugs and sumptuous leather furniture, with framed movie posters hanging on the burgundy walls, Tatiyana whistled. "Wow, great digs. Your man cave smells like a florist shop, and there isn't a dirty dish in sight. Nice."

"I'm glad you like it. I don't usually bring dates in here, but you're special to me, and I wanted you to see where I spend my free time."

Tatiyana gave a nervous laugh. "I am?"

"You have to ask? Isn't it obvious?"

"No. You're hard on me, and I never know where I stand

with you," she said. "Take yesterday for example. You snapped at me twice, then kicked me out of your office."

"That's because I'm an ass."

A smirk tickled her lips. "You said it, not me."

"I know I'm not the easiest person to work for, but I'm trying to change."

"Ha!" Tatiyana barked a laugh, couldn't believe Markos thought he could sweet talk her. He was just telling her what he thought she wanted to hear, but she wasn't buying it. "No, you're not. You're a Morretti, and winning is all that matters to you."

"Not anymore. Helping my clients means more to me than having a winning record."

Raising an eyebrow, she searched his face for signs of deception. "Really? Why the sudden change of heart? You were singing a very different tune three weeks ago."

"I ran into Mr. Zapata this afternoon at the country club," he explained, a pensive expression on his face. "He credited me with saving his marriage and promised to name his second child after me if it's a boy—"

"They're trying to get pregnant? No way!"

"Yoshiro said they're happier than ever. I told him you're the one he should thank, not me, so I suggested they name their next child, Tatiyana. Perfect, right?" Markos wrapped her in his arms. "Because of your example, I'm a better attorney, and a more thoughtful, compassionate person, so thank you for teaching me how to effectively support my clients."

His smile stole her breath away, and her thoughts scattered. Driven by desire, Tatiyana made the first move. She kissed him hard on the mouth. Tatiyana feasted on his lips, mating desperately with his tongue. Her desire for Markos couldn't be denied or contained, threatened to consume her, and in that moment, all she cared about was pleasing him.

To her surprise, Markos abruptly pulled away. "Tatiyana, what are you doing?"

"Giving you an early birthday present."

"I didn't invite you here to have sex."

Her hands fell to her sides and shame flooded her skin. Tatiyana wanted to run and hide, but her legs wouldn't move. They felt weak, as if they were shackled with eighty-pound weights.

"You make me laugh, and there's never a dull moment when you're around." Touching her face, he caressed her cheek with his thumb. "I think you're an incredible woman, one of the most authentic and genuine people I've ever met, and I don't want to mess things up by jumping back into bed."

He is—water filled her eyes, and her nose twitched—*rejecting me?* Gathering herself, she nodded in agreement. "You're right. I don't know what I was thinking. We're just friends." Marching across the room, her vision blurred with tears, she hid her disappointment. "I'm going to turn in. It's been a long day."

"No way. Not so fast." Markos captured her arm and pulled her to his side. "The night's still young. What would you like to do?"

Tatiyana shrugged. "I don't know. It's your estate."

"Let's grab some snacks and relax in the media room," he proposed.

"I'll come, but *only* if you make homemade popcorn, and gelato."

"One strawberry-chocolate gelato coming right up." Chuckling, Markos took her hand in his and kissed her palm. "I'm glad you're here, Tatiyana."

Me, too, she thought, returning his smile. *Me, too.*

Chapter 19

Markos rolled onto his back on his king-size bed and sniffed the air. Starving, he licked his lips and rubbed his stomach. Chef Igor was a wiz in the kitchen who made scrumptious, elaborate meals at his request, and Markos was looking forward to having breakfast with Tatiyana on the patio. He was excited they were spending the weekend together, but feared what would happen if she kissed him again. It was damn hard to keep his hands in his pockets and off her body, but Markos was determined to be a perfect gentleman while she was at his estate.

His cell phone buzzed, alerting him that he had a new text message. Grabbing his iPhone off the side table, Markos punched in his password and accessed his inbox.

Morning, Birthday Boy! Ready for your birthday breakfast?

Reading Tatiyana's text made Markos grin so wide his jaw ached.

Good morning, Beautiful. I'll be downstairs in ten minutes. Can't wait to see you. I have a fun day planned, filled with plenty of surprises, so don't be late.

Markos sent the text he'd composed, tossed aside his black satin sheets and swung his legs over the side of his platform bed. Yawning, he stretched his sore, aching muscles. Last night, after seeing Tatiyana to her room, he'd worked in his home office for hours. It was a struggle, impossible to focus when all he could think about was his titillating house guest sleeping across the hall, but he'd finished his to-do list and answered his clients' emails.

Feeling his cell phone vibrate in his hands, he read Tatiyana's response.

You're not the only one with surprises up your sleeve, Morretti! I told you this was going to be the best birthday you've ever had, and I meant it.

Eager to see her, he chucked his cell on his pillow and rose to his feet. Inside the master bathroom, he showered and shaved, but his mind was filled with thoughts of Tatiyana. Reviewing the plans he'd made for them, Markos made a mental note to call the tour guide to confirm the details of their afternoon excursion. They were going to do it all: hike at Joshua Tree National Park, explore a world-class vineyard and feast on lobster at a popular seafood restaurant. Tatiyana was special to him, and he wanted to spoil her this weekend.

Returning to the bedroom minutes later in his undershirt and boxer shorts, Markos selected a T-shirt and blue jeans from the walk-in closet and put them on the dresser. Markos heard a knock on the door, and said, "Come in."

The door swung open, and in strolled Tatiyana. Pleased to see her, he admired her strapless dress, her lace-up sandals and her gold ankle bracelet.

Carrying a silver tray, her smile radiant and bright, she sashayed toward him with the confidence of Miss Universe. "Happy birthday to ya," she sang, rocking her shoulders from side to side. "Happy birthday to ya. Happy birthday!"

Amused by her off-key rendition of the Stevie Wonder classic, Markos cheered. "Wow, breakfast and a song? Tatiyana, you shouldn't have."

"I had to. It's your birthday. What kind of friend would I be if I didn't go all out for your big day?" she replied. "I made all of your favorites—smoked bacon, Belgian waffles, pesto-scrambled eggs and zucchini muffins."

Confused, Markos pointed at the tray. "You cooked? But Chef Igor is here."

"He was, but I sent the poor guy home. His wife broke her leg yesterday playing Frisbee with their daughters, and since his family needs him more than you do, I gave him the day off. He was worried you'd be pissed, but I told him you'd understand."

"You're not happy unless you're running the show, huh?"

"You know it," she said with a wink and a smile. "Don't be mad. I wanted to cook for you. It's a special day. Turning twenty-one is a big deal!"

Chuckling, he plucked a piece of bacon off the tray and took a bite. "Hot and crispy, just the way I like. I'm impressed. I didn't know you were a world-famous cook," he teased.

"There are lots of things you don't know about me."

"Really? Like what? Fill me in."

"I don't know where to start. There's so much to share."

The allure and charm of her laugh captivated him, awakening his desire.

"I'm an avid chess player, my family members say I cook better than a professional chef and I love biking."

"That explains why you have such a gorgeous body."

"If I have such a gorgeous body, then why did you reject me last night?"

"Reject you?" he repeated, baffled by her outrageous statement. "Are you kidding me? Why would I reject the woman I've been fantasizing about for weeks?"

Tatiyana shrugged. "You tell me."

"I didn't reject you. I'd never reject you."

"Sure seems that way to me."

Markos closed his gaping mouth. He couldn't believe that Tatiyana—a bombshell who had men chasing her down at every turn—doubted his feelings for her. "Let's sit down and talk. It's obvious you're upset."

"No, later. Your food's getting cold."

"It can wait." Markos took the tray from her hands, set it on the raised glass table and sat on one of the leather chairs. Pulling her down onto his lap, he wrapped his arms around her. "Umm," he murmured, inhaling her scent. "You smell like heaven."

"Thanks. After my morning jog, I treated myself to a long, relaxing bubble bath."

"You went out without me? What's up with that?"

"I didn't want to disturb you. You work long hours, and I know you need your rest."

"No," he argued, meeting her gaze. "I need you."

Caressing his face with her warm, soft hands, she whispered against his ear, "Then let's make love. It's your birthday, and I want it to be a memorable, passionate day."

Guilt troubled his conscience, making him feel low, and he confessed the truth. "It's not my birthday. My birthday was in July, and I celebrated with my brothers and cousins in Cozumel."

"I can't believe you tricked me."

"I wanted to spend time with you, so I lied," he confessed, wearing an apologetic smile. "I'm sorry. I should have been honest with you. Do you forgive me?"

Markos held his breath. He thought she'd be angry, expected her to curse him out for tricking him, but to his surprise she nodded in understanding.

"Apology accepted, and since we're being honest with each other, I have a confession to make, too." Wearing a contrite expression on her face, she dropped her gaze to her lap, and fiddled with the gold bracelet on her wrist. "I taped the conversation we had in my suite our last night together in Tampa."

"Good one!" he said with a hearty laugh, patting her thighs. "Sure you did!"

"It's true. I was going to use the tape to blackmail you that morning I showed up at your office..."

Markos gulped, and his hands fell from around her

waist. Filled with panic, his body tensed, and a cold sweat drenched his skin. What the hell? This was a nightmare. He was a Morretti. A successful divorce attorney. A future mayoral candidate. And if a tape surfaced of him bad-mouthing his celebrity clients it would ruin his reputation, and tarnish his career.

"I hope you can find it in your heart to forgive me."

"How could you do this? Why? What were you thinking?" Suddenly Markos saw the full picture, understood why she'd taped their conversation in her suite. The truth came to him in a flash, hit him hard, like a fist to the gut, momentarily knocking the wind out of him.

"I made a mistake, and I'm sorry. No one heard the recording, and no one will. I deleted it after you threw me out of your office."

"Is that the truth?"

Tatiyana hung her head. "Yes. You called me a liar and a con artist, and I lost my nerve," she said quietly, staring down at her hands. "I wanted to help my sister, and I didn't know what else to do, so I befriended you on the flight to Tampa."

Anger shot through his veins. Weeks earlier, he'd contacted his friend who worked at Pinnacle, but the marketing director had never met Tatiyana, and couldn't tell him why she was terminated. "Do you have a history of blackmailing people? Is that why you lost your job at Pinnacle? Because you blackmailed your former boss? Is that your modus operandi?"

Tatiyana shot to her feet, but Markos captured her arm.

"Let go of me," she said, struggling to free herself from his hold. "I shouldn't be here. Coming here was a mistake. I'm leaving…"

"Answer me, dammit. I deserve to know."

A tense silence filled the room.

"I said, let go of me."

"Tell me what happened at Pinnacle first."

Her hands curled into fists, and for a moment Markos feared she'd punch him for holding her against her will. Staring at the window, her eyes dark with pain, she spoke in a somber tone, and the anguish in her voice made him want to hold her in his arms again.

"My boss made a pass at me, and when I threatened to go to HR he fired me."

"You should sue the company for wrongful dismissal. Need my help?"

"No way. Why look back when I can go forward? Life's good. My family's closer than ever, I have an interview at Center of Hope next week, *and* I met a great new guy who's smart, romantic and dreamy. Did I mention he's an incredible golfer, too?"

Chuckling, he reached out and caressed her cheek. "I want to be with you, Tatiyana."

"Me too, Markos. I have a good feeling about you. About us."

"Then no more secret recordings," he admonished. "Thank God it wasn't a sex tape. That would ruin me, and my future bid for mayor, if it fell into the wrong hands."

"Sex tapes aren't sleazy. They're sexy and hot and I think we should make one."

Desire sparked in her eyes, and a seductive grin curled her lips.

"Tatiyana, we can't. It's too risky."

Standing, she unzipped her dress, let it fall on the floor and kicked it aside. "Baby, are you sure, because I *love* living on the wild side. In fact, the riskier the better…"

At the sight of her naked body, Markos salivated. No bra, no panties, no problem, he thought, eager to touch her. He couldn't resist her, even if he tried. "Fine, we'll make a video," he agreed, swiping his cell phone off the side table. "But *I'm* calling the shots."

"Good," she quipped. "I'm ready for my close-up."

Chapter 20

Excitement pricked Tatiyana's skin, flooding her body with heat. She helped Markos out of his undershirt and boxers, and tossed them over her shoulder. Kneeling between his legs, she parted her lips, and sucked his erection into her mouth. She licked it eagerly, hungrily, as if it was coated in caramel chocolate. His groans filled the room, playing in her ears like a song, turning her on. The harder she sucked, the louder he grunted. Markos praised her skills, told her how much he desired her, adored her, and her heart inflated with pride.

Throwing his head back, his eyes pressed shut, he groaned. Markos grabbed fistfuls of her hair, playing in her loose, lush waves. He knew how to excite her, and used his hands to stroke, tease and caress her flesh. Tatiyana wished his fingers were buried inside her sex, his tongue, too, pleasing her like only he could.

"Tatiyana, baby, this is torture…you're killing me… I need to be inside you…"

Looking up at him, their eyes met. His words were a desperate plea, filled with longing and angst, music to her ears. Holding his gaze, she swirled her tongue around his length, wetting and tickling the tip of his erection. His hard, muscled body quivered. Watching Markos come undone, lose control, made Tatiyana feel powerful, as if there was nothing she couldn't do.

"Enough. I can't take any more," he growled, seizing her wrists. "Come here."

Taking her hand, he helped her to her feet. Kissing, they tumbled onto the bed in a heap, shrieking and laughing. Pressing his mouth against her throat, he told her in explicit, graphic detail what he wanted to do to her, and Tatiyana enjoyed every wicked minute of his X-rated confession. Couldn't get enough. Wanted more. His words made her tingle, giving her a rush.

"I love your lips," he whispered, staring deep into her eyes. "They're irresistible."

"Then kiss them."

He did, nibbling and biting and licking until she didn't know left from right.

Tatiyana was wet, and as he rolled on top of her and slid his erection between her legs, she cried out. Bolts of lightning struck her body, leaving her speechless. Hiking her legs in the air, he thrust and stirred his length inside her, over and over.

Watching his erection moving in and out of her sex was a turn-on. His stroke was incredible, oh-so-good, a sensual treat. Tremors, fiery and hot, consumed her. Cupping her breasts in his hands, Markos tweaked and sucked her nipples, licked and rubbed them. The man was a beast, the most expressive and explosive lover she'd ever had. Her eyes closed, sealing her in the moment. They played and teased each other, and Tatiyana couldn't remember ever having so much fun in the bedroom. Since her breakup, she'd been reluctant to get involved with anyone, but Markos had proved to her that he was a good man, someone she could trust, and Tatiyana was willing to take a chance on love.

"I can't get over how beautiful you are, how passionate you are. Baby, you amaze me." Tenderly, he brushed his lips across her cheek and mouth. "I wish I knew how to resist you, but I don't. One look at you and I'm utterly captivated."

Shocked by his confession, Tatiyana couldn't speak.

"Baby, you're it. The one, the woman I want to marry…"

"Markos, don't joke about things like that. It's not funny."

"Who's joking? I'm serious. We can go ring shopping

at Cartier first thing tomorrow," he said, nibbling on her earlobe. "Hell, we can go right now if you want."

Tatiyana froze, staring at him with wide eyes, convinced she'd misheard him.

"I think you had too much Jamaican rum last night," she teased with a nervous laugh.

"I'm sober, and I know what I want. You."

"Markos, we haven't known each other long—"

"It doesn't matter. In case you haven't noticed, Morretti men waste no time putting a ring on it when they find Ms. Right, and I'm no exception."

The defiant expression on his face made her body hum and tingle. *Oh, my,* she thought, wetting her lips with her tongue. *I'm so turned on right now I can't think straight!*

"The first time I saw you, I knew you were special, and I was right. You are. That's why I want to marry you. Why I *will* marry you some day." His voice was firm, as if the matter was decided and there was nothing she could do about it. "Baby, you're it for me."

"Markos, I get it. The sex is off the charts, but—"

"How many times do I have to tell you my feelings for you have nothing to do with sex, and everything to do with who you are?" he asked, interrupting her. "You're right. The sex is amazing, and you're an exquisite lover, but that's not why I love you…"

Her ears perked up, and joy bubbled up inside her. *You love me? Seriously? Even though you have models, and Hollywood actresses throwing themselves at you on a daily basis?*

"All these years, I've been living in the dark and didn't even realize it." Cupping her chin in his hands, he slowly and tenderly kissed the corners of her lips. "The moment I met you, it felt like someone had flipped on the lights, and now my world is a brighter, better place."

"Really? Because of me?"

"Yeah, baby, because of you. You challenge me, you

take care of me, and when you're around I smile more than a kid at Disneyland." Markos laughed. "I've never felt this way before, and I know in my heart you're the only woman for me."

Overcome with emotion, Tatiyana couldn't speak.

"I know a good thing when I see it, and baby that's you. Will you marry me?"

Tatiyana bit down on her bottom lip to ward off the tears pricking the backs of her eyes. His words filled her with unspeakable joy, but she couldn't resist teasing him. "Markos, I can't believe you. You can't propose during sex! Who does that?"

"Damn right I can. Anything goes!" Wearing an impish grin, he wiggled his eyebrows. "And I did my research. I read *Proposals for Dummies*, and according to the authors, there's never a bad time for a man to propose."

Tatiyana cracked up. "Liar! That isn't a real book, and you know it."

"Does it matter? I love you, and one day I'm going to marry you. Just watch."

He kissed her deeply, thoroughly, with a savage intensity. Cradled in his arms, they moved together as one body, locked in a sensual, passionate embrace. They were polar opposites who couldn't be more different, but it didn't matter. They'd found each other, and having Markos in her life was a wonderful gift. Tatiyana felt protected, cared for and closer to Markos than ever before. As an orgasm ripped through her body, the truth fell from her mouth.

"I love you, Markos, and I want to be with you. Meeting you is the best thing that's ever happened to me, and I'd be honored to be Mrs. Markos Morretti."

"I love you, too. Never forget that. What we have is rare, and I'll always cherish it."

Breathing in his scent, Tatiyana reveled in his warmth and his closeness. Being in his arms was paradise, the only place she ever wanted to be. He kissed her, and his tongue explored her mouth, searching, teasing, and electrifying every inch of her body.

"Dannazione," he rasped, through clenched teeth. "I can't hold back any longer…"

His head fell forward, and his shoulders tensed. Growling, Markos palmed her ass, grinding his groin against her pelvis. Her walls contracted and she arched her back, offering more of herself to him. His erection throbbed, expanding inside her. Returning his kiss, she screamed with pleasure as he pumped his hips and increased his pace. His breathing grew louder, heavier as spasms rocked his body.

Wanting more, Tatiyana hooked her legs around his waist and clung desperately to him. Markos stilled, but his breathing was loud and labored. Spent, sweat dripping from his face, he collapsed on the bed and gathered her in his arms. "I can die now. I'm so damn happy and content," he said with a crooked grin. "I'm exactly where I want to be, with the woman I love, and there's no greater feeling."

"Markos, baby, that's so sweet." Moved by his confession, Tatiyana kissed his lips. "I didn't realize I was dating a poet."

"You're not. I heard that line in an old Italian movie, and I've always wanted to say it!" he joked.

They shared a laugh.

"Man, I'm hungry. You wore me out, Ms. Washington."

"You're welcome." Springing to her feet, Tatiyana crossed the master bedroom with a smile on her face and a bounce in her step. She used the bathroom, then returned to the bedroom seconds later.

Locking eyes with him, she picked up the tray on the table and returned to the bed. "Try the waffles." Tatiyana picked one up with her fork and held it under his nose. "I made it from scratch, and it's one of my most popular recipes."

Markos took a bite and chewed slowly. "Babe, wow, that's good!"

As they ate, they discussed their plans for the day, and her upcoming job interview at Center of Hope. Markos offered to give her a reference, and Tatiyana whooped for joy. Working at a nonprofit center had always been her dream, and although she'd miss working at the law firm she wanted a permanent, long-term position helping impoverished communities. Markos had asked Tatiyana to be his date for the Governor's Masquerade Ball at the end of the month, and she accepted, was pleased that he wanted to make their relationship public. Tatiyana wanted to ask Markos about Mayor Glover's return, but sensed it wasn't the right time. High on life, she wanted to enjoy their romantic breakfast, not argue about the mayor's lies.

"Baby, that was delicious, especially the waffles," he told her, wiping his mouth with a napkin. "Thanks again for my birthday breakfast."

Laughing, Tatiyana climbed onto his lap, pinned his arms to the headboard and rocked her hips against his groin. "Now that you've eaten, let's pick up where we left off."

"What do you have in mind?"

"More lovemaking. Then a quickie in the shower."

Tatiyana lowered her mouth and licked his earlobe with her tongue. "How does that feel?" she whispered. "Do you like it? Do you want more?"

"Yeah, baby, but take it easy on me this time. I don't want to end up in the ER."

Chapter 21

"Welcome to the happiest place on earth," the tour driver joked with a hearty laugh.

Seated in the backseat of the Hummer with Markos, enjoying the scenic drive through Joshua Tree, Tatiyana smiled to herself. The guide was driving like a speed demon, but his larger-than-life personality amused her. With skill and expertise, he maneuvered the vehicle through the rocky, rugged terrain, pointing out objects of significance in the lush landscape filled with spiky plants, cacti and wildflowers.

"There's nowhere quite like Palm Springs, and you're going to love it here."

I believe you, Tatiyana thought, reliving the highlights of her day with Markos.

After their morning tryst, they'd watched their sex video—twice—and although Markos said she could keep the footage, she'd deleted it. He was right. If it fell into the wrong hands, it could ruin him, and she didn't want to do anything to jeopardize his career. Once showered and changed, they'd jumped into his Bugatti and headed downtown. In the car, they'd talked about their plans for Thanksgiving, the outrageous characters they worked with at the firm, and the social events Markos wanted them to attend together next month.

They'd spent the afternoon, wandering in and out of the souvenir shops and boutiques along North Palm Canyon Drive. On a whim, they'd taken a city bus tour with a large, gregarious group from Australia, followed by dinner at a posh seafood restaurant. Markos was charming and attentive, but his cell had rung incessantly while they ate their meal. Half-joking, Tatiyana had threatened to toss it into the aquarium, and he'd apologized with a kiss for the constant interruptions. After dinner, she'd challenged him to a game of pool in the adjoining bar. Winning with an improbable trick shot, she'd celebrated her victory by doing the Electric Slide, drawing chuckles from Markos and everyone inside the lounge.

"How long have you two kids been married?"

Tatiyana felt her skin warm. Before she could answer the question, Markos spoke, and his response floored her, leaving her speechless.

"We're not married yet, but we will be, soon," Markos said, oozing with confidence.

"Then let me be the first to congratulate you." Lowering the volume on the radio, he stared at them in the rearview mirror. "Eloping with my girlfriend to Atlantic City last year was the smartest thing I've ever done."

Tatiyana glanced at Markos, saw the amused expression on his face and couldn't resist snuggling against him. She coiled her arm around his and put her head on his shoulder. Leaning over, he kissed her forehead. Tatiyana felt close to him and reveled in their newfound love. She loved how affectionate and romantic he was, and couldn't have asked for a better day.

"Tatiyana Morretti has a nice ring to it, don't you think?" he whispered into her hair. "Because of my horrible track record with women, I never thought I'd ever settle down again, but that's exactly what I want. You and me, together forever."

Giggling, she rolled her eyes at him. "You're silly."

"As long as I make you laugh, I'm doing my job."

Gazing up at him, Tatiyana recalled something the Morretti wives had said in Tampa while the group was partying at Applause Nightclub. *The women weren't kidding*, she thought, admiring his handsome profile. *Morretti men are masters of seduction*. It was more than just the things Markos said. It was the way he looked at her, the way he touched her, the feelings and emotions that stirred inside her when they kissed. He was a dream, one of a kind, and Tatiyana was ready to take a chance on love.

"I don't see anything but wide-open space. Are we lost?" she asked aloud, peering out the backseat window. Hanging low in the sky, surrounded by thin, wispy clouds, the orange-hued sun dripped toward the horizon. A blustery wind blew dust in the desert air, and the scent of pine flowed through the open driver's window. "Where are we going?"

Markos's eyes smiled, and a mischievous expression covered his face. "On an adventure."

"You've been saying that since we left the restaurant over an hour ago." Straightening in her seat, she playfully jabbed his side with her elbow. "Fess up, Markos. The suspense is killing me. I can't take it anymore. I'm dying to know where we're going."

"Be patient. You'll find out soon enough."

Spotting a hot-air balloon in the distance, her eyes widened in alarm. It felt as if her seat belt were choking her, and she struggled to catch her breath. "*Please*, tell me we're not going in there." She pointed at the windshield, her limbs quivering with fear, and swallowed hard. "I don't do well with heights...or balloons...or falling from the sky."

"You have nothing to fear. I won't leave your side."

Her stomach dropped to her feet with a thud. "I think I'm going to be sick."

"Baby, trust me, you're going to love it."

"Why? Because your other women did?"

"I've never been in a hot-air balloon," he confessed. "I thought it would be an exciting new experience for both of us, so I booked the champagne night tour."

An exciting new experience? More like chilling, scary and stressful.

"And for the record, there are no other women. Just you."

The pictures of Markos she'd seen weeks earlier on several LA gossip blogs days before her trip to Tampa came to mind, and she couldn't resist asking him about them. "What about the women you were linked to this past summer?"

"I want you, and no one else. I thought I made that clear this morning. You're the most selfless, compassionate woman I know, and I admire how you care for others." Markos winked. "Especially me."

His gaze zeroed in on her, and her heart sighed.

"You're right. I *am* fabulous!" she joked with a laugh.

"Yes, you are, and I want you to be my girl forever."

Tatiyana leaned over and caressed his face with her hands. "I'd love nothing more, Mr. Morretti!"

"Morretti?" The driver slammed on the brakes. Twisting in his seat, his eyes bugging out of his head like a cartoon character, he spoke in a loud, animated voice. "You're not related to baseball phenom Demetri Morretti from the Chicago Royals, are you?"

Nodding, Markos wore a proud smile. "He's my first cousin."

"Holy crap! That means you're Emilio Morretti's brother!"

"Right again. Are you a fan?"

"Hell, yeah, I'm a fan! Demetri is an outstanding baseball player, and Emilio's the greatest Formula One driver of all time."

"I agree, and they're great guys, too. Talented, hardworking and ambitious."

The driver returned his attention to the road but continued questioning Markos. "Do you have any advice for a young, aspiring businessman like myself?"

"Success doesn't happen overnight. You have to be disciplined and determined to be the best in your field, no matter the cost."

Hearing her cell buzz, Tatiyana fished it out of her purse. She had three missed calls from her mom, and a text message. It was obvious her mom was upset, annoyed with her for leaving town on the fly, but Tatiyana didn't call Lena back. Markos was sitting beside her, and she didn't want him to overhear their conversation. Reading the message made her feel low.

Where are you and why aren't you answering your phone? I hope you're not off with Markos Morretti, because he's bad news. Just like his friend the mayor.

Annoyed, Tatiyana tossed her cell in her purse. Her mom was wrong. Markos wasn't bad news. He respected her, made her feel safe and protected, and Tatiyana was hopeful about their future. He was her man now, and she wasn't going to let her mom disrespect him.

Your man? asked her inner voice. *That was fast! One minute you're avoiding him and the next he's your man. Are you* sure *you know what you're doing? What you want?*

Her thoughts returned to the day they met. From the moment she'd laid eyes on Markos, she'd been smitten with him, and couldn't fight their attraction any longer, wasn't strong enough to resist him. And why should she? Markos was a catch, the kind of guy she'd always dreamed of marrying, and she hoped her family wouldn't come between them. Ice spread through her veins, chilling her to the bone. Pushing aside her fears, Tatiyana told herself not to worry, but she couldn't shake the feeling that trouble was right around the corner.

Chapter 22

"Baby, we're here," Markos said with an easy smile. "Ready for the adventure of a lifetime?"

Hearing his smooth, sexy voice, Tatiyana snapped to attention and nodded.

"This is the launch site. The team's ready for you," the driver announced. "It was a pleasure driving you this afternoon, Mr. Morretti, and behalf of everyone at Ultimate Sightseeing Tours, thank you for your business."

The men shook hands, and Markos stuffed a hundred-dollar bill into the driver's tip jar. In many ways, he reminded her of her Uncle Byron—strong, dependable and generous—and for the second time in minutes, she wondered what her family would think of her dating him. Tatiyana was confident her mom and sister could put the past behind them and embrace Markos the same way his family had embraced her in Tampa. It wasn't every day she brought someone home, and it was important to her that her family and her new boyfriend got along.

Markos stepped out of the Hummer, came around the passenger door and helped Tatiyana out of the vehicle. "Your hands are ice-cold. Are you okay?"

"I don't think I can do this."

"You can do anything you put your mind to."

Fear flooded her body. "But I'm scared."

"Baby, trust me. I've got your back, so let's do this!"

His enthusiasm was contagious, and as he tenderly stroked her arms, her legs stopped shaking and the butterflies in her stomach disappeared.

"Welcome Markos and Tatiyana. I'm Arielle Jospeh, and I'll be your pilot today…"

A redhead, rocking a white Jimi Hendrix T-shirt and

skinny jeans, waved in greeting. Speaking with a Southern drawl, she explained what would happen, what to do and how to be safe during the ninety-minute tour.

In seconds, they were inside the basket of the balloon, flying high in the sky. Tatiyana soaked in her tranquil surroundings. The air was warm and fragrant, the mountains majestic, and the sunset as beautiful as a postcard. The ride was smooth, exhilarating and romantic. It was the experience of a lifetime, and Tatiyana was glad Markos was at her side, holding her close. Watching the sky change colors, she admired the golden-hued landscape. The pilot answered their questions, pointed out various landmarks and educated them about the history of Joshua Tree. Ninety minutes after takeoff, the balloon reached the landing spot. Exiting the basket, hand-in-hand with Markos, Tatiyana was shocked to see a round table decorated with fine linens, candles, and trays topped with tropical fruits and pastries.

"It's time for dessert," Markos announced, pulling out her chair. "Have a seat."

"You've thought of everything, haven't you?"

"Of course. I'm a Morretti. That's how we roll!"

Seated at the table, eating chocolate-dipped fruit, gourmet cheese and decadent minicakes, Markos and Tatiyana looked at the souvenir pictures taken by the photographer and discussed their favorite moments of the flight. "Markos, thank you for an incredible day," she said, overcome with love and gratitude. "It's refreshing being with someone who accepts me for who I am, and who isn't trying to change me."

"Why would anyone want to change you? You're perfect just the way you are."

"Tell that to my ex." Thirsty, Tatiyana picked up her flute and tasted her champagne. "The more I tried to please him, and his family, the more they tried to change me. His sisters made me feel like an outsider, like I wasn't good enough, and nothing I ever did was right. Just because I was raised in the inner city doesn't mean I'm not smart or sophisticated. I am."

"Of course you are. And you're feisty, too!"

"Markos, don't make fun. I'm serious."

He wore an innocent face, but Tatiyana didn't laugh.

"I shouldn't have said anything. You're a Morretti. You don't know what it's like to be rejected. Everyone wants you. You're a catch."

Scoffing, he barked a loud, bitter laugh. "Emme Silva-De Luca doesn't think so."

"The fashion designer? You guys dated?"

"Yeah, for five years."

Tatiyana felt a twinge of jealousy, but she wanted to hear more. "What happened?"

Silence fell across the table.

"Markos, talk to me. I want to know what happened."

"She chose her career over me." His smile was sad, and he spoke in a quiet tone of voice. "I thought Emme was the one, so I hired the best party planner in the country to help me orchestrate the perfect proposal on our anniversary."

Stunned, Tatiyana gawked at him, unable to believe what she was hearing. Markos had been engaged before? Why didn't he say anything? And most importantly, was he still hung up on his ex? Is that why he's been single all these years?

"I went all out, spared no expense," he continued, pushing a cheese ball around his plate. "I had it all. A ten-piece band, a diamond, a heartfelt speech, and all of our friends and family in the private dining room of Beverly Hills Boutique Hotel."

Captivated by his story, Tatiyana leaned forward in her chair, eager to hear more.

"Before I could even propose, Emme stopped me. She said she wasn't ready to get married, that she wanted to focus on her career, then fled the room with her sisters."

"That must have hurt."

"Like a bitch. I've never been so embarrassed in all my life. I felt like such an idiot."

"Why? You took a chance on love. That took guts."

"You sound like my brothers. They told me the exact same thing."

"Where is Emme now?" Tatiyana asked, curious about the competition.

"In New York, living the American dream. According to mutual friends of ours, she has three kids, an executive husband and a die-hard celebrity following obsessed with her line."

"I believe it. Her couture gowns are timeless and elegant."

Markos picked up his flute. "You know her work?"

"Yes, she's incredibly talented." Tatiyana sank back in her chair and crossed her legs. "Every time I wear the yellow mermaid gown I bought from her spring collection I feel like a million bucks. I had to save for months to buy it, but it was worth every penny."

His phone lit up, then rang, but Markos didn't answer it.

"I screwed up with Emme. I took her for granted, and I didn't support her dreams the way she championed mine, and by the time I realized the error of my ways, it was too late. She was gone." He spoke with fierce determination. "I won't make the same mistake twice. I want a woman in my life who I can grow with, and take care of, and do things with—and Tatiyana, I want that person to be you."

Needing a moment to gather her thoughts, Tatiyana forked a heart-shaped strawberry into her mouth and chewed slowly.

"My life has been all about the firm, but being with you makes me want so much more. I want us to sleep-in on weekends, play hooky from work and take road trips around this vast, beautiful state of ours."

"So do I, Markos, but we have to take things slow. Right

now, my focus is supporting Jantel and Allie. Things are stressful at home, and I need to be there for my family."

"Don't let your sister come between us."

Her fork fell from her hand. "Jantel isn't lying, and the paternity test will prove it."

"And if it doesn't?" he challenged.

"It will. I know my sister. I practically raised her. She wouldn't lie to me…"

For the second time in minutes, his cell phone rang, and Tatiyana trailed off speaking.

"Someone really wants to talk to you," she pointed out. "Answer it. I don't mind."

Picking up his cell, he smiled apologetically. "This will only take a minute."

"No problem. Take as long as you need."

Tatiyana picked up her fork and finished eating her dessert. Markos's comments about Jantel bothered her, but she decided not to dwell on it. It didn't matter. She knew her sister, trusted her and supported her wholeheartedly.

She watched as the color drained from Markos's face and knew he'd received bad news. The caller was shouting, speaking in a loud, booming voice, and Tatiyana suspected it was the oil tycoon. He'd called earlier in the day, demanding to meet at LA Family Law to discuss his divorce, but Markos had refused his repeated requests.

"No, Sir, I'm not in LA. I'm still in Palm Springs with my girlfriend…"

Girlfriend? Gosh, I love how that sounds! Tickled pink, Tatiyana couldn't stop a smile from exploding onto her mouth.

"Eight o'clock tomorrow morning? Yes, Sir, that will work. See you then."

Markos ended his call and dropped his cell on the table. "Sorry about that."

"So, we're returning to LA tonight, instead of tomorrow evening?"

"Yes, unfortunately. I hate that we have to cut our romantic weekend short, but if I don't meet with my client before he travels to Saudi Arabia tomorrow, he'll complain to the other partners about me being distracted and unavailable."

"Jeez, I could never be an attorney. I'd hate people calling me day and night, and making unreasonable demands on my time."

"When you're passionate about what you do, it doesn't feel like work."

"The only thing I'm passionate about is dessert!" Tatiyana quipped, licking the vanilla icing off her fork. "Do we have to leave right now?"

"No, you can finish your food. There's no rush."

"Good, because I want another mini cheesecake. I swear, it's heaven in my mouth!"

Markos chuckled. "After my morning meeting, I should make an appearance at the LA Career and Business Symposium. I wasn't planning to attend since I thought we'd be in Palm Springs for the weekend, but if I'm in town I might as well."

"Will you be at the symposium all day?"

"No, just for a couple hours, but after that I'm all yours. We can have a late lunch, get a couple's massage at The Peninsula and play a couple rounds of golf at the country club."

"I can't sleep at your place tonight. I need to go home and check in with my family."

"Call them."

"Babe, I have schoolwork to do, as well."

"I'll help you. As they say, two heads are better than one."

"You said that yesterday, but you never helped me study for my quiz, or write my paper," she told him, cleaning her hands on a napkin. "And I can't afford to fail."

"You won't. You're an incredibly smart woman, and I have faith in you."

Cupping her chin in his hand, he kissed her softly on the lips. For the first time in Tatiyana's life, she felt completely and thoroughly loved, as if Markos would do anything for her. The realization stunned her, flooding her body with fear, but instead of pulling away, Tatiyana linked her arms around his neck, inclined her head and deepened the kiss.

Chapter 23

On Sunday morning, Markos sat in the conference room of LA Family Law listening to his client complain about the revised draft of his divorce agreement. But his thoughts were a million miles away. He couldn't go five seconds without daydreaming about Tatiyana, and when he wasn't fantasizing about his girlfriend, he was thinking of things to do to make her smile.

His thoughts returned to yesterday. He'd had an amazing time in Palm Springs with Tatiyana, sightseeing, and creating memories, and Markos was looking forward to their next road trip. Feeling guilty for cutting their romantic weekend short, he made a mental note to call his favorite florist, and order flowers for his lady love. Marcus wished they were still in Palm Spring, but the oil tycoon was the firm's richest client, and it was his job to make the billionaire happy.

Sunshine spilled through the floor-to-ceiling windows, filling the space with warmth and light, and the scent of coffee lingered in the air. The conference room was a soothing, relaxing space, but Markos could feel a headache form behind his temples.

"Do something," the oil tycoon demanded, tossing the document down on the table. "This is ridiculous. We have to go back to court, or my ex will rob me dry."

Dread churned in his stomach, coiling it into a suffocating knot. In the past, when his clients complained about their spouses Markos would side with them, even when they were wrong, but not this time. He didn't have it in him to lie. Not anymore. The conversation he'd had with Tatiyana weeks earlier about the Zapata case came to mind, her voice echoing in his thoughts.

Markos straightened in his chair. He knew what he had to do. Returning to court meant more money, more billable hours for the firm, but he had to do what was right for his client, not his bank account. "The agreement is fair, Mr. Boswell, and I suggest you sign it."

"Why?" he snapped. "She's trying to ruin me."

"Mrs. Boswell helped you build your investment company from the ground up, and like any other business partner she's entitled to half of the profits."

He banged his fist on the table. "Dammit, Morretti. Whose side are you on?"

"Yours, Sir."

Sighing in relief, he nodded his head. "Good. That's what I wanted to hear."

"That being said, you've been to court numerous times over the years, and I'm worried if you reject the agreement this case could drag on for several more months, if not years."

Mr. Boswell scowled, and shrugged. "Fine by me. I have nothing to lose."

"Your hatred for your ex-wife is consuming you, and if you're not careful it could have a negative impact on your children."

"My children are fine…"

Painful memories filled his mind—memories Marcus couldn't escape. To regain control, he took a deep breath.

"They're too young to understand what divorce is. They're only four and seven."

"They know what's going on, trust me," he said, in a somber tone of voice. "Unfortunately, I've been in their shoes."

"You have?"

"I was only six-years-old when my parents split up, but I still vividly remember how they used to yell and scream at each other. Their bickering had a negative impact on me, and I've been cynical about women and relationships ever since."

As the words left his mouth, realization dawned, and a cold chill snaked down his back. He'd had two failed relationships, and if not for the support of his brothers he never would have survived. In spite of his disastrous dating history, Markos loved Tatiyana and wanted to build a life with her, but deep down, he feared they'd fall out of love one day—just like his parents had—and he'd be a three-time loser at love. The thought terrified him, so he drank some water to alleviate the lump in his throat.

"What do you expect me to do? Just sit back and let her win?"

"I know you're angry that your ex filed for divorce, but for your children's sake sign the agreement, and put the past behind you."

Nodding slowly, his stroked his jaw. "I still think her demands are excessive and unreasonable, but you've certainly given me something to think about."

"Ultimately, it's your decision on how to proceed, and I will support you no matter what you decide, but I hope you'll consider what I've said."

"I will." Glancing at his gold wristwatch, Mr. Boswell stood and buttoned his gray suit jacket. "I hate to cut our conversation short, but I have a plane to catch."

Markos led Mr. Boswell out of the conference room, down the hallway, and into the reception area. Shaking hands, the men made plans to meet next month. "Have a safe flight, Sir. I'll see you when you return from your trip."

"I look forward to it, Markos. And thanks again for your honesty."

Mr. Boswell strode out the door, and entered the waiting elevator.

Feeling a rush of pride, a grin claimed his mouth. He didn't know if the oil tycoon was going to take his advice, but he'd done the right thing, and it was a great feeling.

Walking back through the reception area, his gaze fell across Tatiyana's desk, and Markos stopped. Framed pictures were positioned beside the computer, and Markos admired them all. The childhood photograph of Tatiyana, and Jantel opening presents on Christmas Day. Tatiyana, with her family at a corn maze. And the selfie of Tatiyana cuddling baby Allie.

Seeing the images touched his heart. He wanted to tell her everything—about the pain of his parents' divorce, and the toll his past relationships had had on him—and decided to go see Tatiyana after the business symposium ended.

Questions rose in his thoughts as he stared at the pictures. Was he wrong about Jantel? Had he made a mistake? Was she telling the truth? Markos felt guilty for the way he'd treated the single mom, and knew he owed her an apology. Just because other women had deceived him in the past didn't mean Jantel was lying about her affair with mayor Glover. It was time he spoke to his friend, man-to-man.

Anxious to get to his office, Markos returned the pictures to their rightful place, and marched down the hallway. He was determined to right a wrong, and once he uncovered the truth he was going to see the woman he loved, and tell her everything that was in his heart, because she meant the world to him.

Tatiyana walked onto the deck, sat down at the patio table and opened her management textbook. Birds chirped, the neighbor's dogs barked incessantly and car horns blared in the distance.

Determined to study, Tatiyana read page eighty-seven aloud, committing the necessary information to memory. Returning to LA last night had been bittersweet. She'd missed Allie and had tons of schoolwork to do, but Tatiyana wished she was still in Palm Springs with Markos. They'd done it all: strolled the streets hand in hand, dined at celebrity hot spots, danced in the light of the moon after their romantic balloon ride and even made love in his sports car. But what she'd enjoyed most were their heartfelt talks.

He'd opened up to her about his hopes for the future, and she'd felt closer to him than ever before.

Trembling, Tatiyana wrapped her sweater around her arms. She'd returned home in the wee hours of the morning, tiptoed into her room and after a quick shower fell into a deep sleep. Up by 6:00 a.m., she'd done laundry, made chocolate chip pancakes—Jantel's favorite—prepared Allie's bottle and cleaned the kitchen from top to bottom.

Her gaze strayed from her textbook to her cell phone, and cherished memories of Markos filled her mind. Tatiyana wanted to call and thank him for a great weekend, but decided not to. They'd had their fun in Palm Springs, but Tatiyana was home now and had to focus on her studies.

"Were you with Markos Morretti?"

Tatiyana glanced over her shoulder, spotted her mom standing in between the French doors and smiled. Wearing a short, black wig and denim overalls, Lena looked trendy and youthful. "Morning, Mom. How are you? I'm fine. Thanks for asking."

"Don't get cheeky with me, young lady. *You're* the one sleeping with the enemy, not me." Sitting, she put her smart phone on the table and folded her arms. "How long have you been sneaking around with Markos Morretti?"

"No one's sneaking around. We're dating."

"What about Jantel?"

Confused by the question, she frowned. "What about her?"

"It's been weeks since you went to Tampa, but you still haven't arranged a meeting with Mayor Glover. Why not?"

Exasperated, Tatiyana dropped her highlighter on her textbook. "Mom, we've discussed this a million times. The mayor's out of town on business, but as soon as he returns, Markos will set up a meeting at LA Family Law."

"You're sure? How do you know he's not playing you?"

"He's not. Markos knows how important this is to me, and he won't let me down."

"Good. That's just what I wanted to hear."

Eyes narrowed, Lena inclined her head to the right. "So, what's it like dating a millionaire? Does Markos have his own jet? Is his mansion bigger than Oprah's? Does he have dozens of servants at his beck and call?"

"No, Mom, he's just like you and me," Tatiyana said with a laugh. "He's easygoing, laid-back and ridiculously smart, and once you get to know him you'll see he's a great guy."

"I doubt it. I met him once, and he was a smug, condescending jerk."

Tatiyana winced, as if she was in physical pain. "Everyone makes mistakes—"

"Yeah, but men like Markos Morretti *never* change. It's his way or the highway!"

Jantel appeared, holding Allie in one hand and a plate of fruit in the other. Thrilled to see her sister, and niece, Tatiyana smiled. She took Allie from Jantel and held her close. Tenderly rubbing her back, she stroked and kissed her chubby cheeks. "My sweet baby! I missed you so much. Did you miss me?"

Allie touched her face and giggled when Tatiyana nibbled on her tiny, plump fingers.

"What are you guys arguing about? I could hear you all the way upstairs."

"Your sister's secret boyfriend."

Tatiyana shook her head. "Mom, he's not a secret. You've been so busy going on marathon dates, we haven't had a chance to talk."

"You're dating Markos Morretti," Jantel said.

It was a statement, not a question, surprising her. "How did you know?"

"It's obvious. Heck, baby Allie can see it!"

Jantel picked up a piece of cantaloupe, tossed it into her mouth and plopped down on a chair. Fresh faced, in a white lace peasant-style dress her sister looked like the girl-next-door.

"You don't have to be a genius to put two and two together. You talk about Markos nonstop, and you're excited to go to work every day." Her eyes smiled. "Do you love him?"

Yes, with all my heart, and my feelings for him are so strong they scare me!

"Don't say 'I love you' first. It's bad luck," Lena advised. "And whatever you do, don't move in with him. Get him to put a ring on it first."

"Mom, you're getting *way* ahead of yourself," she said, fixing the pink bows in Allie's hair. "We're getting to know each other, not sprinting headfirst to the altar."

"Really? Could have fooled me. You light up every time you say his name."

That's because Markos makes me happier than I've ever been. Standing, she put Allie in her activity jumper and turned it on. Lights flashed, music played and her niece giggled.

"I adore Markos, but I'm worried we don't have what it takes to go the distance," Tatiyana confessed with a heavy heart.

"You'd make a great couple."

Touched, Tatiyana smiled at her mom. "So, you two are okay with me dating Markos?"

"It's your life," Jantel said with a shrug.

"I know, but I want your support."

"Why? Who cares what I think?"

"Don't talk like that," Lena scolded, swatting Jantel's arm. "You're beautiful and smart and your opinion matters to this family."

Jantel smiled, and seeing the jovial expression on her face warmed Tatiyana's heart. These days, her sister was a hands-on mom, and Tatiyana was pleased with the progress she'd made in recent weeks.

"Good news, Munchkin! Tatiyana spoke to Markos, and he's agreed to help you. In fact, you have a meeting with Mayor Glover next week."

"Really?" Hope sparked in her eyes. "Wow, that's the best news I've had in a long time!"

No! Tatiyana's mind screamed. Mouth agape, she stared at her mom in disbelief.

"I can finally introduce Allie to her dad," she said quietly, stroking her daughter's face. "What date and time is the meeting? I want to write it down on the kitchen calendar."

Feeling a burning sensation in her chest, Tatiyana picked up her glass and sipped her ice water. It didn't help. It hurt to breathe, and she couldn't swallow. She tried to catch her mom's eye, but Lena was too busy on her cell phone to notice her. "Jantel, the mayor's out of town, but as soon as he returns from Asia—"

"He's back!" Lena shouted. "One of my friends on social media just uploaded pictures of the mayor at the Career and Business Symposium. Hey, Markos is there, too!"

Shocked, Tatiyana plucked the phone out of her mom's hand and stared at the screen. Sure enough, there were photographs online of Markos with his brother Dante and Mayor Glover. What the hell? *Why didn't Markos tell me the mayor was back in town? Is that why he insisted we leave Palm Springs last night? Because he wanted to meet secretly with the mayor?* Pissed, her mind racing from one thought to the next, Tatiyana surged to her feet. "Mom, we're leaving. Watch Allie," she said, snatching her cell off the table. "Jantel, let's go."

"Where are we going?"

Tatiyana marched toward the French doors. "The Career and Business Symposium."

Chapter 24

The upscale steakhouse, located a block away from the Los Angeles Convention Center, had a red-hued interior, a lively bar and more windows than a cathedral. Taking off her sunglasses, Tatiyana scanned the upscale restaurant in search of Markos. In a stroke of good luck, they'd bumped into Izzy, at the Career and Business Symposium, and she'd mentioned Markos was having lunch at Figueroa Bar and Lounge with his friends.

"Hello, ladies," the female hostess said in greeting. "How many in your party?"

"My boyfriend, Markos Morretti, is having lunch in the private dining room."

"Yes, Miss, right this way."

Walking through the restaurant, Tatiyana spotted several celebrities talking, laughing and snapping selfies with their wide-eyed, star-struck fans.

"I can't do this." Jantel gripped Tatiyana's forearm. "I'm not strong enough."

"Yes, you are. Munchkin, don't worry. We're in this together."

At the end of the corridor, a slim man sat to the right of the door, clutching a plate topped with food.

"They're with the Morretti group," the hostess announced.

"Okay, no problem." He wore a sheepish smile. "Give me a minute to clean up, and I'll bring you inside the private dining room."

"Not a problem," Tatiyana said. "Take as long as you need. We'll wait right out here."

"I'll be right back."

Licking his fingertips, he marched down the corridor and into the men's washroom.

Tatiyana gripped the door handle, and turned it. Quietly, they entered the private dining room, and stood flat against the far wall. Oil paintings hung on the alabaster walls, and the air held a savory aroma. Her gaze landed on Markos and love flooded her heart. He was sitting at a round, wooden table with Dante, Mayor Glover and a man with wire-rimmed glasses, and to her surprise they were talking about her sister.

"I hold myself, my administration and my family to the highest ethical and moral standards, and I would never do anything to tarnish my reputation," Mayor Glover said, his voice strong and convincing. "I don't know this Jantel woman, and I'm not the father of her child."

"Are you willing to take a paternity test?" Markos asked.

The man with the wire-rimmed glasses snarled like a pit bull. "A paternity test? Hell, no! He might as well hold a press conference on the courthouse steps and invite his rivals!"

"Kassem, do it," Dante advised. "If you don't, this situation could drag on for months."

"This is ludicrous! I don't know her, I never slept with her and I won't allow this strange woman to bully me," the mayor argued.

In a flash, Jantel marched across the dimly lit room. She spoke with such poise and confidence Tatiyana wanted to cheer.

"I'm Jantel Washington, the strange woman in question," she announced, raising a hand in the air. "And I'm not leaving here until this matter is resolved."

Entering the room, Tatiyana noticed the shell-shocked expression on Markos's face and swallowed hard. Guilt troubled her conscience, but when she remembered his lies and deception, Tatiyana knew she was doing the right thing for her sister and niece.

Behind her, a male voice shouted, "Wait! Stop!" but Jantel ignored the security guard's commands and marched up to the table with her hands on her hips, challenging the mayor to take her on.

Utensils dropped, clanging against plates, and mouths sagged open. Quiet descended over the room, and tension polluted the air.

"Tatiyana, what are you doing here?" Markos asked.

"We came to talk to the mayor," Jantel answered, staring at her one-night stand. "And since you've already brought him up to speed about me and Allie, this shouldn't take long."

"You tricked me!" Glowering, the security guard folded his bony arms. "Mayor Glover, do you want me to escort them out? I have pepper spray in my pocket, and I'm not afraid to use it."

Ha! Tatiyana thought, patting her purse. *So do I, security boy!*

"No, everything's fine. Please return to your post."

The security guard quickly exited the room.

"I'm Christopher Nelson, the mayor's chief of staff," the man with the glasses said, straightening his pin-striped tie. "It's obvious you're upset, Miss, but this isn't the time or the place to have this discussion. Let's set up a time to meet in the New Year—"

"No," Tatiyana answered. "This meeting is long overdue. We'll talk now."

Markos reached for her, but Tatiyana pushed his hands away.

"Baby, please, lower your voice. You're yelling."

Eyes wide, the mayor and his chief of staff shared a bewildered look, and Tatiyana realized they didn't know who she was. Markos didn't tell his friends about her? Why not?

"Ms. Washington, I'm not trying to be mean, but I don't recall meeting you at my bachelor party," the mayor confessed. "And I never forget a face."

"We did. We spent the night together."

The mayor shook his head.

"Yes, we did. You came up behind me as I was leaving the master bathroom and fondled me through my dress." Casting her eyes to the hardwood floor, Jantel fiddled with the silver ring on her index finger. "We had sex twice on your bed—"

"That never happened. You're confusing me with someone else."

"No, I'm not. It was you. You asked me to call you mayor. You said it turned you on."

"This is bullshit!" Christopher raged, surging to his feet. "Kassem, let's go. We have better things to do with our time than argue with these two."

Tatiyana wanted to lunge across the table at the mayor's chief of staff but she didn't want to cause a bigger scene for her sister or for Markos.

The mayor stood. "This conversation is over."

The men headed for the door, but Jantel slid in front of the mayor, thwarting his escape. Raising her voice, she revealed intimate details about the night they spent together. "You have a scorpion tattoo on your left shoulder, and numbers tattooed across your chest…" Frowning, she broke off speaking. "It's 113…no…213…no, 313. Yeah, 313!"

The mayor stopped abruptly. "What did you say?"

"You have the numbers 313 tattooed on your chest."

Markos, the mayor and Dante spoke in unison. "Chris!"

"What?" He coughed into his fist.

"What do you mean 'what?' You slept with her and pretended to be me?"

"Hell, no, Kassem! She's lying. Lots of men have the same tattoos as me. Big friggin' deal. It's her word against mine. Nobody will ever believe her."

Tatiyana wanted to punch Mr. Nelson in the face for insulting her sister, but she governed her temper and clasped Jantel's hand instead. Was it possible her sister had been tricked? That she'd slept with Mr. Nelson and not the mayor?

"Kassem, I swear on my grandmother's grave. I didn't touch her."

"I want both of you to take a paternity test," Jantel announced. "My daughter is having heart surgery next month, and I want Allie to meet her father before her operation."

Chris spoke through clenched teeth. "And if we don't?"

"I'll hold a press conference at the courthouse tomorrow morning."

"Very well," the mayor said in a solemn voice. "We'll do it."

Once Markos made the arrangements, the mayor and his chief of staff left the room.

"Why didn't you tell me Allie was sick?" Markos asked, his features dark with sadness.

Tatiyana rolled her eyes to the ceiling. "It wouldn't have made a difference. You never had any intention of helping us. Doing so would have ruined your political aspirations, so you pretended to love me, thinking I'd be easy to manipulate and control."

"That's not true. We both made mistakes, but I never meant to hurt you—"

"You're right," she conceded, interrupting him. "I got what I deserved. I deceived you about who I was, and you betrayed my trust. Now, we're even. We can go our separate ways and pretend the last couple months never happened."

Markos protested, arguing she was wrong, but Tatiyana didn't believe him. A sob rose in her throat, and her voice faltered, but she conquered her emotions. "Markos, we're through."

"What about Palm Springs? What about the plans we made for the future?"

"It meant nothing," she lied, dodging his gaze.

"It meant something to me."

Her heart turned to stone. "If it did, you wouldn't have lied to me."

"Tatiyana, baby, please, don't do this. Let's go somewhere and talk…"

Jantel tugged at her arm, seizing her attention. "I want to go home. I need to see Allie."

"Me, too." Giving her sister a one-arm hug, she leaned over and kissed her cheek. "Munchkin, I love you, and I'm so proud of you."

Jantel smiled through her tears. "I love you, too."

As the women left the room, Tatiyana heard Markos shout her name, but she continued through the corridor, walking hand in hand with her sister. Her emotions were all over the place, impossible to make sense of. Tatiyana was happy for Jantel, but broken inside, shattered by Markos's deception, and feared she'd never be whole again.

Chapter 25

"Wow, look at the jungle gym!" Matteo jumped out of Markos's SUV, and took off running across Van Nuys Park giggling with delight. "The last one to the sandbox is a rotten egg!"

Laughing, Markos took off his seat belt and stepped out of the car. The October sky was overcast, threatening rain, but the park was filled with families and teens.

"I've lived in LA for years, and I know the city like the back of my hand, but I've never been to this park," Jordana confessed, slamming the passenger-side door. "Markos, you're right. This is a great spot for our family barbecue."

"Babe, Markos didn't bring us down here for family time. He's looking for Tatiyana."

Glaring at his brother, he gave him a shot in the chest. "Dante, shut up."

"Will someone tell me what's going on?" Frowning, Jordana glanced from her husband to her brother-in-law. "Markos, I'm confused. I thought you and Tatiyana were cool. You gave her a glowing job reference for Center of Hope and you helped her kid sister, as well."

"Yeah, but he hasn't seen her since she stormed out of Figuerora Bar and Lounge last Sunday afternoon, and it's killing him inside."

"Dante, zip it. I'm not a puppet. I can speak for myself."

"Hey, don't get mad at me because you screwed up. I told you to be honest with Tatiyana and to forgive her for her past mistakes, but you didn't listen."

Sick of hearing his brother run his mouth, Markos opened the trunk, grabbed the picnic basket and shoved it into Dante's arms. "Go make yourself useful. Find a picnic table, unload the food and fire up the grill."

Dante gave Jordana a kiss, then strode off, whistling a tune.

Yawning, Markos sank onto the trunk and rubbed his eyes. He hadn't slept since his argument with Tatiyana. Still couldn't get her accusation out of his mind. Never for a minute did he think she'd leave him, but she had, and his life was empty without her.

What am I going to do when she starts work at Center of Hope? Tatiyana was a spark, a light, and although he was happy she'd gotten the Program Director position at the center he was going to miss seeing her around the office every day. Yesterday, Izzy had invited him to join them for drinks at a downtown pub to celebrate Tatiyana's new job. He'd declined, lied about having motions to proof, but spent hours at his desk looking at pictures on his cell of their romantic weekends in Tampa and Palm Springs.

"Are you okay?" Jordana asked quietly, her features touched with concern.

Nodding absently, he glanced around the park, searching for Tatiyana. A cool breeze was blowing, but his palms were damp, and sweat drenched his button-down shirt. Markos couldn't remember ever being this nervous, not even the first time he'd argued a case in court, but he recognized what was at stake—everything. If Tatiyana rejected him again, Markos didn't know what he'd do. He was miserable without her, and he'd do anything to have her back in his life. "Don't worry about me. I'll be fine. I'm a Morretti. Can't keep me down for long."

"Markos, drop the act. You don't have to pretend with me."

Pensively, he stared up at the sky.

"Talk to me. I want to help."

"I'm scared I've lost Tatiyana forever," he blurted out.

"Then do whatever it takes to win her back."

"You make it sound so easy."

"The next time you see her, put aside your ego and speak

from the heart. Tell Tatiyana how much she means to you, and how much you need her. Markos, prove to her she's your one and only."

"Is that what Dante did to win your heart?"

"Yes, and it worked," she said with a girlish laugh.

Markos chuckled. Suddenly he felt hopeful about his relationship with Tatiyana. Maybe all wasn't lost. Maybe if he apologized she'd give him another chance. Filled with confidence and renewed determination, Markos resolved in his heart to win back the woman he loved. Standing, he gave his sister-in-law a peck on the cheek. "Thanks for the pep talk, Jordana."

"Where are you going?"

"To get my girl," he answered with a broad grin. "Tell Dante I'll be back soon."

Hearing noises behind him, someone frantically shouting his name, he frowned.

"Uncle Markos, come here! I found Tatiyana!"

Markos glanced over his shoulder, and spotted his nephew standing beside the water fountain hugging Tatiyana. Matteo had met her weeks earlier, when he'd stopped by the office with Jordana, and seeing his two favorite people together made him smile.

Eager to talk to her, Markos took off across the field. Love and happiness filled his heart. Tatiyana was there! And what a beautiful sight she was. Her hair was in a French braid, her strapless, floral dress complemented her flawless brown skin and her smile dazzled him. Approaching the group, he nodded in greeting. "Good evening, ladies. How is everyone?"

"What are you doing here? You're supposed to be at the Governor's Masquerade Ball."

Matteo piped up. "Uncle Markos came to see you. He likes you, you know."

Giggles and snickers filled the air. Markos noticed a smile tugging at the corners of Tatiyana's lips, and hope surged inside his heart. All wasn't lost. He still had a chance. He felt it, sensed it and, thanks to his nephew, Tatiyana's mom wasn't glaring at him anymore. *Phew!*

"Matteo, let's go help Dad barbecue." Taking her stepson by the arm, Jordana winked and flashed Markos a thumbs-up as they headed toward the picnic tables.

"Can we talk in private?" Markos asked, taking off his sunglasses. "I have a lot to say—"

"Then you can say your piece right here, Mr. Morretti." Crossing her arms, Lena tapped her foot impatiently on the pavement. "You hurt my daughter, young man, and if it was up to me you'd never see her again."

"Mom, don't be so harsh. If it wasn't for Markos, I wouldn't know who Allie's father is." Jantel wore a grateful smile. "Thank you for advocating for us, and for paying her medical bills, as well. I almost fainted when the hospital called this morning and told me the good news."

Embarrassed by her praise, he nodded in response. The paternity test proved Christopher Nelson was Allie's father, not the mayor, and the Harvard graduate had promptly resigned from his job. "It was my pleasure, and if there's anything else I can do to help just let me know."

Ms. Washington huffed, and Markos knew if he wanted to reunite with Tatiyana, he had to make things right with her mother first. "Ms. Washington, I owe you and your family an apology. I should have taken your concerns seriously when you came to my office, instead of doubting your story," he confessed, wearing an apologetic expression on his face. "I want to marry Tatiyana, and I hope you'll give us your blessing. I'll love her and honor her until I take my last breath."

"Do you really mean that?" Lena asked.

"Yes, Ms. Washington, I do."

Dropping her hands at her sides, Lena's face softened into a smile, and she patted his cheek. "Apology accepted, young man. And if my daughter won't marry you, I will!"

The women erupted in laughter, and Markos knew he was one step closer to achieving his goal. *One down, one more to go.* Stepping forward, he took Tatiyana's hand in his and squeezed it. "Hurting you was the worst mistake I ever made, and if you give me another chance, I promise it will never happen again."

Sadness flickered over her features. "You always know just what to say. How do I know you're telling me the truth?"

"Because you're it for me. I don't want anyone else," he confessed, baring his soul. "You're the number-one person in my life, and you always will be. I love you with everything I am, and I want to marry you more than anything in the world."

"You heard that line in an old Italian movie, and you've always wanted to use it, right?"

"No, baby, that's a Markos Morretti original, and I mean every word."

"You're an extraordinary woman who completes me in every way, and no one else will ever do."

Her mouth covered his in a soft, sweet kiss, and Markos sighed in relief. All was right in the world again. He didn't want the kiss to end, wanted to spend the rest of the night loving her, but remembered they had an audience and reluctantly pulled away. Opening his eyes, he noticed they were alone, and wrapped her up in his arms. Tenderly caressing her shoulders, he kissed her forehead, cheeks and the tip of her nose. "Congratulations on your new job at Center of Hope," he said, brushing a stray strand of hair away from her face. "When do you start?"

"Next week. I'm super excited, but nervous, too."

"You'll do great. I know it."

They shared a smile, then a kiss on the lips.

"I love you," she whispered. "Thanks for showing me that true love still exists."

"We've both made mistakes in this relationship, but the

hard times and challenges we've faced have only made our union stronger."

"Baby, I agree." Tatiyana wrapped her arms around his waist. "You can trust me, Markos. I'll never do anything to hurt you, and you'll always have my unconditional love and support."

Her words touched his heart. "I love you more than anything, and I want to spend my life with you."

Staring deep into her eyes, Markos knew in his heart that Tatiyana was his soul mate. His everything. The only woman for him. And as they strolled through Van Nuys Park, holding hands and sharing kisses, Markos felt like the luckiest man alive. And he was.

Epilogue

Tatiyana put her travel bag in the overhead bin on the Boeing 738 bound for Tampa Bay, closed it, and sat down in her plush, first-class seat. Buckling her safety belt, she glanced around the cabin, and noticed the airplane was half empty. The air smelled of pastries and coffee, and the savory aroma made Tatiyana hanker for something sweet.

Arriving at the boarding gate for Flight 74 an hour earlier, Tatiyana was pleasantly surprised to see Mercedes—the ticket agent who'd checked her in on that fateful flight to Tampa last year—and cheered when the brunette upgraded her to first class free of charge. As expected, the ticket agent questioned her about the Morretti family and they'd shared a laugh.

Tatiyana shook her head. It was hard to believe she'd been dating Markos for nine months. It felt as if she'd known him all her life. He was a part of her family now, as she was a part of his. The more time they spent together—cooking, working out together in his home gym, enjoying the opera and symphony, and taking road trips—the more she loved him. For the first time ever, Tatiyana was blissfully and wonderfully happy and Markos was one of the reasons why she had a permanent smile on her face.

Her cell phone buzzed. Taking it out of her leather tote bag, she read her newest text message from Jantel. A picture popped up on the screen. It was of baby Allie playing at the park, and for the second time that day she marveled at how beautiful her niece was. To everyone's surprise and amazement, Allie had quickly recovered from her surgery and was thriving in her toddler playgroup. And she wasn't the only one exceeding expectations.

Tatiyana had pulled some strings at work, and thanks

to the Human Resources manager at the Center of Hope, Jantel had been hired to work in the kitchen. Within six months, she was the head cook, and everyone's favorite staff. Every day, the sisters ate lunch together outside in the courtyard, and Tatiyana cherished their talks. These days, Jantel was a hands-on mom, who was a hundred percent committed to her daughter, and it was a joy to see. Her sister had risen above the pain of her past, and now they were closer than ever. Being the program director at the Center of Hope—a nonprofit organization that provided services for low-income families—was a rewarding experience. Tatiyana was thrilled she was finally putting her education and training to good use, and seeing Jantel around the center everyday was the icing on the cake.

Excited about the girls-only trip to Tampa with the Morretti wives, Tatiyana signed into her email account, and reviewed the itinerary Dionne had sent her last night. The pilot came on the intercom, but Tatiyana was too busy reading her messages to pay attention. Finished, she turned off her phone and dropped it in her purse. As the airplane cleared the runway and climbed off the ground, she remembered the last time she'd been to Tampa, and smiled.

Tatiyana closed her eyes, pulled the wool blanket up to her chin and crossed her legs at the ankles. Warm, and cozy in her first-class seat, thoughts of Markos filled her mind. *I wish he was here with me*, she thought, with a deep sigh. Last night, they'd had dinner with her family, but he'd been quiet, withdrawn, unlike himself. Walking him to his car after dessert, Markos admitted he was under a lot of pressure at work, and hearing the strain in his voice worried her.

An idea popped in her mind. Maybe she should plan something special for him. Valentine's Day was tomorrow, and although they'd agreed to celebrate when she returned from her trip, Tatiyana loved the idea of surprising her boyfriend. And she knew just what to do. Making a mental note to text Izzy when the flight landed, she decided to also enlist the help of her mother. Lena adored Markos, and told her friends and family she wanted him to be her son-in-law, so she'd jump at the opportunity to do something nice for him.

"The first time I laid eyes on you was nine months ago on this very flight. I knew you were trouble in six-inch heels, and I was right."

Frowning, Tatiyana cocked her head to the side. What an odd thing for the pilot to say? The voice on the intercom sounded familiar—deep, masculine, confident…like… Her eyes flew open, and a gasp fell from her lips. Markos was standing in the galley, talking on the intercom, wearing a boyish smile.

Her mouth agape, all she could do was stare. Dizzy, and confused, Tatiyana feared she was going to faint. At a loss for words, her thoughts scattered, and her mind raced. What was Markos doing on the flight? Where did he come from? Was this for real?

The lights dimmed, and a hush fell over the cabin.

"From the moment we met, you turned my world upside down, but I'm a better man for it. You're a beautiful, compassionate soul, and there aren't enough words in the English language to describe how much you mean to me. You're my world, my everything, and I hope you'll grant me the honor of being your husband."

Tatiyana cupped her hands over her mouth to smother the squeal rising in her throat. Her heartbeat was pounding in her ears, and her legs were shaking, but she stood, and walked down the aisle, toward the man she loved more than anything in the world. Markos looked dashing in his tailored black suit, and the urge to kiss him was so overwhelming she quickened her pace.

A lightbulb flashed in her mind, and suddenly everything made sense. Now Tatiyana understood why he'd been preoccupied last night at dinner. He wasn't stressed out about work; he was preparing for his surprise proposal from forty thousand feet!

Markos hung up the phone, clasped her left hand and dropped down to one knee.

Cheers, and whistles filled the air, adding to the festive mood in the cabin, and Tatiyana noticed passengers were recording them with their smartphones. Her thoughts returned to the day they met, replaying every detail of their encounter. From the moment they'd met, they'd had an instant connection, an undeniable chemistry, but never in her wildest dreams did she ever imagine Markos would propose to her on an airplane. It was the most shocking and outrageous thing that had ever happened to her, and Tatiyana wanted to pinch herself to prove she wasn't dreaming.

"Tatiyana Washington, will you marry me?"

Her lips parted, and the word "Yes" exploded out of her mouth. Moved by his heartfelt speech, Tatiyana flung herself into Markos's open arms, and kissed him tenderly on the lips.

The applause was deafening, and the longer they kissed the louder the passengers cheered. Tatiyana didn't want the kiss to ever end, and relished being in her fiancé's arms.

Water filled her eyes, blurring her vision, but she felt Markos slide the ring onto the third finger on her left hand, then kiss her palm.

"Do you like it?"

Raising her hand in the air, she playfully wiggled her fingers. The marquise-cut diamond was a striking piece of jewelry, and Tatiyana didn't want to ever take it off. The simplicity of the design enhanced the beauty of the ring, and she loved how unique it was. "I don't like it. I love it. It's perfect," Tatiyana whispered, overcome with emotion. "Thank you, baby."

A flight attendant appeared, handed them both a champagne flute, and congratulated them on their engagement. Markos made a toast, and they clinked glasses. Thirsty, and sweating profusely in her burgundy halter dress, Tatiyana quickly finished the drink.

Markos brushed his nose against hers, causing her to giggle, and she snuggled against him. Holding her tight, he led Tatiyana back to her seat, and sat down beside her.

"I can't believe you did all of this for me," she confessed, resting her head on his shoulder. "How did you pull this off?"

"I've been planning this proposal since our weekend in Palm Springs. You teased me about proposing to you in bed, so I knew I had to do something big." Taking her hand in his, Markos kissed her forehead. "It took months of work, and several covert meetings with your mom, but I'm proud to say, Operation Mid-Air Proposal, went off without a hitch."

"Tell me more. I need details."

"I snuck onto the plane after you boarded the flight, sat in the cockpit's jump seat, and waited for the signal from the head flight attendant. Once we reached our cruising altitude, I knew it was showtime, and I was ready."

"I still can't believe we're engaged. It was a wonderful, beautiful moment, and I'll never forget it as long as I live." Tatiyana glanced from Markos to her ring, and squealed. "I can't wait to share the good news with our friends and family."

"You won't have to wait long. Everyone's meeting us in Tampa at the Oasis Spa & Resort to celebrate our engagement."

Realization dawned, and shock flew through her body. "Oh, my goodness! The Morretti wives tricked me!"

His eyes darkened with mischief, and a grin claimed his mouth.

"There is no girls' weekend, is there? It was all a rouse to get me on this flight."

"I'll never tell."

"You better or you'll be sleeping alone tonight."

A cup of coffee and a few questions kept Kamaya and Wesley talking for almost three hours. After sharing more than either had planned, they stood, saying their goodbyes and making plans to see each other again.

"I would really love to take you to dinner," Wesley said as he walked Kamaya to her car.

"Are you asking me out on a date, Wesley Walters?"

He grinned. "I am. With one condition."

"What's that?"

"We don't talk business. I get the impression that's not an easy thing for you to do. So will you accept the challenge?"

As they reached her car, she smiled as she nodded her head. "I'd love to."

"I mean it about not talking business."

Kamaya laughed. "You really don't know me."

He laughed with her. "I don't, but I definitely look forward to changing that."

Wesley opened the door of her vehicle. The air between them was thick and heavy, carnal energy sweeping from one to the other, fervent with desire. It was intense and unexpected, and left them both feeling a little awkward and definitely excited about what might come.

"Drive safely, Kamaya," he whispered softly, watching as she slid into the driver's seat.

She nodded. "You, too, Wesley. Have a really good night."

Don't miss A PLEASING TEMPTATION
by Deborah Fletcher Mello, available April 2017
wherever Harlequin® Kimani Romance™
books and ebooks are sold.

Wesley reached into the briefcase that rested beside his chair leg. He passed her the folder of documents. "They're all signed," he said as he extended his hand to shake hers. "I look forward to working with you, Kamaya Boudreaux."

She slid her palm against his, the warmth of his touch heating her spirit. "Same here, Wesley Walters. I imagine we're going to make a formidable team."

"Team! I like that."

"You should. Because it's so out of character for me! I don't usually play well with others."

He chuckled. "Then I'm glad you chose me to play with first."

Markos chuckled. "Don't be mad. It was for a good cause. I want you to be my wife more than anything in the world, so I enlisted the help of our families to make it happen."

"And I'm glad you did. I love you, baby, and I can't wait to be Mrs. Markos Morretti."

"I love you, too. You're the best part of me, and I'll cherish you all the days of my life."

As the airplane soared high above the clouds the couple sealed the declaration with a kiss.

* * * * *

Summer Loving

REESE RYAN

Next in line as CEO of his family's international luxury-resort empire, Liam Westbrook doesn't play it safe. So when the British bachelor spies divorced single mother Maya Alvarez, he makes a scandalous proposal. Will Liam and their pleasure-fueled fantasy end up as only an affair to remember?

PLEASURE COVE

Available March 2017!

Get 2 Free Books,
Plus 2 Free Gifts—
just for trying the
Reader Service!